MW01125857

A PROMISE
OF
REVENGE

A PROMISE OF REVENGE

The Death of Javier

Terri Kay

To order additional copies of this book, contact:
Xlibris Corporation
1-888-795-4274
www.Xlibris.com
Orders@Xlibris.com
18364

Dedication and Acknowledgments
This book is dedicated to my patient,
long suffering husband Ray.
Special thanks go to my good friend Herman
for his technical information and
my good friend Candy for sharing the light.

Terri

CHAPTER 1

ON TUESDAY, JUNE 1, 1954, the sun rose early, but he did not. The bright yellow light streamed through the six-pane window and fell on his face. Still sound asleep in his apartment at Briggandale University, the large college in Briggandale, Indiana, medical student Brian Tanner had stayed out way too late the night before. The 6 A.M. alarm he had set didn't even make him stir, for he slept right through it. But a single loud ring of the black telephone on the red metal stand outside his bedroom door sent him jumping to his feet. Fully awake now at 9 A.M., Brian was very, very late.

Rushing into the black-and-white tiled bathroom, he moved quickly, preparing for his day. While whipping the soap in the cup with his shaving brush, he chastised himself for his actions the night before.

"Ugh! You look terrible!" He'd finally looked at himself in the mirror. The dark circles under his eyes and his dull skin confirmed what Brian already knew, but had refused to accept. He couldn't continue to juggle two intense lovers and medical school. One of them would have to go—and dropping out of medical school was out of the question.

Short, medium-brown stubble from last night's beard

disappeared quickly as Brian ran the silver straight razor across his face. "Yeowh!" he yelped, suddenly dropping the razor. In the small, cloudy mirror, he peered at the tiny drop of blood oozing from the nick. "That's it! Today's the day—I've got to stop this. I can't go on with both of them any longer." After putting white tissue paper on the nick, he picked up the razor again off the white porcelain sink. His normally smooth routine was interrupted again with another nick and more drops of blood. Shaving usually went well unless he had something on his mind. This morning, he had too much on his mind and his face showed the messy results.

"Well, from the looks of this, I'd better stop thinking about them before I cut my throat," he said aloud. Brian tried focusing on his face but it was no use. Three nicks later, he left the bathroom hurriedly, bumping into Fred on the way out. Fred Butler, his roommate, had come to Briggandale University from England.

"Say Brian, looks like you're growing a bumper crop of tissue paper there! You were trying to shave, weren't you? How will all those pretty girls of yours recognize your new face?" He stepped next to the wall to let Brian pass by.

"Shut up Fred!" Brian insisted, not caring much for Fred's attempt at humor this morning. Usually, Fred was a good roommate. But today, he was being a jerk.

"You know, you only have to dump one of them, old buddy, not scare them both off!" Fred laughed. "But seriously," he paused, "I heard you talking to yourself in there. It shouldn't be too hard to choose." With reddish-brown hair that stuck up in little tufts like feathers on the sides of his round head, a round face, pouting pink lips and black-rimmed glasses, Fred looked like a wise old owl. He always gave advice, most of it very good.

Brian just didn't want to hear it today. "Shut up, Fred!" Brian repeated as he closed his bedroom door to shut Fred out and to be alone with his thoughts again. With a meeting scheduled for that morning with a group of students, followed by lunch with one of the faculty members, Brian couldn't have any prolonged discussions with Fred.

But Fred followed Brian down the hall and continued talking.

"Dyna called last night. I told her you were studying late. I didn't tell her the subject was Sierra Gleason. You owe me, old buddy." Fred sauntered back up the hallway to the bathroom.

As he sorted through the socks in the top drawer of his dresser, Brian found a matching pair. Closing the drawer, he looked up and saw his reflection in the wide mirror atop the dresser. The pieces of tissue paper were still there, stuck to his face. As he pulled the pieces off, Brian thought about Fred's comments. Leave it to Fred to know what I was thinking, Brian thought. Why was it so obvious to Fred and not to these women? They've got to know about each other by now. I love them both, but I can't go on much longer with both of them.

Brian slipped on the pair of socks and walked the few short feet to his closet. Pushing though the shirts hanging there, Brian picked one and held it next to the paisley tie on the oak dresser. The fine, handmade silk shirt Sierra gave him last night matched perfectly with the tie Dyna gave him only two days ago. How strange, Brian thought, that these two items match so well when the women who gave them to me aren't alike at all!

Brian tied his tie and searched the top of his dresser for a tie tack. The silver one would do, it went well with his pale blue trousers. Silver cuff links would complete the look as he finished dressing.

After he grabbed his blazer, Brian Tanner left the apartment still thinking about the two women. Dyna Palpietro was so sweet and kind. She was warm, with the darkest chocolate-brown eyes he had ever seen. She always smelled sweet, like the spicy smell of the hot cinnamon apple pies Mama used to make. When he closed his eyes, Brian could almost smell Dyna and see those eyes. But almost as soon as she was fixed as an image in his mind, Sierra's face would appear.

Brian smiled and got warm all over. Sierra Gleason was sizzling hot. His evenings with her had been fantastic. No, unforgettable. With platinum-blond hair and blue eyes, she was gorgeous. She could make any man think at least twice before leaving her warm, soft, golden-tanned arms. Sierra was, well, "experienced," as Mama used to say.

Brian laughed. "Mama," he said to himself, "That's the kind of experience I like!"

ACROSS TOWN, in the apartment next to Sierra Gleason's, Merritt Hughes put his latest home movie in the thin cardboard box that would hold it, then wrote the date on the piece of tape that would act as the label. He wouldn't put this movie with the rest of his collection, in case one of his friends came across it by accident. This one would join a special group in the bottom of his footlocker, a collection he'd kept secret from everyone.

With his treasure securely hidden, he walked to the end of the hallway. After listening for several moments, Merritt pulled off the vent cover, then pulled the fake panel from inside the vent that separated his apartment from hers. He was certain that she was gone, but had an overwhelming desire to make sure. The vent was his way of keeping in touch with Sierra, even if she wanted nothing to do with him.

When she moved into the apartment next to his last December, Merritt made up his mind to seduce her. After all, he wasn't bad looking and he was a medical student with a bright future ahead of him. But since the first time he knocked on her door, she seemed aloof, almost afraid of him. He had tried everything that he could think of to get her to spend a little time with him, maybe go out for some coffee or on a date. But nothing had worked. Sierra was different. She was the first girl who hadn't fallen for one of his lines and didn't seem impressed by him. Her lack of response intrigued him initially, but in time, he grew obsessed with her in a way that even he couldn't explain.

Within a month after her arrival, frustrated by her indifference, he figured out how he could get a little closer to her without her knowing it. One evening, when he was certain that she was gone, Merritt removed the grate off the cold air return in the hallway of his apartment. He'd lived in the apartment long enough to learn that the vent duct that ran between the two units could be cut, allowing him to see into her unit. Earlier, he had created a replacement panel, with a peephole that could be opened easily from his side. And if he felt like it, he could take the whole panel off.

With the new panel in place, he could spy on her whenever he pleased. And if anyone ever discovered his handiwork, he would deny all knowledge of it.

.

"DYNA PALPIETRO TANNER. Dyna Marie Palpietro Tanner. Dyna M. Palpietro Tanner." She flipped on the makeup light over the white porcelain sink—it flooded the room with more light— and peered deeply into the brown, nearly black eyes of the young, pretty, dark-haired lady looking back at her. With three tiny moles on her right temple and long black eyelashes, Dyna Palpietro, at eighteen, almost nineteen, looked just like her mother did in the old picture hanging in the dining room of their apartment. Each time she said her dream name, her own plus the last name of her lover, Brian Tanner, Dyna paused. She smiled while she listened to the sounds as they resonated in the white-tiled walls of the tiny bathroom. Here, in her bright white meditation place, she took special pleasure in letting each syllable roll from her ruby lips. It was four thirty in the morning in the Palpietro apartment in Briggandale. Only she was awake and she relished these few moments of privacy.

Soon, she thought. Brian is going to propose to me soon, I just know it! I know what he feels for me. And then I'll tell him. I want him to ask me to marry him just because he wants to, not because he feels he has to.

Dyna let the bubbling warm water splash over her small hands into the sink until the worn basin was nearly full. Through the water, she studied the size and texture of her slightly brown hands, especially the ring finger of her left hand. She could almost see her finger with a ring, maybe even a diamond ring, from Brian. With the warm water relaxing her, Dyna mentally drifted away from the small, cramped, three-bedroom apartment she shared with her family. The apartment wasn't very large, but that didn't matter. The Palpietros didn't own much furniture.

She could almost hear her own words spoken the day before to her friend, Nancy. "Of course I want to marry Brian. A couple of days ago, Brian talked to me about an important decision he had to make. But I want him to ask Papa first. If only he would ask soon! I love him so much! I know he loves me, but I really need him to say those words, especially to Papa. We've been going out for months now and it seems about the right time. When? Well, I can't say."

Months earlier, she had met him at the university's bookstore, where she worked full-time. He asked her for some help and as she turned to look at him, she dropped several heavy books on his feet. He should have screamed, but didn't. Both fumbled to pick up the books and as her eyes met his, she knew he could be the one for her. Eight months later, she was deeply in love with him and was three months pregnant.

A jiggle at the door handle followed by pounding at the door startled her. "Dy! Hurry up! I gotta go!" Raphael broke into Dyna's romantic daydreaming as only a seven-year-old with a full bladder pounding on a cheap door could. Sighing, Dyna let the now cold water out of the sink. She stepped out into the dimly lit hallway as Raphael pushed past her into the bathroom. From the end of the hall, Dyna could hear the muffled bass voice of Papa, and Mama's softer, higher tones in response. Daylight was breaking and another June day in the Palpietro household had begun.

CHAPTER 2

JUNE 1953

AS A CHUNKY, pasty brunette with furry eyebrows named Boom-Boom Betty, she wasn't much of a success as a stripper at Jack's club. But the owner, a greasy scumbag named Jack, used her for other purposes, including a few of his special parties. That's how she made extra money, selling drugs and herself, along with setting up an occasional customer for Jack to rob.

A year earlier, she had been Elizabeth Antoinette Belillaber, a nice girl from a poor neighborhood in Octuary, Illinois. Over the protests of most of the people that she knew, she enrolled in Briggandale University. As they predicted, she dropped out of college after her first semester. Going back to Octuary so soon after dropping out was out of the question for Elizabeth. Desperate after being unable to support herself in any other way, she became a stripper at a sleazy club in Enid, Indiana, only ten miles away from the school.

She saw Brian Tanner for the first time at Jack's club in early June 1953. There, with a group of drunk guys from the college, he leered at her, threw a dollar at her and promptly forgot her. But she didn't forget him.

With the other girls from the club, Elizabeth talked about leaving the club and the business. They talked about snaring rich husbands and giving up dancing, drugs and prostitution. But with the crowd that frequented Jack's club, they had little hope of finding husbands or anything else worthwhile there. That is, until the club was shut down after a big drug and prostitution bust in June 1953. Six of the girls, Louie, the bouncer, and Jack were looking at new careers behind jail bars, chosen for them courtesy of the Indiana criminal justice system.

Of all his girls, Jack figured Elizabeth was the one behind his troubles. He guessed she set him up and conveniently disappeared to avoid arrest.

He was right.

Only a week before the bust, as Elizabeth got ready for one of Jack's private parties, Jack promised to step in if the men became too unruly. Two hours later, while Elizabeth begged for help as the men abused her, Jack, who could see everything going on from the peephole in the back of the room, just watched. And one creep even made home movies.

Sending Jack on an extended vacation to jail was the least Elizabeth felt she could do for him. Going home to Octuary wouldn't be fun, but Elizabeth wasn't going to stick around for the round-up at Jack's club in Enid.

JUST AN HOUR after arriving in Octuary, while carrying a shopping basket at the grocery store, Elizabeth saw Michelle, one of her friends from high school. Elizabeth tried crouching near a stack of cans but couldn't hide quickly enough. When Michelle spotted her, she bellowed out a greeting that could be heard two aisles away. Sensing that Michelle really wanted to talk and that escaping from Michelle wouldn't be easy, Elizabeth put the basket on the floor.

In her typical nonstop fashion, Michelle shared the details of her good fortune until Elizabeth felt like puking.

"I'm Michelle Henderson now. Do you remember William

Henderson from the neighborhood? He graduated a few years before we did. I married him. I've got two children now, they're really cute and really smart, like my Bill. I have a house over on Scott Street, you know, the huge yellow ranch Mrs. Clarence used to own. I just redecorated it. Well, I just had to after our month-long trip to Europe. My Bill is working at Uptright Engineering, he's an engineer, you know."

As Michelle went on and on, Elizabeth felt embarrassed and ashamed. What could she say about her own life that was positive? That she dropped out of college and that she was a hooker? Or that she lived in an apartment the size of a shoe box that smelled like cat pee? Boy, Michelle would really be impressed with this news! Elizabeth smirked facetiously. But she stopped smirking as she realized what was about to occur. Eventually, Michelle would stop bragging and would ask for information about her. Elizabeth could either lie or leave, because she knew she didn't have the courage to tell the truth. She decided quickly.

In the middle of Michelle's droning description of her home, Elizabeth gasped, "Look at the time!" She gave an award-winning performance now. "I've got to go, Michelle. My husband is waiting outside in our new sports car. I'll stop by sometime during my visit and tell you about our New York penthouse and our villa in Italy. Ciao, baby!"

She grabbed Michelle in a big bear hug, released her, turned and dashed toward the door of the store. When Elizabeth looked back, she saw her food basket in the middle of the aisle, with the astonished Michelle still looking on. Someone else would have to put the groceries back. For Elizabeth, the items in the basket were not worth losing the shred of self-esteem that she still clung to.

The bus waiting at the corner near the store would take her right to the downtown bus station. From there, she would go back to Indiana.

BACK IN ENID, Elizabeth found that Jack was still in jail and decided it was a good time to disappear. That same night, she packed her belongings and with the money she had saved as a working girl, Elizabeth Belillaber boarded a bus headed for Florida. No one would miss her in Illinois, nor would anyone know about her miserable life in Enid. The ride would be long, but she had plenty to think about.

THREE HOURS LATER Elizabeth bumped along in row seven in the right-hand window seat of a southbound bus. All of her worldly possessions were in a cheap cardboard suitcase stored below her and in her footlocker in the luggage compartment of the bus. With tears flowing down her face as looked out of the window, Elizabeth looked back carefully at her life. She had failed at college, and she couldn't even support herself in a respectable position. She couldn't go back to Octuary, she had too many bad memories there. Going back to Enid was out of the question. Jack would get out of jail sooner or later and would certainly look for her. At times, she wanted to stop the ride, stop the bumping and get to a stable place. Her life was a mess. The success she thought she would have eluded her. She had gone to college but she never expected that it would be so expensive or that life would be so hard. So many people from her hometown expected her to fail, and now she had.

At the stops along the route, the brakes of the bus whined and screeched as if they would give out. Elizabeth was tired of the movement, but she was more tired of the failures in her young life. On that bus ride in June 1953, she decided to end it all. Elizabeth Antoinette Belillaber would have to die.

CHAPTER 3

IT TOOK NEARLY six months, but she finally finished off Elizabeth. At the end of her long bus ride months earlier in June, she wound up in southern Florida. Elizabeth changed her name, dropped forty pounds and now exercised intensively. Now known as Sierra Gleason, she plucked her brows thin and dyed her hair platinum-blond. Her career as a stripper ended and apparently behind her, she returned to Briggandale in the middle of December 1953.

But in starting her new life, one detail remained. Sierra still had to get rid of Elizabeth's belongings. The frumpy old clothing that Elizabeth wore went straight into the trash. Elizabeth's books went there too, but not for long. The books should be worth something, Sierra decided. She pulled them out of the trash.

At the bookstore at Briggandale University, the first clerk available was a petite, dark-haired woman. She couldn't have been twenty. She smiled at the tanned blonde who stood before her with an armload of books.

"I'd like to sell these books back." The blonde piled the books on the wooden counter. "What can you give me for these?"

The brunette looked the books over. "Do you have a receipt or anything to show that you're a student here?"

Looking through her purse as if magically, the receipt or identification would appear, Sierra stalled. "Uh, well, no," she finally admitted. "I don't." What would she do now? Sierra needed the money badly. Although she had a job lined up in an insurance office, she wouldn't start until the following week.

The girl looked at her closely. "Were you a student here in the last year or so?"

"Yes, but I don't have any of my things with me now. I, uh, I had to drop out." Sierra looked down.

Her sad appearance softened the brunette's heart. "Well, this isn't following policy, but," the brunette pulled a yearbook from behind the counter. "What's your name?"

"Elizabeth Belillaber. I was a freshman here last year."

Flipping the pages of the black-and-white yearbook, the clerk found the freshman class pictures. On the second page of the listing of freshmen, the small, black-and-white picture of Elizabeth Belillaber was in the top row.

The brunette looked closely at the photo. The woman in the picture didn't look like the woman standing before her now.

Sierra sensed that the clerk wouldn't give her any money if she didn't speak up. "I lost weight and," she pointed to her hair, "my hair dresser suggested a change."

Convinced, the girl exclaimed, "What a change! But honestly, if you hadn't told me, I wouldn't have ever known." With that, the brunette looked through the pile of books again. "You're lucky. The professors are still using all of these books next semester."

After adding the numbers up on a scrap of paper, the brunette rang the register and took money from the drawer. "We don't give a full refund, only half back." She stuck the paper into the drawer and counted out the money to the blonde.

Grateful, Sierra put the money into her coin purse. "Thank you, miss . . . oh, what's your name?"

"Dyna. My name is Dyna."

"Well, thank you very, very much, Dyna."

As Sierra Gleason left the bookstore in December 1953, Dyna Palpietro looked at the yearbook again, then watched the blonde go. Elizabeth's makeover was impressive and would stay in Dyna's memory for a long time.

CHAPTER 4

CLASSES, STUDYING AND other activities kept Brian busy and tired Tuesday through Thursday. After studying late on Thursday, he fell into bed, exhausted. He really looked forward to getting some rest on Friday morning since he had only one class in the early afternoon.

The next morning, when the telephone rang, Brian didn't budge.

"Brian! Telephone! It's your father!"

"Cut it out Fred!"

"No really, it's your dad."

Behind the closed door, Brian rested on his bed and weighed his choices. His dad never called and Fred always played jokes. So when Fred announced his father's telephone call, Brian refused to believe it and didn't even move. It was Friday morning, well before 5 A.M. He didn't need a practical joke this early.

Knocking hard on the bedroom door, Fred sent Brian jumping to his feet. Brian stepped into the hall and picked up the telephone. Leaning against the door frame, he tried to wake up. To his surprise, it really was his father.

"Son, your ma needs to see you."

"Is she okay?"

"Nope, she's dying. She has cancer."

Leave it to Dad to be blunt, but this was almost brutal. Brian listened, now totally awake because of the news his father provided.

After hanging up the telephone, he walked the few feet to Fred's bedroom and stuck his head in. "Fred, I've got an emergency at home. Can you cover my class today? Oh, and if you see Merritt, please ask him for the book I loaned to him. Thanks."

Now free to leave, Brian hurried to pack a small overnight bag.

WITHIN FOUR HOURS after his father's call, Brian pulled onto the gravel road of the Indiana farm his family called home. He parked his car on the small concrete slab near the carport. In the background, he could hear the sound of a tractor; his father was nearby. But Brian hadn't come to see him. Instead, Brian went straight to his parents' bedroom. He knew he would find his mother there.

"So your father told you. I'm really surprised to see you so soon." Over the black, half-framed glasses she wore, Eva Waterman Tanner looked up from the well-worn black leather Bible she held in her hands. With thick white pillows supporting her back and shoulders, she lay in bed. But she didn't look sick. When his mother flipped back the brightly colored quilts and white sheets, Brian stepped back, startled. She tied on her robe over the long cotton nightgown she wore, swung her feet down to the floor and slipped her feet into the pink knitted slippers at the side of her bed. His eyes widened and his mouth dropped open.

"What is the matter with you? You look like you saw a ghost!" She moved past him and went out into the hall. Brian had expected that she would be bedridden and wondered how she could move about so freely. He followed her like he did when he was a little boy, asking questions the whole time.

"Ma, I thought you were sick! Aren't you sick?"

"I'm not sick, but I am dying."

"Ma!" They went downstairs to the first floor. "Aren't you supposed to be in bed?"

"Brian, come in the kitchen and sit down. I have a lot to tell you."

Everything in the room looked the same as it did when Brian was in high school. The wooden table with the red-and-white-checkered tablecloth, the six dark-brown wooden chairs, and the glass jars on the counter filled with flour, sugar and salt; nothing had changed. The black-and-white metal clock on the wall still ticked noisily. Even the cookie jar on the counter was still there, a gray poodle with an oversized red bow, no doubt filled with big, soft, pale-yellow sugar cookies.

As he sat, Brian noticed it sitting in the corner. She had brought down the little pine rocking chair from the attic. It was his when he was a little boy. As they sat at the table, Brian pulled one of the white cloth napkins from the wicker basket on the table and began twisting it nervously. He never imagined he could have this kind of conversation with his mother. Her frankness surprised him and left him speechless. Good thing, because the details of her illness left him stunned, almost unable to ask the right questions.

"Yes, I have cancer, cancer of the bladder. Yes, it's incurable," she said nonchalantly. "I've been told I have less than a year to live. You know what I think of doctors, Brian. So I got more than one opinion."

She looked at him straight in the eyes, her voice now trembling. "I've considered my medical treatment choices. I'm fully aware of what I'm doing or not doing and the outcome. No matter what, I'm going to die." Eva looked away; she didn't want to see her baby cry.

Abruptly, she stood up. Walking to the little rocking chair, she stroked it, savoring fond memories. She changed the topic, turning slowly to face him. "Brian, whenever you've called or come home, you've told me all about your schooling. But when are you getting married?"

He dried his face with the napkin and dropped it limply from his hand. "Ma, I still have two more years of school and my residency to go yet. I'm going to summer school now just to get ahead on my classes. You know, I haven't even thought about getting married. What woman would put up with all the studying I have to do, let alone the long hours away while I'm working on my residency? Besides Ma, I have loans now, and I know I'll need even more loans before I finish."

"Brian, you don't have loans. Your father and I took out those loans, remember? Those loans for your education are in our names and not yours."

"I know. I meant I have to pay you back."

"You won't have any loans when I'm through. I'm going to sell the store."

Even more startled by her pronouncement, Brian picked up and started twisting the napkin again. The store was one of the most important things in her whole life. And he, too, had spent much of his childhood at the Waterman's Grocery Store.

CINNAMON, PEPPERMINT AND baked goods scents filled the air in Waterman's Grocery. Children ran in across the creaky tongue-and-groove boards of the old wooden floor. Clutching pennies and nickels in their little hands, they bought candy and sweets from the thick, glass display cases and the big round jars on the countertops. The glass jars' lids clinked against the jars as Brian's mother, Eva, or one of her brothers pulled out sweet treats to sell to their eager young patrons. Adults bought fresh fruits and vegetables for sale from the Tanner farm. Waterman's also sold bleach and bluing, lye soap, mops, galvanized pans, cloth on bolts, hand-made brooms and flour in colorful or white fifty-pound cotton bags that could be turned into children's clothing or durable dish rags.

Most of the customers also bought cookies and soft, white, light bread; Grandpa Waterman and later, his only daughter, Eva, baked these. Rich, creamy, hand-dipped ice cream in flavors of chocolate, vanilla and real strawberry sat in big tubs in the freezer chest. Big dill pickles for crunchy, sour refreshment were always available from a huge jar on the counter. The store was busiest on Saturdays, when the farmers and their families came into town.

Customers wolfed down the big, soft cookies and ate thick baloney on light bread while they were in the store, often swigging down cold soda pop at the same time. The store had been in the Waterman family for three generations. It was a symbol of their family's wealth and allowed them a level of influence in their small community. Over the objections of his three sons, Grandpa Waterman gave the store to Eva more than twenty years ago, just before he died.

NOW HER DECISION to sell the store surely would reopen this old, bitter wound between Eva and her brothers. The seriousness of her decision let Brian know she was immovable in pursuing her goal.

"Ma!" He didn't know what else to say, she was staring hard at him.

Leaning on her knuckles over the table, she didn't listen to him. "Which girl are you serious about, Brian?" Her voice was almost pleading now. "I know you've mentioned a few in the last year or two. Are you serious about any of them now?" She leaned back, pulling her hands from the table. Shrugging her shoulders, she turned slightly and added, "You've never brought any girls home to meet us."

"Ma!"

"Brian, I don't want to die without a grandchild. You know that's all I've wanted from you since you finished high school. I'm already very proud of you and all of your accomplishments, Brian. But I really need this from you, please. You're my only child. I've been praying about this since I found out about the cancer. I just want to hold my grandchild before I die." She slid into the chair next to him, still staring intently.

A deep, heavy silence fell between them. Brian squirmed, uneasy about his mother's request. After sitting for several minutes, Brian rose and walked over to the kitchen door. Looking out one of the small glass windowpanes at the thriving green patch garden behind the house, Brian knew what he had to do. This talk with his mother gave him another reason for making a commitment to just one woman. He walked back to the table and then took her hands into his own.

"Yeah, Ma, I think I know which girl I want to marry. Just let me find out if she wants to marry me."

She reached up and touched his cheek with her right hand. Her hand was soft and warm, just like he remembered. "That's all I ask, Brian, just try. I've had my say. Now go and call your father in for lunch. I didn't want him to be here for this."

CHAPTER 5

OPENING HER SLEEPY eyes late on a Saturday morning in mid-April of 1954, she rolled onto her left side on her bed and realized she was not alone. At first, she didn't know whether to scream or to run, but the sudden throb of a massive headache behind her eyes stopped her from doing either.

With dark, curly hair and a slight tan, he was good looking. He spoke first. Good thing, because she had no idea who he was. "You're awake?"

"Mmmh huh," she mumbled. A hangover, she decided. She must have had way too much to drink the night before and this headache and this stranger were the price of her indiscretion.

He confirmed her fears. "Honey, you were really great last night," he said, smiling slyly.

"Thanks, you were great too." Liar, she thought to herself. You don't even remember his name, let alone any part of last night. She propped herself up on one elbow, hoping he would continue talking and somehow she would remember his name.

As he talked, she faked a smile, desperately trying to remember what happened. She looked him over, hoping to remember something. With a hairy chest and strong, muscular arms, everything above the pale blue satin comforter looked pretty good.

"When you looked across the room at me, it seemed like we were the only people at Fat Franky's. You were talking to those girls," he continued talking. As he went on, she picked up a few more clues about their evening together. But she got no hints about his name.

"By the way, when you were asleep, I noticed your tattoo. I've only seen one like that before. But it was on a stripper in Enid." He laughed cruelly, "Boy, she was huge!"

Panicking, she wondered what to do. Did he know that she was that stripper? What could she say?

The telephone on the nightstand behind her rang. Relieved for the distraction, she turned and grabbed it on the second ring.

"Hi! It's me!" The giggling voice on the other end of the line was familiar.

"Oh, hello, Ellen."

"You know that guy you were talking to last night? Wow! Was he good looking!"

"Yeah."

"You and Tony really seemed to like each other."

"Mmmh." Tony? Thanks, Ellen, for the hint, she thought to herself.

"What did you two do after you left? Did you guys go out for a bite or something? Wait—someone's at the door—I gotta go. Bye!"

With the click of the telephone in her ear as Ellen hung up, she suddenly remembered. She'd gone out the night before with Cindy, Mara and Ellen from work. At first, she didn't want to go. Several times during that week, she had refused their invitations, but they persisted. She was dating Brian Tanner, the man she planned to snare. But after a few days of pressure from the three women, eventually she gave in.

Hazy smoke and heavy perfume filled the air in Fat Franky's Bar. With black walls, black ceiling and black floors, the place was dark like a pit. Light from behind the bar, the entrance and the bathroom areas provided the only real illumination. At the tables and in the booths, the flickering flames from wicks in red, globe-shaped candles provided light for those who want to see or to be seen.

He stood at the lighted entrance, as if looking for someone. She stood at the bar, looking over the crowd. She met his stare across the room. Almost instantly, he was there standing at the bar beside her and introducing himself. His tone and style were smooth, almost too smooth. Tony, he said his name was Tony, and he was in Indiana for a day on a work assignment.

Sierra remembered drinking, but she wasn't drunk, and she knew she didn't have enough liquor to get drunk. Bits and pieces of last night's dark puzzle started falling into place in her still groggy head, but not all of the right pieces. Now, she was convinced that going to the bar had been a bad idea.

"Are you okay?" Tony asked.

Tony's comment suddenly snapped her back to reality. This guy was still here, right in the middle of her bedroom, and she wanted to get rid of him. Now. Right away.

"Uh, yeah, I was just thinking about work," she lied, still looking at the wall beyond the telephone.

As she hung up the telephone, she turned back to look at him. He had dressed and stood looking through the silvery white sheers in her front bedroom window. An expensive, imported navy linen suit, a white silk shirt, his gold cuff links now secured in place, his clothing suggested that he might not be a poor man. An awkward interval of silence passed slowly as she tried to figure out how to get him to leave.

He turned and spoke first. "I'll call you." But he didn't ask for her telephone number as he headed toward the door of her bedroom.

"Okay," she answered softly, rising to escort him out. She dressed quickly in her black silk robe, covering the thin, silk, black teddy and tying the robe's thin belt as tightly as she could. At the front door of her apartment, he pulled her close, kissed her passionately while running his fingers through her hair, mumbled something again about calling her and finally left.

As she turned the lock on the door and put the chain into place, she thought about the irony of her actions in locking the door. She leaned against the door and tried to figure out what to do next. Swiftly, with tears streaming down from her eyes, she headed down the hallway directly to the closet across from her bedroom. She took out two pale-pink towels, one for her hair and one to dry off with, stepped into the bathroom and shut the door. Behind the glass door of the shower, Sierra Gleason could not scrub herself enough. Being with Tony made her feel dirty and reminded her of the past she had left. Sierra lathered once, twice, three times, following each time with nearly scalding hot water. Strangely enough, she couldn't feel the pulsing water. She could feel only her own tears rolling down her cheeks.

What have I done? Sierra thought to herself. Did I really spend the night with Tony? He looked so good, but not that good! I just met him and there is just no way I could have asked him to spend the night. Did I give him my number? What else did I say to him? Sierra wondered to herself. He must have slipped a drug into my drink to loosen me up. Should I press charges against him? No, it would be my word against his, no one was here except us who could say what happened. What should I do? What . . . what if Brian finds out? I . . . I . . . I can't lose him. I want him so much. I just know I can get him to marry me, but not if he finds out about this! What am I going to do?

OUTSIDE, IN HIS car, Tony Agriniello opened the glove box of his car and pulled out his black book. He flipped through the well-worn pages until he got to the "G" section. There, he copied Sierra's name, address and telephone number from the back of a business card. He had gotten details about her last night, not long after he had doctored her drink. If she figured out that he had added something to his drink, she didn't seem to mind it. After thinking about Sierra Gleason for a few more moments, Tony entered four small stars behind her name. Done with her for now, he slid the book back into the glove box. The next time he was in the area, he would look her up. That is, unless he ran across someone more appealing.

IN THE APARTMENT next door, Merritt paced angrily. Although Sierra would barely speak to him, last night, she had brought another man home to her apartment, someone whom Merritt had never seen before. This morning, the man was finally leaving.

Upon hearing the two as they came in late the night before, Merritt rushed to his secret place at the hallway vent in his apartment and turned off the light. Slowly, he took the panel off and peered into her hallway.

Sierra staggered down the hallway of her apartment, partly on her own but mainly with the man's help. She sounded giddy, probably drunk, and she laughed more than Merritt had ever heard her laugh before. The man helped Sierra into her bedroom and he closed the door behind them.

Merritt could hear laughter, then muffled voices, then after a while, nothing at all. Angry, Merritt replaced the panel and went outside into the hallway of the building. He listened for a few minutes beside her door, but couldn't hear anything there either. He looked at the fire alarm in the hall. If he pulled the alarm, he could drive the interloper off. Just as he got the nerve to go to the box, someone opened the door to the apartment across the hall from the box. Startled, Merritt decided to abandon his plan and headed back to his apartment. In the months that she had been his neighbor, Merritt knew that Sierra had never brought a man to her apartment, didn't leave very often in the evening and had never spent the night away. Was this an old flame and the reason why she had been unreceptive to him? Merritt wondered. He checked the peephole again. Seeing and hearing nothing, Merritt decided to check in the morning.

Arising a little after six, Merritt removed the panel, but heard nothing. Several times in the following hours, he looked in and listened, but no one was stirring in Sierra's apartment. At ten, he put the panel back in place.

Around eleven, with the morning light flooding Sierra's

apartment, Merritt looked through the peephole just in time to see the man kiss Sierra as he left her apartment. A few moments later, Sierra came down the hallway, her face wet with tears. She disappeared into the bathroom.

Merritt knew that the man had spent the night with Sierra, and he could plainly see that she was crying. But he couldn't ask her about the reason for her tears without revealing that he had been spying on her.

THE NEXT WEEK at work was hard. Sierra lied to Cindy, Mara and Ellen about what had happened. It was easier than facing the truth. She stuck to simple lies, like Tony had dropped her off at her apartment and that he wasn't a very good kisser. She didn't really expect to see him again, she added and besides, nothing had happened. Each time she told her story, it sounded more convincing.

In the weeks following her evening with Tony, he didn't call and she was quite glad he didn't. But by May 1, 1954, she learned she couldn't forget him quite so easily.

CHAPTER 6

BRIAN'S FATHER, ROBERT J. TANNER, or R.J., as he preferred to be called, lived on a farm all his life. Through shrewd purchases, hard labor and some luck, R.J. had expanded his ten acres of clay soil into a large, thriving produce and meat supplier for the local groceries. Over the last thirty years, R.J. poured his energy and vision into developing Sunset Farms into a place where he could provide for his family and where he and Eva could retire.

On the morning after Brian came home in June 1954, as usual, R.J. rose well before sunrise, ate a light breakfast, downed half a pot of coffee and was already outside by 6 A.M. With two thousand acres and more than one hundred head of beef, R.J. didn't have the luxury of sleeping in late. He knew very well how to run a farm. But R.J. didn't know how to help Eva, even though the love of his life was dying. All he could do was keep up the routine of running the farm and pray.

A LITTLE AFTER 8 A.M., Brian stood on the back porch of the farmhouse, listening for the sound of his father's tractor. Brian could hear the cows mooing and the calves bleating as they played.

If he waited long enough, Brian would hear old Valentino, the prize bull his father had bought years ago to service the cows. Old Valentino would snort and bellow when the scent of the cows reached him or if some person were too close to his pen.

From the sound of the tractor, Brian figured that his father was in the back field and headed in that direction. Brian's mother kept a few laying hens and a rooster out in a pen near the barn. As Brian walked past their enclosure, the black, white, gray and specked birds clucked and clattered noisily. They wanted food and he looked like a possible source for some feed. But Brian walked right past the clucking crew of creatures to the open fields behind the barn.

Although Sunset Farms had a small work crew, Brian imagined R.J. would hire additional help by this time. But R.J. still rode the big red tractor, as he always did.

His father guided the rig down the long, brown dirt rows, coming toward him, raising clouds of fine brown dust into the sunny blue sky with each turn of the oversized tractor wheels. The noise of the old tractor and the dust it stirred up increased as R.J. crawled closer and closer. By the time R.J. got within a few yards, Brian didn't even notice the noise of the tractor anymore. He could see tears sliding down his father's tanned, wind-blown cheeks, washing away the thin layer of brown dust. Embarrassed, Brian looked away with newfound interest at the dirt, at the equipment, at anything nearby. He'd never seen his father cry before. Inside, Brian felt an uncomfortable weakness as he realized the two pillars in his life were crumbling.

The rest of the weekend went quickly at the Tanner farm. Brian helped, just as he had done while growing up there. On Sunday, they went to church and sat in the same pew, just as they had done for years. And no one talked about the cloud hanging over them all, that Eva was dying.

As the congregation sang another song, Brian questioned why the god they trusted so much could let his mother die. And he didn't understand why his parents held onto their beliefs even more tightly in the face of her impending death.

His parents' religious beliefs meant little to Brian. As soon as he left for college, he stopped going to church and praying. He had believed that only man could control man's destiny. Now, faced with his mother's terminal illness, Brian struggled with his powerlessness.

After Sunday dinner, when he was sure his parents were resting in their bedroom, Brian mustered up enough courage to take action. Picking up the telephone in the kitchen, he eased into one of the brown wooden chairs and made a call back to Briggandale. Sitting in the golden glow of the late afternoon summer sun, he warmed up to the thought of marriage and of presenting his mother with a grandchild.

On the second ring, she answered. "Hello?"

"Hello baby."

"Brian, I missed you! Why haven't you called?"

He pushed his old, pale-yellow pine rocking chair back and forth with the big toe of his right foot. The tiny chair rocked and creaked, cutting in and out of the golden sunbeam that highlighted it in the corner.

"I've been a little busy. I'm at my parents' place now. Can I see you when I get back?"

"Sure."

"Great, I'll meet you at your apartment. I'll call before I come over."

"See you. I love you."

"I love you too. Bye."

He had decided upon the girl to marry. He felt pretty confident of his decision right then. Staring at the tiny chair, Brian could almost see a little boy just like him sitting in this family heirloom. Grandpa Tanner made the chair for R.J., who in turn, passed it down to him. Now it would be his turn to put a child in that chair.

CHAPTER 7

THE FOLLOWING DAY, June 7, Brian got through his classes and finished his assigned reading early. With the pressure of making a life-changing decision, Brian really couldn't concentrate anyway. Between his call on Sunday evening and going to class on Monday morning, Brian had changed his mind several times about which girl he would ask to marry him. During the afternoon, he called both women and set up dates to meet with each. It was only three now and he would meet with the first girl at seven.

Brian lay on top of the covers of his bed with his arms over his head. As the sun started its slow descent, Brian watched the shadows growing longer and longer on the light pine floor. Over and over, he imagined what he would say and how she would react. He needed plenty of time to think about what he would say to her, the girl he would meet with that evening. With the hard decision he had to make, he was sure she wouldn't make it any easier. Finally, his alarm rang. It was six thirty and almost time to tell her about his mother and about his decision.

Just before 7 P.M., Brian stood outside her door. He stared at the scratches on the brass number on the five-paneled door. When she opened the door and let him inside, she kissed him passionately, drawing her body tightly to his. Instinctively, he responded to her, yielding to the hot flashes of desire. But quickly, Brian pushed her away gently and motioned toward the couch. She walked in front of him then sat beside him, cheerful and bubbly.

I wonder what she'll say? Talking to her about this isn't going to be easy, he thought to himself. As he sat nervously, trying to compose himself, Brian smelled some kind of meat, probably meat loaf. Had she fixed dinner for him? She wasn't going to let him off easily. Noticing his glum face, she asked sweetly, "Brian, you look so serious, so sad. What's the matter?"

He picked up a cream-colored throw pillow from the sofa and pulled at the silk fringe and started slowly. "I just found out that my mother has cancer—it's incurable."

When she learned about his mother's condition, her smile disappeared. Without saying another word, Sierra put her arms around him, leaned back and gently pushed his head onto her shoulder. She waited for a few minutes until she could feel him relaxing in her arms. Only then did she whisper, "Brian, I know you have a lot on your mind and this may be a really bad time, but I have something to tell you too—I'm pregnant."

Startled, he lifted his head and looked at her. His reaction frightened her. His face showed no joy, no anger, no surprise and no expression. But his face was not the face of a man who was anxious to make a commitment to marriage, at least not to her. They sat in silence, with Brian staring straight through her.

Does he know this baby isn't his? Sierra wondered anxiously. Why doesn't he say something? "Brian?"

He stumbled, "I . . . I don't know what to say. Just let me think about it for a minute or two." He waited, as if he were letting the news sink in.

The silence was awkward. Her tears began to flow and she broke the silence with small sobs. Brian looked down at the fringed pillow.

"Sierra, I really need some time to think about this. Don't do anything. Promise me please. I'll call you." Suddenly, he stood up and dropped the pillow on the couch.

Was Brian leaving for good? Was he going to disappear, like Tony had? Panic-stricken, Sierra wasn't going to take a chance on his leaving. She had done all she could to entice him and she wasn't going to let this prize get away. He was her best shot at some kind of life, and being the wife of a doctor wouldn't be bad at all.

She moaned loudly and bent over, clutching her stomach as if in pain, and from the sofa, she crumbled to the floor. Brian instinctively dropped to the floor beside her. Holding her in his arms, he brushed her hair back from her face and cuddled her. Sierra rested in his arms, eyes closed and sobbing quietly. All the while, she wondered if her act was working.

That night, in his bed, Brian just couldn't sleep. Could he marry Sierra? In the darkness, he looked up at the ceiling, remembering how he had gotten started with this woman in the first place.

HE SPOTTED SIERRA GLEASON in March, at a coffee house near the university. There, with a couple of girls from the insurance office where she worked, Sierra caught his attention immediately. Brian was there with a couple of his friends. One of them, Merritt Hughes, introduced her to Brian after privately describing her as being fun, but a bit loose.

Over the next month, Brian spent more time with her and found she was smarter than most girls he knew. Her memory was almost as good as his and she was very ambitious. She said she was going to go to college to take accounting and other business courses. Now growing close, he learned she had lovers before him, but none for quite a while. In mid-May, he spent his first night with her.

IN LATE MAY, while seated near the front window of the coffee house, Merritt Hughes and Ricky Croft watched as Brian and Sierra walked past outside, holding hands. As Brian kissed her, she giggled. They were oblivious to their audience.

Merritt stood up, jiggling the table and their two cups of coffee in the process.

"Watch it man! This coffee's hot!" Ricky snapped, concerned about being burned by the steaming liquid.

"Can you believe that? I introduced Brian to her and now Sierra's going out with him. The girl of my dreams is going out with him!"

"You just missed out, man. Just forget it," Ricky commented. He blew on, then took a sip of his coffee. "How did you ever meet her?"

"She lives in my building. She moved into an apartment on my floor in January, no, in December last year. I've seen her and gotten to know her a little, but otherwise, she won't give me the time of day. I tried to discourage Brian from asking about her, but he didn't take a hint."

"What did you say?"

"Well, I told Brian that she was loose—that she would use him like she did all those other guys she'd been with."

"Is that true? I mean, have you seen her with a lot of other men?"

"No, I just made that up. I just didn't want Brian to get to her before I did."

"Forget her man, just forget her. She wasn't intended for you," Ricky said.

"I'd like to know why not?" Merritt retorted.

"Where should I start, Merritt?" Ricky said, laughing now, "Those home movies of yours and those pin ups in your apartment would scare any decent woman off. But there are plenty of other women out there who would settle for you."

"Very funny."

"Kick some of your bad habits, Merritt, and the right woman for you might just come along."

"Yeah, and some rich guy like Brian will be there to snatch her away. This is so unfair!"

"Forget Sierra Gleason, just forget her. She wasn't meant for you," Ricky said. "In the meantime, while you wait for Miss Perfect to come into your life, you'll just have to settle for someone normal or one of your home movie girls, like Boom-Boom Betty."

They laughed, but quickly, Merritt grew serious.

"We'll see, Ricky. Maybe Sierra Gleason isn't meant for Brian Tanner either."

ALTHOUGH MERRITT TOLD Ricky about meeting Sierra Gleason, Merritt didn't tell him everything. Since she had moved into the apartment next door to his own, Merritt had studied her carefully. He knew when she left for work and when she came home. As she walked past his door to go to the elevator or to the stairs, Merritt would open his door slightly so that he could see her walk by. When he was sure that she was leaving the building, he would watch her from the window at the end of the hallway on their floor of the apartment building. From where she worked to where she bought her groceries, Merritt Hughes knew her routine, some of her habits, and even the way she walked.

Some of the things that he knew about her Merritt could know only from watching her through his hidden peephole.

Now that Brian Tanner was in the picture, Merritt made up his mind to find out even more about her. He wouldn't give up his dream girl that easily.

ON JUNE 7, AFTER watching Brian Tanner leave her apartment, Merritt still could hear Sierra crying. But those tears might be good news for him, Merritt decided. With Brian out of the way, Merritt figured that finally, he would have a chance with Sierra.

NOW FACED WITH his mother's request, Brian struggled with the idea of marrying Sierra. Remembering Merritt's comment about Sierra and his own experience with her, Brian knew his mother would never approve of Sierra if she knew every detail about her. But with Sierra, Ma would have the grandchild that she so desperately wanted. A baby already coming—who would have ever thought that it would work out so fast? Besides, being married to Sierra wouldn't be half bad. She did have some qualities he really did enjoy.

The darkness lightened eventually and rosy hues from the rising sun broke through the inky darkness. The room grew lighter and lighter.

By 7 A.M. on Tuesday morning, when his alarm went off, Brian was still awake from the night before. Sierra wasn't the one that he had planned to marry at first, but by seven that evening, when he would meet with Dyna, he would have to know for sure.

CHAPTER 8

THAT EVENING, BRIAN stood outside the door to her apartment. After he entered and closed the door, Dyna kissed him shyly, sweetly. He kissed her back stiffly, but held her tightly in his arms for a long time, occasionally stroking her dark hair.

"Brian, please sit down. No one else is at home yet and I'm fixing dinner. I have to go and check on it." She walked through the living room and dining room, disappearing through the swinging door of the kitchen to turn the pot down to a low simmer.

Brian stood looking at the pictures on the walls. Most were of Dyna, her brother, Raphael, and sister, Sally. A few others included Anna Palpietro, their mother. Their father, Joe Palpietro, appeared in only two pictures in the whole room. In both, he wore a frown.

Brian met Dyna's father only three times while he'd been dating Dyna. Brian sensed Dyna's father could be quite disagreeable. He'd noticed Joe's strong, muscular arms and club-like hands, no doubt developed from his work as a stone mason. And Brian knew he never wanted to cross Joe Palpietro.

When Dyna returned to the living room, she sat next to him on the threadbare, brown tweed sofa. In the air, he could smell onions and some kind of sauce. He looked down at his hands as he touched his fingertips to hers slowly.

"Dyna, I've had a lot on my mind lately and I don't know where to start. Sometimes, things don't work out the way we plan . . . ." He stopped speaking, fumbling for the right words.

"Uh, Brian, what is it that you are trying to say?"

"I, uh, Dyna, it's my mother, she has cancer. She's dying. I just found out."

"Brian, I'm so, so sorry." Her eyes filled with tears as she took his right hand. Studying his face carefully, she sensed his mother's illness wasn't the only bad news he was bringing to her.

He continued, easing his hand from hers, "I'm sorry, Dyna, but I can't see you anymore."

She stood up suddenly and turned away from him when he told her it was over between them. Now, he watched her intently. Was she crying? Brian couldn't tell. Unsure of what else to say, he repeated his words. "I can't see you anymore."

She didn't say anything. She had walked to the end of the sofa by then and stood with her back to him to avoid eye contact.

"Dyna, I'm . . . I'm going to marry someone else."

Only then did Dyna speak. Composing herself, she turned to face him, her arms now crossed. "So this is what you wanted to tell me—this was the important thing you wanted to talk to me about."

Her calm, quiet response surprised him. He expected her to scream or cry or something. Brian almost wished she had. He believed he could handle the hysterics better than the painful quiet she had shown. Her actions were unexpected—he thought he knew Dyna better.

Brian stood and then reached out for her. He moved next to her and tried to take her hand, but she snatched it away. They stood less than a foot apart, yet for Brian, the distance was immense.

"Maybe you should go now," Dyna spoke quietly but firmly.

"Dyna!"

"Don't make this harder than it already is, Brian."

"But Dyna, I . . ."

She interrupted, "Brian, all this time you made me think I was the only one. I thought you wanted to marry me. How could you?"

Her reaction surprised him. He thought she would at least beg him to stay with her, or she would respond with hysterics. But she hadn't. Had he made a mistake? Was he throwing away true love for the chance to get a baby right away for his dying mother? He panicked. "But Dyna, I love you. I really, really love you." Did she really love him? He couldn't tell based upon the look on her face or by the sound of her voice.

"Brian, please go." She walked with him stiffly to the door to let him out. He stammered and looked puzzled, but finally he left.

As she locked the apartment door, she felt her knees and then her dignity give way. She crumpled into a small pile on the floor next to the door, sobbing harsh breaths of air without tears. Dyna stayed on the floor for almost an hour until her mother came home from shopping.

CHAPTER 9

OUTSIDE IN THE hall leading to their apartment, loaded with bags of groceries, Anna Palpietro could smell burnt tomato sauce. Panicking, she struggled with her key, afraid of what she would find inside. When she finally got the door opened, she called out, "Dyna! Dyna!"

But still in shock, Dyna couldn't answer.

Grocery bags and all, Anna rushed straight back to the kitchen, right past Dyna, who was still next to the door. After putting the burning saucepan in the sink and running water into it, Anna decided to check the apartment for her family. As Anna left the kitchen, she called out again, "Dyna! Where are you, girl? This place could have burned down! Dyna!"

Only when she walked back through the swinging doors from the kitchen back into the dining room and living room did Anna see her daughter. From a single glance, Anna knew that Dyna was in big trouble, something so serious that her otherwise mature daughter couldn't handle it.

After her mother helped her to the brown tweed sofa, Dyna told her everything—including the news she was pregnant with Brian's child.

"But Ma, I didn't tell Brian I was pregnant. I wanted him to marry me because he wants me, not because he feels he has to." Dyna's tears flowed faster then and her voice began to falter. "Besides, he . . . he wants to marry someone else!"

Her mother, Anna, grabbed her and pulled her close, holding her tightly. After a few minutes of heartbreaking crying, Dyna went on. "I don't want anyone to know he's the father of my child. Ever. Swear to me, Mama, swear you'll never tell a soul he's the one. Swear!"

"Dyna, I won't tell anyone. I promise." With Dyna crying in front of her, Anna Palpietro knew what she must do. She knew her husband would beat Dyna, or even worse. Anna feared greatly for her daughter's safety. Thinking about the danger made Anna clutch Dyna tighter, as if to protect her from Joe's fists.

Sensing her mother's anxiety, Dyna looked up at her and became intensely afraid as she thought about her father's reaction.

"Mama, you won't tell Papa, will you? At least, not right away. Please don't tell Papa! Please Mama! Please!" Dyna sobbed.

Readily, her mother agreed.

But both women knew Dyna's secret couldn't be hidden forever.

As she held Dyna in her arms, Anna thought back over her twenty years of marriage to Joe. She already knew that he would react violently. The only thing she was unsure of was how bad it would be.

CHAPTER 10

"MAMA, PLEASE! CAN I wait? I'm so afraid!"

Twenty years earlier, on the day before her wedding, Anna Sarcesi stood crying in her mother's bedroom in Bellina, New Jersey. Kneeling before her, with a thin needle moving quickly through the white material, her mother, Maria Sarcesi, still had plenty of stitches left to finish the hem of the wedding gown. Any thought of postponing the wedding wouldn't be tolerated, not at this late date.

"Don't be silly girl! Don't you realize what your uncle and I had to do for this? Getting married isn't cheap. And we've already paid for almost everything!"

"But Mama, I've only seen him a few times and I've never been alone with him."

"That's right, that's exactly how it should be."

"But Mama, I don't know anything about him! How will I know what to do when we get married, you know, running a household?"

"You'll manage. Now stand still."

"How will I know what he likes or doesn't like?"

Maria didn't look up. "You'll find out. Now stop moving or I'll stick you with this needle."

"Please, Mama! I'm so afraid. I don't know what my life will be with him. Please, please, can we postpone the wedding?"

Maria sat back on her heels with the needle in her hand and stared at her daughter. "Anna, you've got to trust us. Your Uncle Ed and I know Joseph's parents. We've made the right decision for the two of you. Be a little more understanding please!"

"But Mama," Anna sobbed, "I don't love him. I barely know him."

"Trust me. After you're married, you'll learn to love Joseph. No more talking about this. Joseph's got a good job and he brings his money home." Maria leaned forward and picked up the hem of the dress. "How bad can it be? And besides, what's love got to do with it anyway?"

The next day, on their wedding night, while in a drunken rage, Joe punched Anna in her right eye.

Anna tried to hide the black eye with powder. The following Saturday morning, when her sister, Alicia, came to visit her to see the new apartment and the new sofa Anna and Joe had just gotten, Anna also tried to cover her injury with lies. "I fell, I just fell."

She repeated the lie again when her sister kept looking at her. But Alicia wasn't fooled. She cut her visit short.

About an hour later, Anna could hear the familiar grinding noises of her uncle's old car. Hearing someone knocking, she opened the door. Her uncle, Ed Sarcesi, and her cousin, Vinnie, stood in the hall, looked at her, then at each other, then at her again. To her bewilderment, they wouldn't come into the apartment when she asked. Uncle Ed spoke, "Hello, Anna, where's Joseph?"

Sitting on the brown tweed sofa in the living room, Joe got up and came to the door when he heard his name.

"Joseph, we have something to discuss with you. You need to come outside into the hall."

The door shut behind Joe as he stepped into the corridor.

Through the thin door, Anna could hear them asking Joe not so politely to take a ride with them. She couldn't hear much else, so she tried to open the door. But someone was holding the door from the outside. She stepped back from the door, unsure of what to do next.

In the hallway, Joe trembled. "Uncle Ed, Vinnie, I would go with you at any other time, but I cannot go today."

"Oh?" Uncle Ed.

Joe laughed nervously. "I have a chimney to work on. The repair has to be done today. I was just getting ready to go now. Maybe later, I can go with you, maybe tomorrow." He stalled, hoping they would leave him alone.

But they didn't answer. The looks on their faces let Joe Palpietro know he was going with them whether he wanted to or not. Joe opened the door just wide enough to reach in and grabbed his jacket from the iron hook beside the door. He closed the door.

Puzzled, Anna decided to check the window. As she watched from their apartment window, the men emerged from the front door of the building. Uncle Ed and Vinnie walked quickly to the car with Joe in the middle. Joe turned his head and looked up at their apartment window. Anna thought Joe looked afraid, but she wasn't sure.

Four hours later, while sitting on the sofa mending one of Joe's shirts, Anna again heard the sound of her uncle's car on the street below. Joe let himself into the apartment very quietly. He didn't speak to or even look at her, but walked right past her and went into the bathroom. Her head down, she greeted him, but he didn't answer. Somehow, Anna knew it was best to stay quiet and well out of his way.

Around nine, she arose from the sofa and went to bed. She left the light on his side of the room.

Several hours later, Joe entered the bedroom where Anna pretended to be asleep. He sat on his side of the bed, at the foot. As he pulled off his shoes and socks, he moved slowly, groaning faintly as he reached for his feet. Anna barely opened her eyelids and turned her head slightly so he wouldn't catch her watching him. Joe stood with his back to her. He pulled off his jacket, then his tattered shirt slowly, and painfully sucked in air the whole time. Even in the poor light, she could see red welt marks from a belt or strap, too many to count, crisscrossing his back. As he dropped his shirt, her eyes opened wider in horror. She quickly closed her eyes as he walked to the head of the bed to turn out the light.

Hours passed as both pretended to be asleep. Anna was gripped with fear. Joe was gripped by pain.

In the years after being beaten, Joe rarely drank. They had two babies, Dyna and Sally, while they lived in Bellina. Joe and Anna Palpietro argued and fought as married couples sometimes do, but they never came to blows.

In time, their physical injuries healed. But for Joe, one wound never did. Anna's sister, Alicia Sarcesi, was no longer welcome in his home. Starting with that weekend, Joe conveniently wouldn't tell Anna when her sister called or stopped by. He intercepted as many cards and letters as he could that looked like they had come from Alicia. If they were from her, he destroyed them. But he hadn't stopped the two women from talking on the telephone.

Next, Joe told Anna lies about her sister to try to break the two sisters apart. It took him years to do it and he chiseled away at their relationship like he chiseled away at the stone that he worked with on his job. But eventually, Joseph's plan to separate the sisters worked.

OCTOBER 1935

AS SHE POURED another cup of coffee for her cousin Vinnie, Alicia sniffed and sighed. Her children were in school, Alicia was lonely and had been crying before he arrived. She really needed someone to talk to. Her cousin Vinnie came unexpectedly, but just at the right time.

"You know Vinnie, I miss her. I really miss talking to Anna." She wiped the tears off her face.

He put two teaspoons of sugar into the coffee cup, stirred and then added two more teaspoons. "When did you last speak to her?" His thick, dark-haired hands contrasted sharply with the delicate white porcelain cup.

"It's been three months already. We used to talk every day, but now, nothing!"

"Why did she stop talking to you?" He took a big sip, then smiled wickedly. "Because we roughed Joe up?"

"No. It didn't seem like Anna blamed me for that. What triggered this was that she accused me of sleeping with Joe! Can you imagine that?"

"You've gotta be kidding!" He put the cup down, astonished.

Alicia put her head in her hands and sniffed. "No, I'm serious! She called me and said that Joe had told her that I had made a pass at him. Like I would ever, ever have any interest in that creep! That liar! Joe is just a bald-faced liar!"

Vinnie shook his head as he spoke, "How could Anna believe that?"

Alicia pulled the wadded white handkerchief from her pocket and wiped her eyes. "I don't know. Anna was absolutely convinced that I had been with Joe! She made it really plain that I wasn't welcome in their home anymore."

"Well, I heard that when lovers fight, they sometimes turn on the people who come to help them." He put his right hand down in front of the cup. He could hide the tiny bit of china behind his cupped hand.

She slapped her hand down on the table, now angry. "Well, what should I have done? Vinnie, she's my sister! I couldn't let that gorilla beat her up and sit by and do nothing! She's my sister—I had to do something!" Alicia burst into tears.

"You did the right thing, Alicia," he assured her. "If you had kept quiet, he would have done it again." Vinnie had never seen her cry before. He wondered whether he should put his arms around her; her crying was getting to him. He decided to wait.

Her tears slowed and then stopped. "Still, I feel really bad, Vinnie!"

"What, that we didn't rough him up enough?"

"No, only because she isn't speaking to me now. I couldn't care less about him." Alicia hesitated, trying to hold back more tears.

Anna was more than just a sister. Anna was her friend, her confidant and someone whom she had trusted intimately. And now, Anna wouldn't even talk to her.

"Vinnie, no matter what she says to me now, if Anna ever decides to talk to me or wants help from me in any way, I will never, ever turn her away."

"I'll make sure she gets the message. Joe won't try anything with me. But I can't promise that she'll talk to you again. She's starting to cut all of us off. Joe has her brainwashed."

IN THE YEARS that her sister Anna wouldn't talk to her, Alicia missed her deeply. At Christmas and on Anna's birthday each year, Alicia sent a card to her sister. Maybe Anna would change her mind in time. Some years, her cards came back unopened, but in some years, they were not returned at all.

Ostracized by Anna, Alicia grieved deeply for her sister, Anna, as if she were dead. Alicia hoped her sister would call her and that Joseph would leave them alone. She vowed that if Joe ever tried to interfere with their relationship again, she would keep in touch somehow with Anna through a neighbor or someone. Alicia felt that she could not afford to lose her sister again. It would kill her.

AFTER FIVE YEARS of marriage, Joe and Anna moved to Briggandale, Indiana, where Joe found work as a stone mason on the expansion project at the university. Seven years after arriving in Indiana, Anna gave birth to a son. They named him Joseph Raphael.

Over time, Joe and Anna developed a ritual. Every day when he came home from work, she had a cup of rich, black coffee ready for him. After he took a bath, he lay on the bed while she sat at the foot of the bed, mending his socks or other torn clothing. Each work night, he told her about his day. Joe started with who said what, who got a raise, who got fired, and so on. Anna kept her eye on his coffee cup. Joe told her what level work he was on and what he had done, even down to the tools he'd used. He rarely gave her a chance to ask questions and she never asked any. He took a sip or two more of the rich dark coffee and continued to recite the details of the day. She heard little of what he said and cared even less about what she heard. Most of the time, she was content to let him drone on. Anna learned he needed to let off pressure about his day and she was his safety valve. Besides, it wouldn't kill her to listen to him.

When he was excited or upset, he talked faster and gulped his coffee. Inevitably, they fought or he beat one or more of the children for some minor irritation they caused him. In time, Anna learned to watch his coffee cup carefully. If his coffee went too quickly, Anna stopped what she was doing and put the children to bed early. No sense in upsetting him even more, she decided.

JUNE 1954

SO WITH HER pregnant daughter in her arms, for Anna, the answers were simple. "Dyna, I agree with you, you should marry for the right reasons," Anna declared firmly, "But you're not getting an abortion and you're not putting my grandchild up for adoption. And you know you can't stay here, your father would never allow it."

Anna knew the only solution that would assure Dyna's safety was in New Jersey. While holding Dyna, Anna remembered her cousin Vinnie's message from her sister. It had been years since she last talked to Alicia, but Anna hoped that her sister would still keep her word. "I'll call my sister, Alicia. She'll help us. I'll send you to live with Alicia in Bellina."

Anna sensed that her daughter was extremely vulnerable and Dyna could not hold her emotions inside much longer. "In the meantime," she continued, "Here's what we'll do. Until I can arrange to send you out east, stay in your room as much as possible to avoid contact with Papa. I don't want him to suspect anything is wrong."

CHAPTER 11

ONCE THE ARRANGEMENTS were made, on the third day, Anna went to get the money to pay for Dyna's fare. She had a secret hiding place in which she had been saving for a new living room set. Suddenly, her desire for furniture didn't seem very important anymore in the face of this crisis. Anna picked up the worn chair cushion her husband, Joe, sat on every day, turned it over, unzipped it and pulled out a flattened wad of cash. She had over four hundred dollars saved. Daily, Joe sat on her stash like a goose. He didn't know he had a golden egg just beneath him.

Amazed by her mother's hiding place, Dyna just stared.

Her mother's comment was direct. "Well, your father has never helped me with the housework. What makes you think he would have ever fluffed the cushion in his chair? Besides, it's time for a new hiding place anyway."

That afternoon, Anna took Dyna to the bus station to board a bus bound for Bellina, New Jersey. At the station, she held Dyna tightly, then at arm's length. "Stop crying," Anna said as she consoled her tearful daughter. "It's not like it's across the ocean. It's only New Jersey. You're not too far away."

But neither knew how far the distance would turn out to be.

BY FRIDAY NIGHT, sometime after nine, Brian pulled up in his car in front of the Palpietro apartment. Was Dyna at home, he wondered. He just wanted five minutes alone with her. Maybe he wasn't too late.

Figuring he could get her attention, he threw one pebble and then another at her bedroom window. Brian waited in the dark, believing he could talk to her once he saw the lights go on in her bedroom.

More than an hour later, still waiting, he stared at the darkened window. Had Dyna started seeing someone else so soon? Or had she been seeing someone else all along? Brian didn't know what to think.

IN BELLINA, NEW JERSEY, Aunt Alicia met Dyna at the bus station. She stood less than five feet tall and looked like a fragile ballerina, with her hair in the small bun she wore on the top of her head. But she had the voice, the spirit and the vocabulary of a truck driver. And she didn't mince words. "Get it straight, girl," Alicia Sarcesi Carselli told her. "You gotta be ready to take care of you and yours. You can't always depend on a man, even a good one. You gotta do for you."

Dyna figured her aunt probably knew what she was talking about. Aunt Alicia had been married five times that Dyna knew about. Aunt Alicia even had two of those husbands at the same time.

"By the way, I got you a job at Hebner's Bakery and Deli, in downtown Bellina on Olin Street. It's just a short bus ride back from the deli to my apartment. The baker, Mr. Hebner, he owns the place." She chuckled. "He wants to be my sixth husband, but his wife won't let him."

Dyna started to ask her aunt about the Hebners. But with the look on her aunt's face, Dyna decided against it.

Aunt Alicia and Mr. Hebner planned her days, as if Dyna

were their own child. With them in control, Dyna didn't have
much to think about. Ride the bus, work at the deli, ride the bus,
go back to Aunt Alicia's apartment. Dyna figured her days would
be pretty much the same until the baby came.

SEVERAL TIMES DURING the weeks following their
breakup, Brian tried calling Dyna, but her mother always answered
the telephone. He hung up the telephone each time without saying
a word.

At the end of June, in a small civil ceremony in Briggandale,
Brian Tanner and Sierra Gleason were married. They agreed they
would handle it this way. The next day, they had a small party at
Brian's parents' home in Cellis.

A week after his wedding, Brian Tanner stood at yet another
pay telephone booth at the corner gas station near the university.
He dropped a coin into the slot and watched the rotary dial spin
back as he dialed each number for the Palpietro apartment. He
wanted to talk to Dyna just to hear her voice one more time. But
again, her mother answered the telephone.

"Hello?"

"Hello, Mrs. Palpietro. May I speak to Dyna please?"

"She ain't here."

He sensed her hostility, but he decided to keep trying. "This
is Brian, Brian Tanner. Do you know when she'll be back?"

"Are you stupid or just looking for trouble? Don't call here
anymore. She ain't here and she doesn't need you. Ever. Got it?"

"But . . ." he started.

"Listen, if you ever call here again or ever try to speak to my
daughter, I'll get you! Do you hear me? I'll hurt you just like you
hurt my Dyna! Do you understand? You fancy schmancy college
boy! You used my daughter then broke her heart. She ain't here
and don't you ever call here again or I'll see you regret it for the
rest of your life! Got it?" Anna Palpietro slammed the telephone
down so hard it sounded like a small explosion in Brian's ear.

From the tone of her voice, Brian knew Anna would make

good on her threat. With a heavy heart, he hung up the telephone. He didn't know Dyna was already gone.

But Brian couldn't stop thinking about Dyna. Now, her face came into his mind at different times. Even while he lay with his new wife, Sierra, he remembered Dyna.

AT TIMES AT school in Briggandale, while looking at charts or books, Brian imagined smelling Dyna's faint, sweet fragrance. He couldn't put her out of his mind. He wondered what she was doing and who she might be with.

After class on a Friday in late September, Brian sat with Fred, his former roommate, at their old apartment. The two were there in the kitchen to review for a test, but Brian had other things on his mind.

"Brian, did you look at the materials for this class? You haven't been able to answer many of the sample questions so far."

"Yes, I read them," Brian snapped. Immediately, he was sorry. Fred had a right to expect him to be prepared. "I'm really sorry Fred. I've just had a lot on my mind."

Fred was sympathetic. "Being a newlywed might have that effect." Fred chuckled.

Brian hesitated and then put his book down. He confided, "Fred, what do you think I should do? I still love Dyna."

Fred dropped his book onto the kitchen table. "Are you crazy? I think you should forget her, Brian. Look, you've got Sierra now. You made your choice and you should be happy. Stop worrying about Dyna. Besides, you've got a baby on the way. Isn't that what you wanted?"

"Still, it bothers me. Dyna didn't get upset about breaking up. And so soon after our breakup, she stayed out late with someone else. Where was she anyway? She must have been dating me just for a chance to get at the money I'll make as a doctor."

"Stop it! Don't spend one more second thinking about her, Brian. It's just not healthy. And besides, even if she did use you in any way, what can you do about it now? Nothing! Leave Dyna alone. I'm telling you as a friend."

Brian grew quiet. He knew Fred was right, but still, he struggled with his feelings about Dyna. They made it through the materials for the test and Brian left.

But Brian didn't stop thinking about her. And over time, Brian convinced himself Dyna didn't really love him. She couldn't have loved him and just let him end the relationship so easily, Brian rationalized. She was a greedy witch who just planned to use him, Brian decided. Irritated because he didn't know what she was doing and he had no control over her, Brian began imagining the worst about her. Slowly, with greater intensity than when he once loved her, Brian grew to hate Dyna.

CHAPTER 12

"**M**ISS, I'D LIKE three dozen glazed doughnuts please."
Once a week, always on Mondays in the morning,
the young guy with the bright red curly hair came into the bakery
carrying a newspaper. He sat in his usual spot on one of the red,
vinyl-topped stools at the counter and placed his usual order of
three dozen doughnuts. He was always polite, but he never
expressed any special interest in her, until today. Dyna pulled a
wax paper sheet from the dispenser and grabbed three paper bags.
He watched her closely, especially her face.

"Miss, I'd like a smile too."

Surprised, she looked up. The red-haired guy was talking to
her and it wasn't about the doughnuts.

"I've been coming in for months now and noticed you always
used to smile. But you haven't smiled during the last two or three
times I've been in. Is everything all right?"

Dyna looked about anxiously. She thought she had hidden
her feelings, especially at work. She didn't want Mr. Hebner to say
anything unusual to her, especially about any customer concerns.
He gave her this job as a favor to her aunt, to help her make ends
meet until the baby came. Mr. Hebner was proud of his shop and
always commented on how happy his work crew was. And Dyna

needed this job badly enough to let Mr. Hebner continue his fantasy. She continued putting doughnuts into the bags.

Mr. Hebner stood at the other end of the counter, talking to a long-time customer. He didn't notice this young fellow talking to Dyna.

Dyna hesitated. "I'm—I'm all right, I just have some problems. But I'm okay now." She shared this information and hoped he wouldn't ask any more questions. Dyna quickly closed the bag on the last dozen doughnuts. She slid the three bags across the counter.

"Well, if you were my wife, I would never make you sad. That man must be stupid."

Dyna smiled slightly. If this guy only knew about her heartache, he wouldn't smile either.

"Come on now, that's better. I see a little smile. By the way, my name is John, John Mitchell."

"Pleased to meet you, John. My name is Dyna Palpietro. That'll be a dollar fifty please." She finally gave him a broad smile. He seemed to be all right.

"Here you go. See you tomorrow." He left the money on the counter and jumped off the stool.

"Tomorrow?" Dyna asked as she scooped up the change. She barely had a chance to catch what he'd said before another customer stepped up to the counter.

Hours later, after serving up many more orders, Dyna left the bakery, exhausted and peculiarly nauseated. As she tried to button her oversized coat, she glanced down onto her very pregnant belly, sighed, and stopped trying.

John Mitchell came in next day, and the next.

OCTOBER 1954

IN THE KITCHEN of the farmhouse in Cellis, R.J. Tanner slid into one of the wooden chairs as he waited for his son, Brian, to pick up the telephone in Briggandale. It was five thirty in the morning and R.J. had let it ring six times already.

"Hello?" Brian answered sleepily.

"Brian, I took your ma to the hospital today; she couldn't keep her food down. I didn't know what else to do. She's doing better now and I think they'll let her come home later today."

"What did the doctor say Dad?" Brian was fully awake now. The news that his mother had been hospitalized scared him.

"It's the illness and the treatments. They told us it would be this way. So it's not unexpected. Your mother was dehydrated, but she's better now." R.J. paused and adjusted the telephone on his ear; he wasn't used to talking this much on the telephone. After waiting quietly for a few seconds, R.J. asked, "When will you know for sure about the baby?"

"I don't know, it's really too early, Dad. But I'll call you as soon as I know."

The doorbell rang so loudly at the side door of the farmhouse that Brian could hear it on his end of the telephone.

"Brian, I've got to go, one of the neighbors has stopped by to give me a hand with the herd. Goodbye, son."

"Tell Ma I love her. Bye, Dad."

As Brian slid the handset back onto the receiver, he wondered what he could do this early in the morning now that he was wide awake.

GEORGE TAPPED THE pack of cigarettes and opened it. He'd gone through eight cigarettes since sitting down with Joe Palpietro that evening at the bar in Cal's Grill. But since Joe was buying, George wasn't leaving his favorite spot at the long, glossy, brown wooden bar, not yet anyway.

"I thought you said you were out of smokes. Give me one, George." Again, Wayne bummed a cigarette from George. With free cigarettes from George and free drinks from Joe, Wayne hung around Cal's Grill that evening, even if he didn't want to hear Joe's complaining.

"Wayne, I thought I was, but I double-checked. You know the light is so bad in here." The dim light was fine, but George had given Wayne three cigarettes already and was tired of Wayne's mooching. Wayne never bought his own unless he absolutely had to. And at Cal's, he knew that his mooching would be tolerated, if for no other reason than to keep the peace.

Cal's catered to drinkers who wanted their liquor in relative peace. The men who hung out at Cal's viewed their drinking as a serious activity. Cal's wasn't a pick-up joint or a place for the socially conscious. Occasionally, a fight would break out, but at Cal's, these were very rare and not at all tolerated. Cal's never had a bouncer and never needed one. The patrons would deal with the offenders by casting the bums out on their rears.

Shortly after his daughter, Dyna, left for New Jersey, Joe started drinking with his friends at Cal's Grill. Next, he started hiding a bottle of gin in his big green armchair in the living room. He started with one or two shots in the evening. After two months, between drinking at Cal's and from his stash at home, Joe regularly finished a fifth of gin in a single night without much effort. The more he drank, the meaner he got.

At Cal's Grill, Joe, Wayne and George routinely met after work to drink and complain about their lives. Misery loves company and these three were in misery much of the time. So they drank and sat and complained.

They had picked one of the better watering holes in Briggandale. In Cal's, smoke hung like a haze in the center of the room. With no dart board, no gaming tables or a pool table, the only thing that Cal had to liven up the joint was a jukebox. Many of the tunes were specially chosen by Cal to set the atmosphere for active alcohol consumption. Guitar-twanging, toe-tapping, bass-bumping country music echoed through the bar. Cal's offered a wide selection of dirty deed-inspiring melodies, spanning the spectrum of cheating, beating, lying, stealing and otherwise dirty hearts. The music at Cal's showed that somebody was doing something and somebody was doing some wrong somewhere. These depression-inspiring little ditties helped Cal and his patrons quite a bit. For the customers, the songs renewed memories. For Cal, they increased revenues. Depressed customers drank more.

For Joe, the complaint of the day was about his wife, Anna,

and how she had sent his pregnant daughter, Dyna, away.

"Who is Dyna?" George asked. He knew perfectly well who she was, but since the evening had been boring so far, he wanted to get Joe going. Joe's lively outbursts were always something to watch.

"She's my wife's daughter."

"I thought you said she was your daughter, the unmarried pregnant one." George persisted, "I thought you told us last time that she had run out on you."

"Well. My wife and I had her, but she betrayed me. Now, she's not my daughter anymore, she's my wife's daughter." After finding out where Dyna was and why, Joe Palpietro disowned her.

"I don't have a daughter named Dyna anymore," Joe said loudly with fierce, stubborn pride as he slammed both of his big hands down on the bar countertop. Self-righteous, bitter and unforgiving, he no longer had that child who had betrayed him and ran off to his enemy, Alicia Carselli, without giving him a chance to handle the situation. Joe got quiet after that display of anger. For ten minutes, he didn't even drink his gin.

George watched Joe, figuring that he needed to push Joe a little harder. George had almost finished his beer and would need another soon. Joe usually kept the liquor flowing when he was complaining.

"Joe, you know that your girl couldn't have come up with that idea on her own. Where did she get the money to go? And how did she know that she would have a place to live or even that she would be welcome when she got there?" George knew these questions would get Joe riled.

Sitting on the bar stool between George and Joe, Wayne piped up, "He's right, you know. She couldn't have pulled that off on her own."

"You know, maybe your wife had something to do with it." George threw the last drops of the golden brew down his throat. "Uh, Joe, I could really use another. My throat's really dry tonight."

Joe called to the bartender, "We need more down here." While the bartender poured drinks, Joe decided that his friends were right. Dyna couldn't have done this on her own. She couldn't have even thought of asking Aunt Alicia for help. The last time any of them had seen Alicia was years ago. Dyna would have been under four years old when they left New Jersey.

"You guys are right. Anna had to be behind all of this," Joe agreed.

"You need to teach her a lesson Joe," George insisted.

"Yeah, teach her not to double-cross you again." Wayne added.

Gulping down his gin now, Joe decided Anna had done him wrong. She had arranged for her sister Alicia to take Dyna in. That traitor had a part in sending Dyna beyond his reach, his wrath and his punishment. He wouldn't deal with her tonight, but he would take care of her soon.

"Bartender, set up another round for me and my friends."

"Joe, please be sure to let us know how this all comes out," George said as he looked into the suds in front of him. He figured that Joe's next session at Cal's would be extremely interesting.

LATER THAT WEEK, when the telephone bill came, Joe carefully looked it over. Anna had always paid the bill and never told him when it came. But he picked up the mail from the downstairs mailbox that day. A bottle of gin gave him the nerve, and the weekly calls to Bellina, New Jersey, shown on the telephone bill gave him the excuse. For Joe Palpietro, it was time to set Anna straight about her calls to her sister, Alicia Carselli. He would show Anna who was the boss. He was in control of the household and not Anna or her sister.

Joe struggled from his armchair and staggered to the bathroom, where Anna stood, brushing her teeth. Unexpectedly, he stood in the door, blocking her way out. He gave Anna two black eyes to convince her not to call her sister or Dyna.

MR. HEBNER WAS among the first to notice that one of his longtime customers, John Mitchell, had changed his routine. Every morning now, as Hebner stacked pastries on the cooling racks in the back room, he could see John Mitchell through the swinging doors. Mr. Hebner remarked to Celia, one of the girls in the back, "That John is good for business. Here he is again for his three dozen doughnuts. Now he buys at least a doughnut or two and a coffee on a daily basis besides his Monday morning order."

Dyna counted on John Mitchell for a lot more than the doughnuts. Each day he stopped by to talk to her seemed a little bit brighter, a little bit easier to cope with, despite her advancing pregnancy. He learned about her family in Briggandale, she was nineteen and single, and about Aunt Alicia whom she lived with in Bellina. Dyna learned he was single, he was an only child, he worked as a salesman and his parents were dead. But he had a favorite aunt, Aunt Vernice, and plenty of cousins. She found it easier and easier to talk to him and began looking forward to his visits.

IN NOVEMBER 1954, five months after Dyna left home and after Anna's black eyes had healed, Joe cornered Anna in the bedroom and beat her again. After three cracked ribs and a few bruises, all outward contact with her sister, Alicia, and Dyna stopped.

In time, Anna became afraid for herself and for Raphael and Sally, their two children who were still at home. Anna wasn't about to try to contact Dyna anymore. Nor would she contact the police about her own life. Yes, Joe was in control of the Palpietro household again. They all feared him.

.

SHE CALLED OUT and instantly, he was there. "Please R.J., hold me. I feel so cold right now." Eva had closed her eyes tightly, wincing in pain. With her eyes closed, tears still flowed from the sides.

"Does it hurt very much? Should I get the doctor now? I love you. You know I hate to see you cry."

"No, just wait. I'll be all right."

R.J. sat in a chair at her bedside, holding her, anxious and unsure what to do. After holding her for a few minutes, he released his grip and eased the telephone off the hook. He called for an ambulance. She heard him and opened her eyes. "Thank you," she whispered.

R.J. picked up the telephone again. Eva stopped him. "Don't call Brian, it's only four in the morning. Just let him rest. It's just pain, that's all."

Thirty minutes passed, but the ambulance still hadn't arrived.

"Where are they now? Why aren't they here?" Eva cried, her pain increasing.

"They'll be here soon. Please, honey, just take my hand. I love you. You know I hate to see you cry." He held her frail hand as she tried to squeeze away the waves of pain that flowed through her body.

Eventually, the ambulance came to take Eva to Cellis Memorial. R.J. followed in his car. After she was admitted, staff administered pain relief and she passed out. Once he was sure that she was stable and he had talked to the emergency room doctor about her discharge, R.J. called Brian.

"Brian, I'm at the hospital now. Your ma wasn't doing well. When they brought your mother to the hospital this time, she was in a lot of pain. She had some kind of reaction to the treatments. She's doing better now and I think they'll let her come home after they figure what level of pain relief to give her."

R.J. didn't want to pressure his son; he knew that Brian had been overwhelmed so far. But he'd never seen Eva so weak. "Brian, how soon will it be?"

"Sierra's had some false labor pains, but they stopped. It's really early but it could be any day now, Dad, any day."

CHAPTER 13

O N THE THIRD Monday in December, John showed up at the bakery to order his usual three dozen doughnuts. But Dyna wasn't there. Celia, who now worked at the front counter, stood in her place.

"Where's Dyna?" John asked.

Celia looked about and whispered. "You'll have to ask Mr. Hebner. He'll be out here in just a moment." Sure enough, Mr. Hebner pushed open the swinging door a few seconds later while carrying a huge tray of doughnuts.

"Where's Dyna? Why isn't she here, Mr. Hebner?"

The bald-topped, gray-haired baker dropped his smile immediately, put the tray on the counter and crossed his arms defensively, like an older brother or uncle. His gray, furry eyebrows came together into a frightening scowl. At six feet four inches, with a barrel chest and arms like a weightlifter, Mr. Hebner made it plain he was protective of Dyna. By now, he frowned. "Don't bother her, young man," Hebner cautioned. "She's a nice girl. She just made a mistake, that's all. She doesn't need more trouble. I'm sure you won't give her any, right?"

"Mr. Hebner, I want to marry her. How can I reach her?"

"Are you serious?" Mr. Hebner uncrossed his arms. "Really?"

He pulled a worn slip with a telephone number from a secret place from under the counter. Hebner had hidden Alicia's number very well from his wife, but kept it close enough for his own use. Hebner wasted no time in giving Alicia Carselli's telephone number to John, but added, "Young man, I'm sure Dyna isn't home now." Hebner slid the number safely back into its hiding place.

"How do you know?"

"She had her baby just this morning. Her aunt told me Dyna had a little boy."

DYNA NAMED HIM Javier. She had picked the name from a movie she had seen. No one in her mother's family in New Jersey understood why, even though they asked her repeatedly. Tradition would require her to name her son after an uncle, a grandfather, a brother or a father. But she'd broken tradition by naming the baby after someone none of them even knew.

But to Dyna, with his long lashes, dark hair, dark skin and dark brown eyes, he looked like a Javier. In her eyes, he looked like her younger brother, Raphael, when he was younger, maybe a little fatter in the face. But he was her Javier, her gorgeous man-child. More importantly, he didn't look like Brian Tanner.

Just after lunch on that same day, Alicia picked up the telephone to call her sister Anna. Alicia had waited for hours before making this call. She had to be sure that Joe was at work and not at home. And if Joe answered the telephone or Anna gave her the secret words during the call, Alicia knew to hang up quickly.

Fortunately, on that day of good news, Anna answered the telephone. Joe was at work, allowing the sisters to talk for almost an hour. Obviously, they wouldn't tell Joe about the call. Instead, Alicia would send a letter. Even Joe would be curious enough to let a letter pass through with news about a grandchild.

A week after the baby's birth, he and Dyna slept in a small bedroom in Aunt Alicia's apartment. This great nephew was welcomed with wide open arms by Aunt Alicia the same way as his mother, Dyna, had been. It had been over ten years since Alicia shared her apartment with a teenager and much longer than that with an infant. For the otherwise private person she had become over many years, Aunt Alicia was surprisingly accepting of her pregnant niece, and now her niece's son. For Alicia Carselli, Dyna and Javier represented a tie to the relationship she once shared with her sister, Anna. One man, Joe Palpietro, came between them to separate the closest of sisters. Now many years later, Dyna's son, Javier Palpietro, enabled the sisters to renew their relationship once again.

CHAPTER 14

AUNT ALICIA MADE sure Dyna didn't talk to him when he called the first three times. She was polite but firm. Dyna was not in any condition to talk to anyone now, Aunt Alicia would say. She had a baby only a week ago and needed rest. The last time he called, Aunt Alicia learned another key detail, namely that the caller got her telephone number from Mr. Hebner at the bakery and deli.

Sitting at her oak rolltop desk in her bedroom where she had been working on a crossword puzzle, Aunt Alicia hung up the telephone. At first, she couldn't make up her mind whether she should be angry with Hebner for giving out her telephone number. After thinking carefully about the calls, Alicia decided Hebner had to be up to something good. He wouldn't have taken the risk of upsetting her if he thought John Mitchell meant trouble. If Hebner were wrong, Alicia Carselli decided, she would repay him by calling his wife. Mrs. Hebner wouldn't take kindly to a call from her husband's girlfriend.

Aunt Alicia went back to her crossword puzzle to pass the time. But she didn't fill in many words while she waited.

After ten that same morning, Alicia called the bakery. She knew Hebner had finished with the breakfast crowd and wouldn't start with the lunch crowd for almost an hour. Understandably, John Mitchell was one of the first topics they discussed.

"John's all right," Hebner assured her. In his office, he sat working on the employees' schedules. With Dyna's absence, he had to juggle hours and he found her hard to replace. "John has a good job, he's single, he's an only child, his folks are dead, and he's never flirted with any of the girls at the shop. He never even flirted with Dyna," Hebner added. "John's a good guy and he treats her really well. John Mitchell don't mean no harm. Besides," Hebner continued, "John said he wanted to marry her!"

"What? He didn't say that!" she responded, shocked at Hebner's claim.

Hebner paused, letting John's statement sink in. "C'mon, Alicia, not too many guys say that under any circumstances. This guy is willing to take Dyna even though she just had some other man's kid."

Aunt Alicia found the logic compelling, but not totally convincing. She knew some men would say anything to get a woman they wanted. They might even temporarily forget their own wives. She decided to wait and see how serious this John Mitchell would be.

John called again on the next day, and the next. Even if Dyna couldn't or wouldn't see him yet, he had made up his mind that he would keep in touch. She would have to know how he felt about her.

AT ENID HOSPITAL, ten miles west of Briggandale, after seeing Sierra wheeled into the delivery room on December 30, 1954, Brian decided to call his father. He located a telephone booth and placed his long distance call. The operator connected his call to the operator in Cellis, who in turn reached the Tanner farm. R.J. Tanner answered the phone.

"Dad, we're here! We're at the hospital now. Sierra just went into labor." Barely controlling his excitement, Brian sounded giddy, as if he were a small boy about to open a present at Christmas.

R.J. wasn't as enthusiastic. "Son, I'm glad you called. We, uh, we took your ma to the hospital today. She was really sick. She's home now, but she doesn't look good. She isn't resting well."

Brian's heart sank. "Dad, uh, do you think she might . . . you know." He didn't want to finish the sentence.

"Son, this may be the very news she needs. Maybe knowing her grandchild is almost here will give her the strength to keep holding on." He was quiet for a few seconds.

Brian thought his father might be crying. "Dad, I hope so. I'll call you back when the baby is born."

AT ENID HOSPITAL, just before Sierra and Brian Tanner arrived, a beautiful girl was born to an unfortunate, married woman who had been savagely raped by a stranger. At the mother's request, the child was never taken in to her to be seen.

Dr. Florin Anderson hated these kinds of situations. The older doctor stood at the scrub sink, washing his hands and forearms while he shook his head. In his twenty-plus years at Enid Hospital, he had delivered dozens of unwanted babies. Usually, these babies were born to unmarried girls attending Briggandale who had gotten pregnant and had chosen to give up their babies at birth. Enid Hospital was a small private hospital, unlike the large public hospital in Briggandale.

As the duty nurse, Sheryl Alt, gently sponged the infant, the tiny baby girl wriggled and cried. Dr. Anderson looked at the squirming infant and sighed. A baby born under these circumstances faced an unfortunate future, he imagined. Placement at the children's home was inevitable, unless and until adoption could be arranged. Besides, these kinds of births meant more paperwork for Dr. Anderson.

While Dr. Anderson stood at the sink, Head Nurse Carmen Hill pushed open the swinging doors of Delivery Room A and called for him. "Doctor, we need you in Delivery Room C right away. Mrs. Tanner is delivering right now."

"Isn't she Dr. Lerner's patient?"

"Yes, but she's delivering now and he can't make it here. He's out of town today."

"She can't be ready so soon! Didn't she just get here?"

"Tell that to the baby, Doctor Anderson," Nurse Hill replied dryly. "Doctor, something isn't right with this delivery. Could you hurry, please?" As Nurse Hill walked ahead, pushing through the swinging doors, Dr. Anderson followed, his hands still wet. While they walked quickly to the next delivery room, Nurse Hill gave him the details of what had happened. When the woman became uncontrollable during labor, Nurse Hill administered thiopental sodium intravenously. But the outburst wasn't all.

From the frightened expressions on the staff's faces as he entered Delivery Room C and from the unusual silence, Dr. Anderson could tell something was terribly, terribly wrong. One look at the infant's head and upper torso, partially emerged, revealed only some of the infant's grotesque physical condition. The child was horribly deformed and was dead. The woman was unconscious.

As they worked on the delivery, Dr. Anderson looked the woman over carefully. He noticed her well-manicured hands and that on her very puffy left hand ring finger, she had a wedding ring set. Her diamond solitaire was even larger than the one he'd given his own wife.

After completing the delivery as best he could, Dr. Anderson braced himself for the hard part. Other staff members quickly left the room, for they knew that he preferred to be alone after a difficult delivery.

Dr. Anderson stood at the scrub sink, washing his hands and forearms. They were clean and had been for several minutes. But Dr. Anderson wasn't ready to leave the sink or even the room. It took him some time to prepare. Even with all of his years of experience, Dr. Anderson still felt uncomfortable about what he had to do next. Discussing with the husband all of the details about the birth and the bleak prospects for any future births was the hardest part for Dr. Anderson, especially when the man would break down and cry.

After a few moments, Nurse Hill slipped back into the room

and reminded him about Brian. "Her husband's in the waiting room. Dr. Lerner said this guy is a medical student and that according to the husband, this was going to be their first baby."

"Their first? His maybe, but not hers."

"Doctor . . . ."

Dr. Anderson sneered. "You saw the scarring and the calcified tissue. That woman has been pregnant before and if I don't miss my guess, she's had more than one back-alley abortion."

Nurse Hill was more practical. "Maybe so, but that information might not be appreciated, Doctor, especially not at this moment. Let's call it a miscarriage; the husband obviously doesn't know. Besides, you still have a little problem in Delivery Room A ."

This last detail affected Dr. Anderson in the way she had hoped it would, for he turned his head and stared at her. In her twelve years of working with Dr. Florin Anderson, she had an idea of what he might do next. She hoped he would do it again this time.

Dr. Anderson hated being reminded by Nurse Hill, but he knew she was right. He had to tell the expectant father the bad news. He finally dried his hands, then ran them over his forehead and through his thinning brown hair. No sense in waiting any longer.

As he walked down the hall to talk to the expectant father, Dr. Florin Anderson had a major lapse of ethics and a quick flash of insight. The young couple would have their baby, he decided. And the local children's home would get one less admission.

Opening the waiting room door, Dr. Anderson found five men of varying ages. Unsure of which man was the father of the dead child, Dr. Anderson stood at the door and called out, "Brian Tanner?"

A well-built young man of medium height and with short, medium brown hair turned from looking out the window. He stepped forward nervously, with the wide grin of a new father. Dr. Anderson looked at his shoes and clothing for a quick financial assessment. The young man wasn't starving and his clothes and shoes were of fine quality. He wasn't poor by any means.

"Hello, I'm Dr. Florin Anderson. Your wife's stable now. May I talk with you in my office?"

As he followed the doctor out of the waiting room, Brian asked, "How's the baby?"

Dr. Anderson said nothing.

Maybe the doctor hadn't heard him. Brian asked again. "How's the baby?"

Dr. Anderson stretched his long legs and walked faster.

Brian asked repeatedly about the baby, but Dr. Anderson only mumbled, "Not yet."

As he moved quickly through the hall toward his office, with Brian following close behind, Dr. Anderson pretended not to hear any more of Brian's questions.

In the privacy of the cluttered office, Dr. Anderson broke the news about the dead child. "Have a seat please. Brian, Dr. Lerner said you're a medical student right?"

"Yes."

"I feel I can level with you. The truth is your baby died of spina bifida—an extremely severe case. She never had a chance. She had other problems too." Dr. Anderson recited the list of obvious defects.

"I understand," Brian interrupted.

"No, I'm afraid you don't. It's a miracle that your wife even carried the baby this long. How many times had your wife miscarried before?" He studied Brian's face.

"I don't know." Prior miscarriages? This was news to Brian.

"Well, this pregnancy was hard on your wife. During delivery, she lost a lot of blood. She wasn't strong enough for this pregnancy. With what we in the medical community know now about spina bifida, I wouldn't advise her to have another child."

The face of Brian Tanner showed his mixed feelings. He turned away from Dr. Anderson, biting his lips to keep from crying out, his shoulders shaking. Brian gripped the edge of the desk hard, as if he would crush the mahogany top between his fingers in his grief. Brian knew his mother had a number of stillborn children and had half expected some bad news from Dr. Anderson. But the number and severity of birth defects surprised him.

Dr. Anderson didn't want the news to sink in too deep. He

continued. "We have a delicate situation here, Brian. But there's something I want you to consider. I have a possible solution here, if you're interested."

Brian almost didn't hear as he could only hear the words of his dying mother. She just wanted to hold her grandchild, and now he had failed. He needed a baby now. Brian opened his eyes, wiped his face with one hand and looked at Dr. Anderson, his eyes still red and blurry. "What? What are you talking about?"

"Brian, I can get a baby for you and your wife."

"You don't understand," Brian started, his voice rising as he lifted slightly from the chair. "I needed this baby, my baby, Doctor. I can't adopt a baby! I can't wait that long!"

"Calm down. Listen. I'm proposing a kind of unofficial adoption here, Brian. You can take a baby home when you take your wife home. A baby was just born here whose parents don't want to keep her. You just need to come up with a little money to cover the costs, expenses, you know. A thousand should do it. I can arrange everything."

Brian sat on the edge of the chair, staring intently now. "What are you talking about? What about the parents of the baby? Won't they be involved?"

"You won't have any problems from them, either now or later. There won't be any record of this. They'll never know your name. And they'll never show up on your doorstep. Their baby looks strong and healthy. And this will be our little secret, just between you and me." With his thumb under his chin, Dr. Anderson tapped his long nose with his long, bony finger. "But if you're not interested, well, there'll be another couple who would take this baby in a heartbeat. What do you say?"

Brian hesitated. If what Dr. Anderson said were true, what were the risks? Money wasn't a problem; he could get the amount that Dr. Anderson asked for without any trouble. Could he pass this baby off as his own child to his own dying mother? And what were the consequences, professionally or otherwise, of his participation in this deception? From what Dr. Anderson said, the secret of this baby's identity would never be revealed. Their joint participation in a baby switch and falsification of the records of the birth and death could remain hidden. Brian felt almost certain that he wouldn't be caught. But if the details did come out, he could kiss his medical career goodbye. The big question remained— what would he do?

AFTER THREE MORE telephone calls from John, Aunt Alicia finally agreed to let him come to the apartment to see Dyna and Javier.

When she opened the door, Alicia Carselli knew this man could be the right one for her niece and her great nephew. The chocolate-brown plush teddy bear in his right hand and the dozen cloth diapers in the bag in his left hand melted the stern look on Aunt Alicia's face and got him past her and into the living room, where Dyna sat, holding the baby. As soon as John sat on the sofa, Aunt Alicia went into the kitchen. There, the radio still blared, but she quickly turned it off. Naturally cautious, Aunt Alicia sat at the kitchen table with her latest crossword puzzle in front of her. She sat just beyond sight, but not beyond her keen hearing. She peeked into the living room every few minutes or so, pretending to do some housework or looking for something. She wanted to have a clear picture of what was going on, without looking too nosey of course.

CHAPTER 15

H E HAD DECIDED. Brian grabbed Dr. Anderson's right hand and began pumping it rapidly with both hands. "Yes, I'll take her! Thank you, Doctor!"

For the sake of his wife and his dying mother, Brian rejoiced at getting a healthy baby to bring home. He could hardly believe that the tragedy turned out so well. He would participate in the fraud. And he would never tell Sierra.

Visibly relieved, Dr. Florin Anderson relaxed. Brian listened carefully to Dr. Anderson's instructions. With Sierra still sedated and expected to sleep, Brian could go on home. After all, Dr. Anderson needed a little time to take care of the switch.

After Brian left, Dr. Anderson called for Nurse Hill.

"Well?" she asked as she stepped into his office.

"It's all set."

DOCTOR ANDERSON UNOFFICIALLY moved other babies out to families during his years at Enid Hospital, especially when a healthy baby was bound for the children's home. Selling a child to a childless couple was nothing new for him, especially if the price were right and if the couple were financially able.

But whenever he switched babies, Dr. Anderson never informed the receiving parents of the switch. He enjoyed being the stork in a medical jacket, delivering unwanted healthy infants to couples who had lost a child or whose child had been born with disabilities. The young single mothers had given up the children anyway. "Why not let the couples go on believing that the little ones they received were actually theirs?" Dr. Anderson would tell Nurse Hill.

Taking a calculated risk, Dr. Anderson made an exception in Brian's case. He wouldn't have even told the young man about the death if it hadn't been for the extensive birth defects and the substantial risks to his wife. Dr. Anderson would inform Sierra about the substantial risks and advise her to avoid future pregnancies. He had his standards, as flawed as they were. But he would not tell her he had substituted her dead baby with a living child.

Sierra Tanner awoke a few hours later, moaning softly in pain. The intravenous drip had carried her through the delivery. But she needed something now for the pain. And she wanted to see her baby. Flat on her back, Sierra hovered between consciousness and unconsciousness.

As she passed Room 322, Nurse Hill checked on Mrs. Tanner again. The woman had been sedated since the delivery, but she should be awake by now. Nurse Hill knew she had to be present when the young woman awoke, in case Dr. Anderson had encountered any problems in making the baby switch.

As she opened the door, Nurse Hill noticed Sierra was stirring, and slipped into the room quietly. She didn't want Sierra to know that she was there, let alone that she was giving her an additional dose of sedative. Creeping closer, Nurse Hill gave Sierra an incremental dose of thiopental sodium intravenously. She wouldn't enter this dose in the charts. As Sierra slipped back into a deep sleep, Nurse Hill watched, hoping that Sierra wouldn't roll over to look at her. After a few minutes, when she could hear Sierra snoring lightly, Nurse Hill left the room.

Nurse Hill had done her part, but she wanted to make sure Dr. Anderson had plenty of time to do his. Finishing her rounds quietly, she waited for the confirming signal from Dr. Anderson. By the end of her shift, she had her answer.

WELL INTO THE second shift, while sitting at the third-floor nursing station, Nurse Amy Wainder wondered why the woman in Room 322, Sierra Tanner, was still asleep. If there had been any complications or trouble during the birth, surely Nurse Hill would have informed her. But Nurse Hill said nothing unusual in her update at the shift change. As the head nurse on duty on the obstetric wing, Nurse Wainder normally knew everything important that had happened on the previous shift. Puzzled, she decided to check Sierra's chart. The only unusual entry in the chart was that Sierra and her baby would be transferred to Briggandale University Hospital the first thing in the morning, if both were stable enough.

Twelve hours after giving birth, Sierra awoke again. Brian wasn't there. Unaware of the time, Sierra worried he had learned something about the birth he shouldn't have. She hesitated, but after a few minutes, Sierra pressed the bell to call for help.

Nurse Wainder answered the call bell.

"May I see my baby now?" Sierra asked and threw the covers off, as if she would stand up. Immediately, she grimaced with pain. Moving so quickly had hurt intensely.

"Stay right there. I'll bring her to you."

With a small bundle in her arms, Nurse Wainder quickly returned.

Sierra gently took the baby into her arms, cradling the infant's tiny head in the crook of her right arm. She wanted to ask questions but feared her nervousness might tip the nurse off to her inner turmoil. Holding her breath, Sierra gently lifted the blanket from the sleeping infant's face and smiled broadly. She had nothing to fear. The baby didn't look like Brian, but at least she didn't look like Tony. Brian would never learn from her that this child wasn't his own.

Only when she had looked at the baby's face did Sierra's voice and courage return. "May I feed her now?"

FROM HER SPOT in the kitchen, Aunt Alicia decided that she had better find out more information about the stranger in the living room. As she sneaked another peek, Aunt Alicia was amazed. John held Javier with ease. She had known too many men who wouldn't touch a baby, let alone volunteer to hold one. But John didn't seem afraid or overwhelmed in handling the newborn. He cuddled, he cooed, and he juggled the baby like a pro.

Did he have children of his own? Aunt Alicia started to wonder. She knew he was an only child, Hebner had told her that. John looked up at the door and caught Aunt Alicia, her eyes wide and her mouth open. He looked lovingly at Javier and explained simply, "I was the oldest among twelve cousins. My family always made me the baby sitter. I learned to love them early. And I want at least four or five of my own." He looked at Dyna shyly. She looked away, blushing deeply.

THE NEXT DAY, Eva managed to hold the telephone although she wondered whether she might drop it. R.J. had dialed the number for Brian's apartment for her and stood nearby at the head of the bed. He'd been outside to feed the herd already. Now, he was back inside to warm up and to check on her.

At the apartment in Briggandale, Brian had just returned from running errands. He hoped to get a few hours of sleep before going to the hospital. He could barely stand up, he was so tired. But with his mother's illness and with Sierra and the baby still in the hospital, he couldn't ignore the telephone. Brian answered it on the fifth ring. "Hello?"

"How's Sierra today?"

"Ma! It's good to hear your voice! Sierra's doing better now and I think they'll let her come home by the end of the week. But the baby isn't nursing very well yet. The doctor said we should leave her there with Sierra for a few more days. She needs to nurse to be healthy. But Ma, how are you?"

"I'm fine, doing well today. When will you know for sure, Brian?"

"I'm checking with the doctor about the baby every day. I should know something in two or three days. I'll call you in two days for sure. Okay, Ma?" He sounded as if he would hang up the telephone.

"Wait, Brian! Don't hang up. I want some details about my grandchild. What's her name? How much did she weigh?"

Brian had given the details to his father, but his mother wanted to hear the news herself.

"Sorry, Ma, I was so tired that I wasn't thinking. We named her after you, plus a name that Sierra liked. Her name is Andrea Eva Tanner. She weighed seven pounds, three ounces when she was born. Oh, and she's twenty inches long."

"Congratulations son!" She paused now, breathless for joy, then whispered, "Thank you, Brian, thank you." They didn't talk for a few moments, for he heard his mother's soft sobs on his end of the telephone.

Eventually she spoke. "Do you really think it will be two days? I'm really looking forward to it, Brian. Call us as soon as you know. I can hardly wait! I love you son. Give Sierra my love too." Eva handed the telephone to R.J., but by then, Brian had already hung up.

"Help me to sit up, R.J."

He lifted her gently and held her upright as he adjusted the pillows behind her. "Just think, Eva, our first grandchild! You asked for a grandchild and got what you wanted." He lowered her back onto the pillows and kissed her on her forehead.

"Thank you dear, that's much better." Eva smiled. She had more strength today. "Yes, our first grandchild, a baby girl!"

Now seated on the other side of the bed, R.J. looked at Eva and commented wryly, "She must be a pretty fertile heifer to pop out a baby that soon!"

Eva frowned. "Stop talking like that, R.J.!"

"Come on Eva! That girl must have been pregnant when you asked Brian to get married. Our son was already working on what you wanted, even before you told him about the cancer."

"R.J., you know I don't approve of the order that they did it."
The prospect of holding the baby had tired her and Eva paused to
catch her breath. "But I'll take the results." She smiled as she
snuggled down into the pillows.

"It all worked out, Evie, it all worked out! Let's just be grateful
for that."

But after one in the morning, R.J. took Eva to the hospital.
She had thrown up several times after midnight, but her heaves
continued, racking her frail body. When Eva passed out twice, it
was almost more than R.J. could take. For several hours, staff at
Cellis Memorial ran tests and administered fluids and eventually
stabilized her.

At seven thirty that morning, R.J. called Brian. "I took your
ma to the hospital early this morning. She was really sick. I didn't
know what else to do. She's doing better now and I think they'll
let her come home."

"When will you know for sure?"

"I can't say. Your mother's resting now. I just came home to
change and to call you. I'm going back in a few minutes. How is
the baby?"

"She's doing better now and I think they'll let her come home."

"And Sierra?"

"She's ready to come home too."

CHAPTER 16

O N A TUESDAY in early January 1955, after work, Joe sat at the bar at Cal's Grill. With his gin half gone and his two buddies' glasses nearly empty, it was time for another round. For Joseph Palpietro, the complaint of the day concerned the name of his grandson.

"Javier. Javier. What kind of name is that?" He took a mouthful of gin, but swallowed it slowly. "I'll tell you what kind of name that is. It's the kind of name that my daughter, Dyna, used just to hurt me. She didn't honor me by naming him the right way, you know, respecting tradition. That's what kind of name that is."

Not more than an hour earlier, Anna told Joe about the letter from Alicia and that Dyna had named his first grandchild Javier. She had the gall to name the boy after someone not even in the family! Joe could hardly wait to go to Cal's Grill to tell Wayne and George.

"Who is Javier?" George asked and tipped his drink up.

"Who knows?" Joe answered scornfully.

Wayne pulled his cigarette from his lips, but still held the smoke as he talked. "Is that the baby's father's name?" Now, he let the gray smoke curl out from both sides of his mouth.

"I don't think so, but I don't know." Joe sat quietly, swirling the remaining gin around in his glass. Could it be? Joe thought about it and found that Wayne's question had some logic behind it. Brian hadn't come around since Dyna left home. Come to think of it, Brian hadn't even called that Joe was aware of. Maybe Brian had dumped his daughter when he found out that she was seeing someone else. Maybe Javier was the name of the baby's father.

"Well, what does your wife think?" Wayne continued. Now he practiced making smoke doughnuts, blowing out ring after ring after ring.

"Yeah, what does she think? Better yet, what does she know?" George asked, instigating. He glared at Wayne. The smoke rings were the main reason why George hated giving cigarettes to Wayne. When Wayne had his own cigarettes, he rarely shared them and wouldn't waste a good puff. But after mooching cigarettes from George, Wayne got creative with his sticks, seeing how many rings and the kinds of shapes he could create. With free cigarettes, Wayne liked to play around. The cigarette Wayne was using now for making smoke rings was the fourth he had gotten that evening from George.

But George and Wayne enjoyed provoking Joe about his wife. Joe's comments about Anna would provide plenty for Wayne and George to talk and laugh about long after Joe had gone home.

"My ex did stuff like that. She kept all kinds of things to herself." George added, looking at Joe and smirking. George didn't tell Wayne or Joe that his ex-wife had a secret affair for years. "People who keep secrets sometimes want to hurt you. They wait until you least expect it and boom! They hit you with the bad news."

George learned about his wife's secret when she ran off with the ice cream man two years ago and took all the furniture in the process. He really didn't miss his wife too much. But he really missed his furniture, especially his television set. The set was his first, and he had worked hard to get it.

"Well Joe?" Wayne asked, "What do you intend to do?"

"Right now, I'm going to order another round. I'll deal with Anna when I get home." Maybe Wayne and George were right. His wife, Anna, had kept Dyna's pregnancy secret. She didn't tell him that she had sent Dyna to New Jersey to live with her sister. Maybe this was another one of her secrets. Joe intended to find out if Anna knew who the father of Dyna's baby was, even if he had to beat it out of her.

THE DAY AFTER her discharge from the hospital, Eva had to go back after throwing up blood. She resisted at first; she didn't want the ambulance to take her. If she were going to die, she wanted to do it at home. Eventually, R.J. convinced her to go.

As soon as she was admitted, R.J. called Brian from the hospital. "Son, it doesn't look good. I'm at the hospital now."

"How is she? How's Ma?"

"When they took your ma to the hospital this time, she was unconscious when she arrived."

"Should I come now?"

"No, just stay by the telephone. If something happens, the doctor said it would be soon. You could never make it here on time. She's awake now, but barely holding on."

"Dad, what should I do?"

"Son, just wait. And pray."

Standing beside her bedside, R.J. held Eva's hand. He leaned over her and whispered into her ear, "Evie, you can make it. The baby is almost here."

"R.J., I don't know if I can hold on much longer." She could barely whisper the words. "I can't keep my food down now. After all this, will the smell of baby lotion and powder make me throw up?"

"Hold my hand, sweetheart! You can make it. The baby is almost here."

After a long pause, she whispered, "Even if I survive, I don't think I can hold her. I feel so weak right now."

"Don't talk like that, Evie! You'll make it just so you can see the baby." He kissed her bald head, squeezed her hand gently and tried to hold back his tears. "They'll be here any day now. That old doctor, he's just trying to make sure the baby's all right."

"Could you give me some water please? I'm so thirsty." She was barely whispering now.

He held the cup to her lips as she took a tiny sip, then grimaced.

"Could I have some more, some . . . cold water this time?" She grabbed his arm weakly and closed her eyes. "And R.J., no matter what, don't let me die in this place. Take me home, honey, please. Promise me that you'll take me home."

He stood over her until her hand slipped from his arm. Whispering to control the tremor in his voice, R.J. finally answered, "I promise, honey, I promise. Now, let me get you some cold water."

Standing in the bathroom as he ran cold water, R.J. couldn't hold back his tears any longer.

ABOUT AN HOUR later, R.J. called back to Briggandale from the hospital in Cellis. "Brian, your ma's awake now and she's resting. They don't know why she got so sick, but she's better now. The doctors are talking about sending her home, but they still want to check her over. I'll call you if anything changes."

THEY RELEASED EVA from the hospital later that day. Back at the farm, after making sure that she was asleep, R.J. called Brian. "Son, we're back home now. Your ma's upstairs, asleep." R.J. desperately wanted to break down and cry because of the ongoing strain and disappointment, but he forced himself to ask, "How's it going there?"

"The doctor will take a look at them first thing in the morning. We may be able to come then."

"That's good, Brian. I wondered if your ma would be able to hold on much longer. I mean, that baby seems to be the only reason why she's still here."

"Dad, I know. Every day, I worry whether we can make it there, you know, before she . . ." Brian paused, not wanting to finish the thought.

The two men waited in silence for a few moments, then Brian finally spoke. "Dad, how can you handle the pressure of Ma's being sick and knowing that she's going to die? I mean, just in the short time that Sierra has been in the hospital, I haven't slept well and my appetite is almost gone."

R.J. laughed gently. It had been a while since Brian had asked for advice. "I don't always manage everything, your mother's illness, running the farm and all the other things that come along. A few times, I did wonder if I could go on."

He wiped his face with his big, rough hand and took a deep breath. "But I pray and God gives me the strength I need. Sometimes, it's just strength for the hour, sometimes, it's just enough strength for the day. When I feel that I'm running low, I just ask him for some more." R.J. paused now, trying to choke back the tears. "And in all these years that I've been asking, he's never told me no."

CHAPTER 17

THREE WEEKS AFTER Javier's birth, on a Monday when Dyna returned to work, John met her at Hebner's Bakery and Deli at his usual time. Instead of his normal newspaper, he carried a handful of flowers and a small box. He'd already called Aunt Alicia and explained what he had planned. In front of the entire bakery staff on duty, John put the flowers into Dyna's hands and dropped to one knee. Opening the box, John asked, "Dyna, will you marry me?" The black, leather-wrapped box contained a wedding ring with a real diamond that sparkled under the bakery's bright lights.

She stood dumbfounded for a split second. Then Dyna smiled broadly and laughed joyfully. "Yes! Oh, yes, yes, yes!"

"Wait, I'm not done yet." He swivelled on his knee to face Mr. Hebner. "Mr. Hebner, is it okay with you too?"

Mr. Hebner had to sniff and clear his throat to say yes. The sentimental old bear had been listening while he stood behind the silver metal counter, his eyes filling with tears. "And today John, no charge for the doughnuts."

Within the hour, Aunt Alicia called Mr. Hebner with her idea. Recognizing a golden marketing opportunity when he saw one, Hebner quickly agreed.

A little over a month after Javier's birth, Dyna Marie Palpietro became Mrs. John Mitchell at the main counter of Hebner's Bakery and Deli. Mr. Hebner sponsored the wedding. With all the free press and publicity, even Mrs. Hebner attended the ceremony. Aunt Alicia sat on the far end of one side of the main counter, while Mrs. Hebner sat on the other. Wisely stationed in the middle was Mr. Hebner. He stood out of the reach of his wife and his girlfriend, in front of the reporters, the photographers and the huge, four-tiered wedding cake. He gave Dyna Palpietro away in marriage to become the wife of John Mitchell.

CHAPTER 18

BACK AT BRIGGANDALE University Hospital, when Brian went into her room after six that evening, he found her crying.

"Sierra, what's wrong?"

"Our first baby . . . and she's sick! And I can't have any more! Oh Brian, this is so unfair!" She burst into tears anew.

"Now don't give up hope now! What happened?"

"I saw the doctor today and it doesn't look good. He said that the baby has lost some weight and has a slight temperature. It may be just a minor infection, but he doesn't want to take the chance. He wants to keep the baby in the hospital for a few days more with me nursing her, you know, to try to build up her strength and weight."

"Please, honey. Stop crying. You know I hate to see you cry."

"But Brian, what can we do? How can we get her to your mother on time?"

Brian turned, trying to hold back tears. "I don't know. But I'll call Dad and let him what has happened."

IN THE APARTMENT that evening, Brian called the farm. He was afraid to speak to his mother; he couldn't handle her disappointment right then. Fortunately, his father answered the telephone.

"Dad, it's Brian."

"Hello. How is it going there?"

"Sierra's okay." Brian paused. He hated disappointing his parents.

"Uh, Dad, I have bad news for you. They're going to keep the baby for a few more days. She has an infection and isn't nursing well. I'm sorry, Dad, but we can't do anything for two or three days."

"That's all right Brian, just do what you think is best for the baby."

"How's Ma?"

"She's asleep. I'm in the bedroom with her now. She's a little weak, but she'll be all right."

"Dad, I'll call you tomorrow with any details if anything changes."

Noticing that Eva was stirring, R.J. decided to end the call. "I'll talk to you later. Goodbye."

Even though she had been dozing, Eva knew that R.J. was talking to Brian about the baby. In a very weak voice, she asked, "What did the doctor say? Will they let her out today?"

R.J. touched her face gently with his hand. "The doctor says for Sierra to rest and keep the baby near until they both are better. Sierra's really protective of the baby, this being the first and all."

"R.J., listen. I don't blame her one bit, knowing that she can't have any more. I felt the same way about Brian."

ALMOST TWO WEEKS after the baby was born, as soon as Dr. Lerner released Sierra to travel to Cellis, Brian called his father. It wasn't too late; his mother was still resting from coming home from the hospital the day before. Brian quickly made the drive to Cellis with his precious treasure.

Four hours later, when Brian turned onto the gravel driveway, his father's car was gone. Panicking, Brian wondered if he should even get out of the car or drive straight to Cellis Memorial. He turned around to the back seat, where Sierra and Andrea were sound asleep.

Brian exclaimed, "No! Dad must have taken Ma back to the hospital! He said she was weak but she could hold on! Sierra, what are we going to do?"

As they sat in the driveway, the front door of the farmhouse opened and R.J. stood there, gesturing for them to come inside. He slipped on his shoes and walked out to the car. "Good thing I looked outside the window! I thought I heard you drive up."

Brian got out of the car, trembling. "Dad, where's your car? Where's Ma?"

"Son, one of our friends wanted to do a favor for us, with your ma sick and all. Mike at the garage came by earlier and picked up the car to give it a tune-up and to check the brakes. Sorry to scare you! Your ma is inside. We knew you'd be coming and your mother wouldn't have missed this moment for anything in the world."

R.J. helped Sierra out of the car, but Brian quickly left them outside. Carrying the baby girl in his arms, Brian strode through the house, going straight to his parents' bedroom. He hesitated at the open door, unsure of what he would see inside.

Pale and still in the bed, Eva was propped up with bright, white pillows. She appeared unconscious. But at that moment, Brian thought his mother looked better than she had in months. He had visited her routinely during Sierra's pregnancy. All the while, Brian feared that his mother would die before seeing her first grandchild. Now that the special moment was finally here, Brian couldn't help reflecting as he stood quietly at the bedroom door. How ironic, he thought, my baby died, but Mama's still here.

Brian entered the room only when R.J. and Sierra made it to the bedroom. Eva woke up slowly, then looked up. She was very much alive and had beaten the doctors' predictions. Though extremely weak, she beamed radiantly from beneath the pale blue cloth scarf covering her now bald head. She had demanded and gotten radium therapy, even though doctor after doctor had advised against it, given the incurable nature of her bladder cancer. Therapy had left her scarred and very ill, but not cured. Clinging to life, Eva just had to see and hold her grandchild.

Brian lifted the blanket flap off the baby's face. "Ma, I'd like to introduce you to your granddaughter, Andrea Eva Tanner."

As he gently lowered the sleeping baby to his mother's chest, both Brian and Sierra had the same unspoken fear. Would Eva Tanner know this baby wasn't Brian's child?

Lotion and baby powder fragrance gently rose from the baby's warm body. Eva inhaled deeply and smiled broadly. Eva had waited so long for this moment. Only days before, Eva had feared she would be too weak to hold the baby and the very smell of baby lotion and powder would nauseate her. But today, with her grandchild in her arms, Eva had no nausea. Plus, she had all the strength she needed.

The baby had ten fingers and ten toes. She had two ears, puffy little cheeks, and a perfectly shaped head. The baby yawned and opened her eyes. In the doorway, Sierra and R.J. stood, eyes misty from the significance of the moment. Eva cried. Brian cried. Little Andrea started to cry softly.

Brian and Sierra had given her a perfect grandchild. For Eva Tanner, that gift was enough.

CHAPTER 19

JOHN AND DYNA moved into an apartment in Bellina. They lived downtown, near some of the noisy, small factories. By the time Javier was five months old, Dyna started looking for quiet places in their frequent excursions. Often, she found it in one part of Genesee Park. There, she could get away from some of the attention seekers in the more popular sections of the park. Old-time regulars went there, old men and old women who sat for hours in the same spots they had held for years, feeding the squirrels and pigeons. The area had no play areas for children, only rows of benches set up for feeding the park animals.

At first, many of the old women and a few of the old men hobbled up to Javier's carriage just to look at him. But in time, the regulars stopped coming over to look. Soon, Dyna was left alone with Javier.

Dyna talked to Javier and sang softly to him as he lay, gazing up at her. Cooing and gurgling, he stretched out his little arms. The early morning sun shone down upon her face, while her baby lay protected by the black carriage hood. From a distance, Dyna seemed to glow as golden sunlight reflected off her creamy brown skin. She savored these moments; they allowed her to think about her family in Indiana and her new life in New Jersey. Her marriage to John was great and Javier was a good baby. Javier seldom cried and often, before he started, he let her know with those expressive eyes of his when something was wrong or he needed something. Javier gave Dyna such joy that she almost forgot her painfully embarrassing pregnancy. He was Javier Mitchell now, for John and Dyna had changed his birth certificate to claim John was the father.

One Thursday while in the park, Dyna noticed her. She was one of those elderly ladies who had once hovered near Javier. But this old one didn't sit with the park regulars. With a long black dress and tattered, black wool shawl, she looked like a storybook witch. Dyna never saw her feed the squirrels or the birds. The old one just sat there alone and rocking on the bench. She looked one way, then another, as if she expected some long-lost lover or child to come walking down the stony path to meet her.

Once, as Dyna pushed Javier's carriage past the old one, Dyna thought she heard the old one counting, but she wasn't sure. Dyna decided she wouldn't let that one come too close to Javier. You can never be too safe, Dyna concluded.

A week later, Dyna came to the park at noon. The sun had been shining for hours, warming up the benches that sat in the direct sunlight. The heat from the benches would cook an egg on that day, let alone the delicate skin of an infant. Dyna took refuge under a large oak tree just beyond her favorite bench in Genesee. She marveled at the diehards who still occupied their usual spots. Sitting under a tree in the presence of so many birds and squirrels carried its own special hazards, so Dyna adjusted the hood of the carriage to shield her baby from visitations from above.

Suddenly, the old one stood right beside her. Dyna hadn't heard her approach. Startled, she looked up into the old woman's dark, fiery eyes and heard her speak.

"Seventeen but not eighteen. Seventeen but not eighteen. Seventeen but not eighteen. Beware of the healer and the one of blood and cloth."

"What? What did you say?" Dyna gasped, eyes wide. She expected gibberish in response. To her surprise, the old woman spoke clearly, but not words Dyna wanted to hear.

"I said seventeen but not eighteen. Your son will live to be seventeen but not eighteen, but—" She didn't finish her sentence, for Dyna angrily interrupted her.

"What? How dare you! What do you know, old woman?" Dyna jumped up, angry, surprised, fearful and yelling. She wanted to confront the old woman. But she also wanted to know why the old woman could say something so awful. The old woman stepped back as Javier began to shriek. Instinctively, Dyna looked down at her son. She looked up to curse the old woman for scaring her and her child. But to Dyna's surprise, the old woman was gone.

The old women and men sitting nearby stared at Dyna as the squirrels scattered and small birds flew up to the shelter of nearby trees. Even the greedy pigeons scurried and flapped their noisy gray wings to get away.

Dyna reached into the baby carriage and picked up Javier, patting him on the back and gently rocking him. As she comforted her son, Dyna recalled what had happened. She put Javier back into the carriage and quickly gathered her things to leave. Kook, seer or prophetess? Dyna didn't want to take time right then to find out which the old woman was. All she knew was she and Javier had to leave the park right away.

For more than three weeks, Dyna didn't bring Javier back to the park. In the meantime, she anxiously pondered the old woman's words.

IN BRIGGANDALE THAT day on an assignment, Tony Agriniello went to the building where he had taken Sierra Gleason to two years earlier and knocked on her door.

The woman who answered the door was chunky, with dark hair.

"I'm looking for Sierra Gleason."

"She doesn't live here anymore."

"Do you know her? I mean, do you know where she lives?"

The brunette opened the door a little wider, but kept the chain on the door. "I've lived here for almost a year and a half. I never met her, but I heard that she married a guy named Danner, no wait, his name was Tanner. Merritt, her neighbor who used to live next door, he told me."

"Married? Sierra?"

The woman noted Tony's surprise. This guy couldn't have been very close to Sierra or he would have known about her marriage by now. Suspicious now, she decided to end the conversation and began closing the door.

"Wait, miss! Which apartment is Merritt's?"

She paused. "Merritt? He's gone now too. Neither of them lives in this building anymore. I've got to go now, I've got company." With her last comment, she shut the door. This guy was asking too many questions. If he planned to cause any trouble for Sierra or Merritt, she didn't want to get mixed up in it.

Tony stood in the hallway for a few moments, then checked his watch. He would have to try to find Sierra Gleason some other time.

CHAPTER 20

EXACTLY FOUR YEARS to the day after Dyna left Indiana, Joseph Palpietro sat in his big armchair. He had finished one bottle of gin but wanted more. He was too drunk to drive, but too angry to sit around in the apartment anymore. All he could think about was that his wife Anna had done him wrong. She had arranged for her sister to take Dyna in. That traitor had a part in sending Dyna beyond his reach. Anna had to know the name of the father of Dyna's baby but claimed that she didn't. In his mind, Anna deserved punishment, now, right now, for everything.

Joe staggered to the bedroom where Anna slept. He locked the door behind him. Anna screamed only once, as Joe poured out the rage he had held since the beating that her uncle and cousin had given him nearly twenty-four years before. In their rooms down the hall, the couple's children slept, unaware of what their father was doing to their mother.

TO THE OUTSIDE world, the Tanners looked like the perfect family. After finishing medical school, Brian joined an older practitioner named Smertz in a small clinic in Cellis. Beautiful, slim and tanned Sierra looked like the perfect wife. When attending social events necessary to build up his practice, they appeared quite happy.

That charade was for the public.

Brian and Sierra went on for years, never revealing to each other their own secrets involving Andrea, their daughter. They loved their pretty little girl. But they didn't love each other. Except for Andrea's needs and the required social events, they lived lives together, but worlds apart.

After Andrea started school, Sierra spent most of her days in drunken stupor, working on her tan. Occasionally, she sought quick affairs with anyone who interested her. She preferred brief relationships with men who would never consider leaving their wives and who wanted to keep their relationship with her very, very secret.

Sierra had become a doctor's wife, as she had dreamed. In exchange for giving Brian and his mother a child, she got money, prestige and a good name. As long as she kept her activities out of sight, Sierra could do as she pleased. Secure in what she was doing, Sierra felt she wouldn't be caught.

THEIR FIRST HOME was a small house in town near his practice. But in Sierra's mind, the three-bedroom house wasn't good enough. The golden brick ranch had a little over twelve hundred square feet, a partially finished basement and a detached, one-car garage, also brick. A sliding glass door allowed them to go from the kitchen to the screened-in rear patio. The patio was added by the prior owners as part of a renovation, but it was well constructed and not unsightly.

But to Sierra, the house was a dump. She had expected a house at least four times that size with a pool for their first real home.

One Monday evening, as Brian collapsed on the bed, dog-tired from a long day at the clinic, Sierra walked down the short hall to their bedroom. She had been in Andrea's room at the other end of the hall. The sight of him just lying there, plus the half pint of liquor she had finished earlier, convinced her to start in on him. She leaned against the door frame with her arms crossed. "Brian, with everything you make, why can't we have a better house?"

"We can't afford it right now, Sierra, so stop talking about it!" All he wanted was to make her shut up so he could rest. He needed quiet; a nag-free quiet.

She pointed her finger at him and shook it. "You aren't trying hard enough! That's why!"

"Like all the men you had before you married me? Did they try hard enough for you, Sierra?"

She hesitated. He was treading on dangerous ground here. What did he know about her past? "And what do you mean by that smart remark?" She had her hand on her hip, her voice growing louder with each word.

He was on his feet by now and moving toward her. "You heard me! The doctor told me about your miscarriages. I know I wasn't your first!"

Furious now, she decided to set him straight and hurt him in the process. But he had never come toward her when they were fighting. "Miscarriages? Those were abortions, you fool!" She started backing up toward the bathroom. By now, she stood in front of the open door to Andrea's bedroom, right next to the bathroom.

Sierra dug deeply at him, "And if it wasn't for your dying mother, I would have had one more abortion!" Backing up into the bathroom, laughing, Sierra slammed the white door in his face.

"Sierra!" Now deeply wounded, Brian yelled as he rushed toward her.

"Daddy! Please!"

Only Andrea's cries stopped him from revealing the truth about Andrea and from punching Sierra's lights out. Brian pounded on the door as Andrea held onto his leg, shrieking in fear.

Now, he was absolutely sure and equally as heartbroken. Sierra married him for convenience and not for love. He hit the door hard once more and slid down to the floor to comfort his young daughter. Holding his little girl tightly, Brian Tanner broke down and cried.

AS BRIAN SPENT more time at the clinic, Sierra spent more time drinking. But when she was sober, she was indifferent to him and passively angry. When drunk, she was cruel to him or sexually aggressive. And Brian never knew what mood she would be in when he would get home at night.

One Thursday before he left for work, they fought about Andrea, money and sex. Later, when he came home, as soon as he opened the door, Brian knew that Sierra was in a particularly foul mood. The first hint came from the heavy book that she hurled his way, creasing his forehead. The book crashed into the wall beside the front door and landed at his foot. Sierra had found out about Fred's bachelor party.

Fred Butler's bachelor party was coming up in three weeks. Brian planned to keep the party a secret from Sierra. But Ricky Croft, one of Brian's friends from Briggandale, called to speak to Brian and inadvertently told Sierra about the party. Well experienced with those kinds of parties, Sierra imagined the worse. She had waited in ambush for Brian.

"You are not going to one of those sleazy things! The guys get drunk and act really stupid with some girl!"

"But Sierra, I said I would provide some of the entertainment."

"Some entertainment!"

"Look Sierra, it isn't going to be like that. There won't be a girl in a cake or anything like it," Brian lied as he picked up the thick book and returned it to its place on the bookshelf.

It was easy for Brian to lie about the party. He wanted to spend time with his buddies from college. But more importantly, he wanted to get away from Sierra, at least for a little while.

"Please believe me, Sierra. I wouldn't lie to you about something like this."

ON FRIDAY EVENING, Brian met with Ricky at his apartment back in Briggandale. For a party of this size and kind, they would need plenty of room. Ricky had lined up the place months ago. With some work, Ricky and Brian got most of the details of the party taken care of, but Brian decided to double-check.

"How did you find out about this place, Ricky?"

"The owner and I go back a few years. I knew him when he had a bar in Enid."

"Oh yeah?" Brian sipped his cola. He would need the caffeine for the drive back to Cellis that evening.

"His place there was called Jack's."

Brian finished his drink and wiped his mouth. "Jack's? Didn't we go there once?"

"Good memory. I went there with you once, but I went quite a few times on my own. His place here is called Murphy's. It's in the name of his brother-in-law, but Jack runs it, just like he used to run his own."

"So you'll take care of the other entertainment?"

"There's not much else to do, Brian. The girl will be coming later on, but we need to set the mood. I've got these movies that we can use, but I think someone else should look at them first. I've got my favorites, but everyone might not like them."

"How many do you have Ricky?"

Ricky laughed.

"That many, huh? You pervert! That's why no woman in her right mind would marry you!"

"Say what you want, Brian. Some of these are homemade movies from Merritt. When we were in school years ago, Merritt and I used to hit the bars in Enid and Briggandale to film the strippers, most of them secretly, of course. Some of them were shot at private parties after hours. I'll lend you four or five. Look at those and let me know if you want more. I only have a few, but you should see the collection Merritt has."

"Merritt? Whatever happened to that guy? He dropped out, didn't he?"

"For some of the stuff he did, he was lucky that he wasn't expelled. There was this one time when he got picked up for some trouble with a girl. She dropped the charges, you know, her word against his. But after that, he wasn't the same."

MONEY STOPPED HIM from continuing in college. After hiring a lawyer and making a quiet settlement offer to the girl who had complained about him, Merritt Hughes was wiped out. By the end of 1954, Merritt Hughes had to drop out of school and move out of his apartment into a cheap flat. Eventually, with what he'd learned in school, he found work in Enid as a sales representative for a pharmaceutical manufacturer. As a sales rep, he traveled frequently, met plenty of people and made money. Merritt figured that in time, he could return to school and become a doctor, just like Brian Tanner had.

THE NEXT NIGHT, back in his basement den in Cellis, Brian loaded the first film into his projector. By the third film, he was sick of looking at the moving bodies until he noticed a rose tattoo on the right cheek of the rear end of a fat, pasty-looking brunette. He stopped the film and rewound it slowly by hand. He played the section of the film repeatedly until he was absolutely convinced.

Although the men on the film called the woman Boom-Boom Betty, he recognized the tattoo and the butt. It was Sierra, his sleek, tan and platinum-blonde Sierra. But in the tacky home movie, she was chunky, pasty and brunette.

He sat in the dark for hours, trying to figure out what to do.

FRED BUTLER'S STAG party was a hit with the guys. Brian used four of the five films to entertain the group until the cake girl arrived. But he didn't return the fifth film.

"Ricky, I'm really sorry about the one film, you know, the one with Boom-Boom Betty. I wrecked it, so I didn't bring it back. The film jammed and melted in the projector. I tore it trying to get it out before Sierra could catch me."

Ricky seemed to believe him, especially about the part about Sierra's reaction. "I'm not surprised."

"You don't know what she's like, man. Sierra would have killed me if she caught me looking at it."

"I'm really sorry to hear that. It was one of my favorites. I got that one from Merritt. We made a special trip to Enid just to catch her act. Don't worry about it, the reel was well worn before I got it. Merritt must have watched that film dozen and dozens of times before he gave it to me."

"Well, maybe you two can make another, like Boom-Boom Betty part two?"

"No, we shot that one at Jack's in downtown Enid. The club was shut down years ago."

The truth was, Sierra hadn't caught him. She didn't even know Brian had the film. As Brian hid the film, he hoped he had the original, that Ricky hadn't made any copies, and that Merritt didn't have any other Boom-Boom Betty films.

But Ricky's comment that he and Merritt had seen the film raised a new concern. Brian wondered how many more of his friends from the college had seen it. Brian had never thought about looking at the men in the film when he had looked at the film before. But now, he would have to watch the film once more to see if he recognized anyone else.

RICKY STOPPED BY Merritt's apartment on his way home from work. Merritt answered the door with a beer in his hand.

"What were you doing, Merritt?"

"Practicing for the Couch Olympics, what does it look like?" He had been sitting in the darkened room watching television.

"Anything new?"

Merritt had been drinking a lot since losing his job in pharmaceutical sales. He hadn't found a job that paid anywhere near the money he used to make. At least he had been smart enough to keep the studio apartment. The cheap flat was all he could afford now. Merritt swallowed a big swig of beer and burped. "No, no new job leads."

Ricky hoped to cheer him up and get him out of the apartment that evening. Ricky slid into the armchair nearest the door and tried to think of something to say. "Guess who I saw last month. Brian Tanner! He came to Fred Butler's bachelor party."

"How's he doing?"

"Just great. He lives in Cellis now. He's still with Sierra and they have one kid—a little girl."

"It figures. He's rich, good looking, and he gets the girl! It's so unfair!"

"Some guys have all the luck!"

"Yes, and some have rich daddies who buy their luck for them."

"You sound jealous Merritt."

"Yeah," Merritt said and chugged his beer. "Shouldn't I be? He marries the girl of my dreams. Then he moves into her apartment, right next door to me. Can you believe that? Then right away, he moves from that apartment to a better one. He got to finish school. I had to quit school and I had to move out of my apartment into this crummy studio. Eating and having a place to live are kind of important, you know!"

"Maybe you can go back, you're still young."

"Yeah, I'm young and up to my eyeballs in debt. Obviously, 1954 was a very bad year for me. Oh well, maybe it's for the best." He laughed bitterly and finished his beer. "Maybe it's my destiny to work for peanuts at a job I hate, and to be alone."

"This isn't pretty man! Maybe you should get up and go out somewhere!"

"What isn't pretty is that guys like Brian never have any trouble. They live perfect lives, have perfect wives and don't even get a little dirt on their hands. It just isn't fair. I wonder how he would act if he had the slightest bit of trouble, or his wife wasn't doing right. That would be fair man, that would be fair."

Staring at Merritt, Ricky shook his head as he rose from the chair. "You need a change, man, and you won't find it in that bottle. I gotta go. I'll see you around."

CHAPTER 21

DYNA, YOUR AUNT'S on the telephone." The words were simple, but to Dyna, her husband John sounded funny, as if something were wrong. Something was wrong, terribly wrong. He stood in the doorway, silhouetted by the bright light in the kitchen, where he had gone to make a peanut butter and grape jelly sandwich for himself. In the darkened living room of their apartment, Dyna rocked their red-haired twin infants, trying to get them to go to sleep. Fortunately, Javier was already sound asleep. It was nearly 8 P.M., Dyna had a backache, she was tired and she had struggled with the cranky twins all day. Most of all, she didn't want to talk to anyone, not even Aunt Alicia. Dyna gestured John to get rid of her.

"Dyna!" He called again from the kitchen.

She put the twins down on the soft blanket on the floor. Trying to shake the stiffness out of her back, she walked slowly to the door, where John stood, holding the telephone. He sat down at the table, took a bite of his thick sandwich and watched her.

Dyna leaned against the frame of the door. "Hello?"

"Dyna, sit down, honey." Aunt Alicia whispered in a barely audible voice. She was quiet, too quiet and not like her usual boisterous self.

Unable to sit, Dyna stood still while looking back at the twins on the living room floor. She wanted to lie down in a warm tub more than anything else right then. Maybe Aunt Alicia was having one of her spells, or she had a fight with Mr. Hebner. Hopefully, it would be only a quick discussion. Dyna leaned against the door frame. She didn't have the strength for much else. "Aunt Alicia, what? What is it?"

"It's your mother, she . . . she's dead." Whispering now, Aunt Alicia could barely speak the words.

"What? No! No! No!" Heart-wrenching anguish erupted from Dyna's throat as if her chest would explode. John jumped up from the table, dropping his sandwich and took the phone back from Dyna, who by now stood rigid in the doorway. He pulled her close, wrapping one arm tightly around her as he put the telephone to his ear. She buried her head in his chest and wailed. Over her cries, John tried to find out what had happened.

"Aunt Alicia, what's going on over there?"

Aunt Alicia sat in the dark, in her bedroom in her apartment. The light from her bedside lamp hurt her eyes, because she had been grieving so much. Aunt Alicia took a long, deep breath. It was the only way she could get the words out. "John, she's dead, John! My sister is dead! Sally called me. But John, it's worse than that. Joe . . ." Aunt Alicia stopped. After gasping for breath, she continued, "Joe beat Anna bad last month. She . . ." Aunt Alicia stopped again, took a deep breath and struggled to finish. "They never even took her to the hospital. Sally said Anna didn't want to go, but I don't believe that. Sally said she never got over it, something was wrong with her side. They found her dead. She's dead, John, my sister is dead!" The tears started flowing so heavily Alicia could barely speak.

"What? Where is she now?"

"Joe . . . Joe buried her, they didn't even have a real funeral for her." Her speech punctuated by sobs, Aunt Alicia went on. "They put her in the ground last week and didn't even call me until now. Dear God! Dear God!" Sobbing uncontrollably now, Alicia Carselli couldn't speak anymore.

"Aunt Alicia, stay put. We're on our way over," John said and listened for her response. But he didn't know whether she heard him or not, Aunt Alicia was sobbing so hard.

Within minutes, John and Dyna bundled up their three small children and went to Aunt Alicia's apartment.

Aunt Alicia had left the door unlocked and the lights off, but John and Dyna could hear her sobbing in the bedroom. The two made their way slowly through the living room and hallway, turning on lights as they went. They eased the light on in her bedroom and found her, huddled up in her bed.

With her hair down from its usual bun, showing gray streaks in her dark brown tresses and with eyes red and puffy, Aunt Alicia looked frightened and very old. As John put the children on the bed in the spare bedroom, Dyna and Aunt Alicia walked haltingly to the living room, sat on the sofa and hugged each other. Dyna tenderly took her aunt's hands as John slipped into a nearby chair. Aunt Alicia told them what had happened.

Dyna's sister, Sally, had called Aunt Alicia to blame her and Dyna for the trouble that the family had suffered in Briggandale. But more importantly, Sally wanted to make it clear—the family in Indiana wanted no further contact with Alicia or Dyna again.

Aunt Alicia repeated Sally's last hurtful jibes, "Dyna broke my dad's heart. He killed himself, right after Mama's funeral. We buried him today. Dyna can't ever be a part of our family again. And don't you call here either. Ever again." Aunt Alicia began weeping again.

As she held her sobbing aunt, Dyna's tears gave way to stony silence as the finality of the message sank in. She had no mother, no father and no family in Indiana. Although she had a husband, children of her own and other family in New Jersey, Dyna felt a dark emptiness in her soul, as if she were totally alone in the world.

EIGHT MONTHS LATER, Dyna sat at the oak desk, holding the package with the pale yellow ribbon. Letter after letter, she held them in her hands. All were from her. None were opened. She could tell Papa had written on most of them, but on the last two or three letters, her sister Sally's handwriting appeared. On all the envelopes, the message was clear "Refused—return to sender."

The cryptic messages brought back wave after wave of painful memories for Dyna. She wept. In the years since she left their small apartment in Briggandale, she had gotten few letters from her immediate family. It had been more than four years since Mama's last call. Papa had made sure of that. Dyna sat in front of the oak rolltop desk. She knew Aunt Alicia and Mama had kept in touch in a special way that close sisters sometimes do. Now, those two had to be chattering away at each other, Dyna imagined. They were in a much better place now and there was no way for Papa to interrupt them. He was dead too, but Dyna was sure he wasn't in heaven with them.

Dyna ran her fingers back and forth along the wooden slats of the desktop, like she used to do when she lived with her Aunt Alicia. When words wouldn't come or she needed to reflect on the events to write about, Dyna used to touch the wood and feel its glossy finish. Today might be her last time to touch this treasured piece of furniture.

Scenes of the life she had with her aunt in this place seemed to play in Dyna's mind like faint images from an old movie. She remembered the times when Aunt Alicia danced like a wild and crazy teenager to some bouncy tune on the radio. She remembered when Aunt Alicia started a pillow fight with her to cheer her up when she felt especially blue. Fine feathers flew everywhere and the two women romped like children, until the neighbors below banged on the ceiling and yelled for them to be quiet.

Dyna recalled the especially tender moment when she and Aunt Alicia brought Javier home from the hospital. Dyna cried because of the beautiful bassinet and decorations that Aunt Alicia had bought and set up in their room for the baby. Pastels and dark wood, the corner set up for the baby was just darling.

Her tears flowed so hard at this point that Dyna realized that her hands were now wet. An hour had passed while she sat at the desk, reflecting on her time with her aunt. With the memories, Dyna realized that she wasn't just losing her aunt, but also a place of shelter, love and protection. This was a place where she was loved and belonged and where her mistakes weren't something to be hidden, avoided or feared.

In Aunt Alicia's bedroom, Dyna tied the pale yellow ribbon back around the unopened letters. Her tears kept flowing even as she smiled sadly. She knew Mama and Aunt Alicia had protected her in so many ways while she lived in New Jersey. But Dyna never expected this. Finding the unopened letters she had written to her family among Aunt Alicia's important papers was the last thing Dyna had expected. She put the packet down beside her, and then put it back in the drawer. Dyna started sorting through the drawer again and found the insurance policy she had come for. It would more than pay for the expenses of the funeral. After dropping the policy into her purse, Dyna pushed the packet of letters to the very back of the desk, behind all the rest of the clutter. She closed the desk, gathered her purse and walked slowly toward the door, crying.

Pausing for a few moments in the doorway of Aunt Alicia's bedroom, Dyna returned to the desk. Aunt Alicia probably intended to take the secret of the letters with her to her grave. Throwing the packet away was the next best thing under the circumstances. No sense in telling anyone else about the letters, she decided. Dyna's family in Indiana had cut her off months ago. That day, Dyna did the same to them. She opened the rolltop desk again. Dyna pulled out the packet by its ribbon and tossed the packet into the oversized trash can at the door. Flipping off the light, Dyna shut the door behind her. She only had a few minutes left to get back to Tangelo's Mortuary to finish the arrangements for Aunt Alicia's funeral. No one would know the extra reason for her sorrow.

·

CHAPTER 22

IN THE APARTMENT with John, Dyna had few occasions
for long baths. One tiny bathroom and three small children
meant she was rarely alone. She treasured the times that one of
Aunt Alicia's children would take the boys, even if only for an
hour. Dyna could wash her hair in peace and relax somewhat in
the cramped bathtub.

Sometimes, after she had filled the tub, she would discover
the water was cold, ice cold. The building in which they lived was
old. Other tenants would take baths and showers in the hours
before she could get a chance to run water for her bath. But hot
water or not, she soaked anyway, desperate for the relief the few
minutes of privacy gave her. As she lay back, the water coming up
only to her waist, Dyna dreamed about her favorite fantasy—the
one in which she and John would get their own single-family home.
Even if they had no furniture to put inside and they had to sleep
on the floor, she would get her dream home and her dream
appliance. It would be a thirty-gallon, no, a specially installed
fifty-gallon hot water heater. And she would fill the tub and soak,
over and over until she ran all of the hot water out.

With John and the boys gone today, she started to run water

for her bath. Today was a good day, she could tell. The water came out hot.

WITH THE DEATH of R.J. during their fifth year of marriage and the inheritance that passed to Brian, he and Sierra moved from their small house in town to a much larger one in a better neighborhood. This house was well over five thousand square feet and had an in-ground pool, all located on seven well-manicured acres. This place had everything she had wanted, all the things she imagined a young doctor should have.

Brian made the best of his poor marriage by focusing his energy on his medical practice. In time, he turned the two-person office into Tanner, Meyer and Smertz, one of the largest clinics in the four-county region. By the time Andrea was a little older and the clinic was well established, Brian figured out a way to make the clinic meet more personal needs.

"DYNA, HONEY, JUST hear me out on this!"

"I'm listening, John."

In the five minutes he had been home, he had turned her world completely upside down. John took off his tie slowly to stall, hoping somehow she would calm down a little.

He had come home and found her in the kitchen, preparing dinner as usual. The twins, Alfred and Benjamin, were in their high chairs, eating carrot strips. Javier sat at the kitchen table, coloring quietly. John came in as he always did and pecked her on the cheek. She continued stirring the food until he told her they were moving to Indiana and soon. Understandably, she was upset.

"Sorry I didn't talk to you about it first honey, but Ed Harrison put me on the spot." John studied her for a second or two. Her mouth was closed, but her crossed arms and tapping right foot said plenty. He had some serious explaining to do.

"Ed gave me the choice of a regional position in Indiana or letting me go. They just don't need so many salesmen here. The northern Indiana region is wide open. Reserpico has only a few salesmen in Indiana. Only two of those work in the northern part of the state."

While he continued, Dyna took quick inventory of their situation in New Jersey. With their twin sons, Benjamin and Alfred, during their marriage plus Javier, she had her hands full already. But here, Dyna could count on at least two or three of Aunt Alicia's adult children to help her with her young boys. In a pinch, Dyna could even call on some of the ladies from the church they attended. How in the world could she raise three children in Indiana with no family or friends to help her? Other questions flooded her head and she only half listened to John. Could they afford to live in Indiana? The apartment they had now wasn't big enough. How could they afford to move? Where would they live?

"Ed promised me a raise, plus moving expenses." He caught her attention. "It's a lot cheaper to live in Indiana than here. The price of almost everything is less expensive there than here, Stan told me." Stan was Stanley Hood, one of John's co-workers who had moved out to Indiana last year. Stan had been good to them while he lived in New Jersey. At least they would have two friends, Stan and his wife, Loretta, to count on in Indiana. But Dyna wondered if these two would be enough.

"Stan's already found a couple of really nice houses, some of them are single-family homes, Dyna. We can stay in a house there for a lot less than we pay here for renting this apartment. They even have backyards for the boys to play in."

A single-family house with a yard! Dyna slowly uncrossed her arms and leaned forward to listen closely. No more Genesee Park— it was changing anyway. There would be no more complaints from the neighbors about how her boys jumped up and down in the apartment building. No more catty comments from Mrs. Schneider, their neighbor in Apartment 7, about how she would never let her children cry so loud at night. With Aunt Alicia's death last year, Dyna felt less and less like New Jersey was her home. Here was a chance to leave New Jersey and live in a real house of their own.

"We can do a lot better there than we can here, Dyna. I just know that we can."

Dyna still didn't answer right away. She thought about one more reason why they should move to Indiana. Reconciling with her family there might be possible. Surely, if they could see how cute the boys were and how Javier looked just like Raphael, maybe they could get over whatever bad feelings they had toward her. Maybe they could be close again, like they were when Dyna lived with them in Briggandale. The move to Indiana didn't seem half bad now.

Dyna finally smiled a little and asked, "Where will we live?"

Noticing her slight smile, John took her into his arms and kissed her passionately. "Cellis. A place called Cellis, Indiana. And on our way there, I'll take you to meet my favorite aunt, Aunt Vernice. She's my only close relative on my dad's side of the family. She lives in Todda, Ohio, near Toledo. You'll like her."

As he stroked Dyna's hair, John giggled, relieved she was willing to make the transition gladly with him. He kissed her cheeks and forehead and then took her chin in his right hand. "And I promise you'll love Indiana. I'll make it good for you. I promise."

•

CHAPTER 23

MORE THAN TEN years after she had left Briggandale, Dyna had nearly everything she had ever wanted. With a husband who adored her and four healthy, beautiful children, in Cellis, she lived in a lovely single-family home, a three-bedroom cottage with a bath and a half and a den. A white picket fence surrounded her yard. Dyna even had a small garden and a few flowers in the back. Javier, her eldest son, was ten. Benjamin and Alfred, her twins, were six, almost seven. Her youngest, Steven Jacob, was four going on five years old. She and John even had started taking their family to church regularly. Except for the lack of contact between herself and her siblings, her life was complete. She even got to enjoy her fantasy, except now, it was a reality.

In the green-tiled bathroom of their Indiana home, Dyna hid from her children and even from her husband, John, at times. Dyna didn't get to escape very often. But when she could, Dyna would soak in the tub, surrounded by warm, bubble bath-scented water. If she pulled her knees up, she could lie back in water up to her neck; otherwise, she got the water just past her waist. She would pretend that the maid would make the dinner and the nanny would bandage the latest scraped knee. The boys knew to leave her alone during those moments. Inevitably, a squabble over a toy, or a demand for food from an obviously starving child, or a cry for medical attention for a bloody finger or skinned limb, or a telephone call would end those peaceful retreats. But at least the water was hot every time she wanted to take a bath.

THAT DAY STARTED like many other winter days in the Mitchell home. Gray skies were overhead and the sun wasn't shining; heavy rain and snow were in the forecast. The day started out in the forty-degree range, but dropped twenty degrees. The older children were at school. John had the day off and he was in a really good mood. Only Dyna seemed out of sorts. She had a cold or some minor sinus infection. But she still had errands to run, including taking Jake to the clinic for a checkup. John came to her rescue.

"Just get some rest, honey. I'll take Jake to the doctor. It's just a routine check-up, right? We'll be back soon, so go back to bed, Dyna."

With John taking charge of Jake, Dyna thought she could get some much-needed rest. She stood before the wide picture window in their living room to watch them go. Dyna saw John buckle Jake's seat belt, but not his own. As she waved goodbye to them, Dyna made a note to remind John to buckle his own seat belt. Those seat belts were the latest thing in car safety and they picked that model because of them. After all, she needed him in her life and in the lives of her children.

Dyna got back into bed and in minutes, she was sound asleep. While she slept, the snow storm started.

Four hours later, an officer rang the doorbell at the Mitchell home. As he stood at the golden door of the white cottage with the black shutters, he wondered about the people who lived there, especially who would answer the door. He hoped it would not be a small child. The officer rang the doorbell and braced himself for the inevitable scene that was sure to occur.

Still half asleep, Dyna stumbled from their bedroom to the front door and yanked it open. She was irritated that John hadn't used his key.

But John wasn't at the door. A tall, thin police officer stood on the porch, his dark uniform silhouetted by the falling snow. Dyna's heart leaped to her throat. Her ears ached from the unbearable pounding of her heart. "Please come in," she said fearfully, although she really didn't want to see him.

As he stepped over the threshold and stood on the entry rug, knocking the snow off his clothing, she couldn't help noticing his color.

The officer was very pale. His color contrasted sharply with the dark blue of his uniform. He started slowly, "Ma'am, are you Mrs. John Mitchell? I'm Officer Melvin Drake."

"Yes, I am. What's wrong?" She stood trembling; she felt as if she were about to faint.

"Ma'am, I'm afraid I have some bad news for you."

To Dyna, the rest of what happened seemed like a nightmare. But she could not wake up. She could barely take the bad news in. John was dead. Her baby was at Cellis Memorial Hospital. Even as they spoke, hospital employees were working on Jake. The news was horrible, too horrible to comprehend. But it was real.

Dyna called Kathy, a neighbor girl who was attending college part-time, to come and wait for the other children to come home from school. The officer waited in the car. Dyna grabbed her purse and coat and ran out the door as soon as Kathy arrived.

For Dyna, the rest of March 23, 1965 was a dark, swirling blur.

CHAPTER 24

LONG AFTER THE rest of the clinic staff had gone home, Brian Tanner sat in the lower level of the clinic in the records room. Normally, by this time in the evening, he would be home, asleep in his easy chair. But tonight's activity energized him. Of the file cabinets lining three sides of the room, Brian had picked through three drawers that evening. With a pencil, some paper and a cup of water in front of him, he sat at the long table in the room, skimming through patient files.

"Mrs. Ketters?" She met most of Brian's criteria but she was too ugly. Since he could choose, he felt he should do a whole lot better than her.

Occasionally, he consulted the payment ledger beside him. He had chosen two already, and had only three more files to look at this time. The clock on the wall showed it was already nine.

He flipped through the next file quickly. "Mrs. Gunderson, no husband around. Pass on her."

For the next file, he took a little more time. "Mrs. Ferris, well, she's rich but she doesn't need the kind of services I want to offer." He thought about her for a few more minutes, and then put her file into the discard pile.

"Mmmh, Mrs. Grisher's a possibility. She looks okay, doesn't have much money and has an unemployed husband who spends more time drinking in bars than looking for work. Her daughter badly needs reconstructive surgery." Brian put her file into the "yes" pile.

Three were enough for now. He settled back to take a closer look at the three manila file folders he had kept out. After reviewing the file on top, he stuck a pencil in it to keep it open and he made his first call for the evening.

"Hello, is this the Grisher residence? Oh, is this Mrs. Grisher? Well, this is Dr. Tanner from the clinic. Yes, I'm fine, but I was just sitting here reviewing your daughter's medical history and had some questions. No, no, sometimes I do work late, and tonight, your daughter's situation was on my mind. Do you have a few minutes now to talk? Were you aware that our clinic sometimes performs surgery at no cost for needy children? Oh, I see. Your daughter's condition is so special to me. I wondered if you and I could get together privately to talk about it."

Brian began his pitch innocently. As with other mothers, he started each time by focusing on the child's need for help and his supposed compassion. But he wouldn't discuss what he really had in mind until he had the woman alone in front of him.

Brian's scheme was simple but effective. The clinic periodically performed reconstructive surgery for children from needy families. Most of the clinic's patients knew this. Some had become patients in hope of improving the chances of their children being chosen.

Usually, the local newspaper, the *Cellis Courier*, ran a couple of articles about the clinic and a feature article about the child they had selected, along with a few details about the surgery. When the charity surgery was done, another article would appear. After each article, the clinic's business would increase predictably. It was a great public relations move, the partners had decided.

But for Brian, the services give away netted some fringe benefits that would never make the newspapers. Occasionally, he targeted some of the mothers of children needing surgery and hinted he had some control over the selection process. He, in fact, did not.

The decision was made by the partners in a blind draw, followed by discussion and evaluation, all done in secret.

In picking his victims, Brian chose pretty, married, underinsured or financially strapped women whose children desperately needed reconstructive surgery. He knew they had the need and were less likely to blow his cover. Brian picked the most emotionally vulnerable ones, figuring they were the most willing to yield to his requests without a whole lot of trouble.

A few mothers had taken Brian's hints and offered him anything, including their own bodies, in exchange for influencing selection. To some women, he didn't even hint he could influence the selection—he lied outright about his power to choose the recipient.

When he found a woman who was even slightly receptive, he pursued her slowly, almost imperceptibly, until she made an offer to him. After each of his private sessions with the woman, Dr. Brian Tanner marveled at how far the woman would go with him for her child. After four of five private sessions with Dr. Brian, he assured the woman that her child's selection was almost in the bag, but the partnership would have the final say.

For any woman who seemed dissatisfied with his representations or overly anxious about the selection process, he reminded the woman that he was nationally known for his expertise and hinted that no one would believe her if she ever complained. He would remind her that she had initiated the relationship, hoping to shame the woman into silence.

By now, he was confident that no woman would ever contact the medical board about his antics. No husband would confront him either. Invariably, within six months or so, even if the child was selected for surgery, the woman cut the child's visits, and then dropped out of sight.

The scam served Brian well for years.

CHAPTER 25

WITH HIS WIFE, his mistress and his expanding business, Everett Q. Sears led a busy life. The wife he loved dearly had been sick for almost a decade. Too ill to work or to socialize much, Ellen Sears stayed at home, hidden behind the pale pink plaster of their villa-style home. On bad days, she lay in their bedroom in an oversized poster bed, dozing, often too ill to leave the room.

But today was a good day. Arising before him, she had dressed and left their bedroom early. Everett awoke and walked through their home to find her in her favorite place.

Ellen sat in the central plaza of the home, soaking up sun. She looked like a fairy princess, her wispy, pale-yellow hair flowing down on her gauze-like pink chiffon robe. Multiple gowns covered her thin frame as she sat out in the bright light. She had cut blossoms from the lilies she had planted the year before. The pale yellow and pink petals moved in the early morning breeze while the crystal vase holding them sparkled. As he stood in the doorway, beholding her in her surreal setting, his heart stirred. He loved her for her gentleness and beauty.

Throughout her lengthy illness, Ellen still managed their household, paying bills, decorating their home and doing minor tasks as she felt able. She demanded to keep these responsibilities. Ellen claimed they helped to maintain her dignity. Even during her illness, Ellen liked to know how well they were doing financially. Everett let her do as much as she could—he knew she wouldn't be around much longer.

As he ran his right hand through his silvery hair, Everett struggled with the hard choices he had to make about his two women. His mistress was pressing him to provide for reconstructive surgery for their young son, Zachary. Everett loved his little boy. The sickly little boy was the only child Everett had produced so far.

But he couldn't pay for the surgery out of his own pocket. That was the problem. How could he come up with that kind of money without his wife finding out about it? He knew he couldn't with his regular business; opening the last shop had drained all of his available cash reserves. But he could come up with the money if he went back to the type of work he had left long ago.

HE HAD SERVED as a contract enforcer for years for a minor Chicago hoodlum. Insurance hits were his specialty.

Everett's boss, Mike Hoffer, made seemingly legitimate loans with high interest rates to struggling small businesses. And with each loan came accident and life insurance policies naming Hoffer's company, IBIN Loan, as the beneficiary. When the borrowers fell behind or could not pay, the boss contacted Everett. As needed, Everett caused injury to or the death of the victims chosen by his boss. In turn, Mike collected insurance proceeds based upon the policies. Failure to pay loans to Mike Hoffer under those circumstances could be quite costly.

But Mike and two of his top underlings were killed seven years ago, in a bloodbath that made national news in 1963 as the New Libertyville murders. Everett knew that, unless he dropped out of sight, his days were numbered too. The grisly slayings just gave him the incentive to relocate quickly. Everett and his wife moved to West End, Indiana.

Two years after leaving Chicago, Everett met the girl who would become his mistress—Gina Minear, a waitress at café near his north side Cellis store. Dark-haired with violet blue-eyes, she was gorgeous, simple-minded and very attentive to his needs. With her, he had found someone to take care of him. Gina had come to West End from a little town in Utah. She knew about his wife and his commitment to stay with her until her end, but was willing to spend time with him anyway. It was during this time of high stress that his only child, Zachary, was born.

Neither of the women knew about Everett's underworld ties. He tried his best to make sure these women were kept in the dark about his past murderous activities.

From West End, as he had in Chicago, Everett ran a chain of dry cleaning establishments. His business covered the West End, Abbeville and Cellis area. While he still had some minor illegal activities going on with his nephew, Dieter Hunt, he had nothing that generated the kind of money needed for Zachary's care.

AS HE SAT in his main office in West End in early April 1970, flipping through the *West End Gazette,* Everett saw a story about the charity surgery the Tanner, Meyer and Smertz Clinic had performed for some little girl. He read the article carefully and learned that the girl had the same deformities as his son had and that Dr. Brian Tanner headed the team that had performed the surgery.

Everett didn't want charity. He just needed some help for his son, done in a way that couldn't be traced to him. And he couldn't let his wife know about it. Ever. Finding out about the little boy would kill Ellen and Everett couldn't bear that thought. He had to come up with a solution.

And Dr. Tanner was that solution, if Everett could help it.

Checking through his customer lists, Everett learned Dr. Tanner was a customer of one of his locations in Cellis, as was the clinic. Everett made a note to visit him.

But he didn't have to make much of an effort to meet Dr.

Tanner. Two days after the *West End Gazette* article, Brian Tanner walked into one of Everett's Cellis stores at the same time Everett did. Carrying several shirts and two wine-stained dresses, Brian made a petty remark to the counter girl about his sloppy wife.

Recognizing Brian from the articles, Everett introduced himself. "Aren't you the doctor who does free surgery on little needy children? Sure, you're that guy! You're making a big difference in so many lives. Stay with it. Wonderful work you're doing there!"

Flattered by the recognition, Brian warmed up immediately to Everett. Within minutes, the two talked as if they were old friends. The men found they shared the same attraction—being in total control of their lives.

"Brian, it's been nice meeting you. I've got to get going. I've got to take care of some business here and at one of my other shops. But I'll be in contact with you soon."

Although he was anxious to present his need to Brian, Everett knew he had to wait. What he had in mind would take time and trust.

CHAPTER 26

"GIVE MAMA ONE more leg lift."

"No!" He shouted. "It hurts too much!"

"Jacob!"

"Please, Mama, please!"

"Jake!"

"Ugh uh!" he grunted. "Mama, please, no!"

"Steven Jacob Mitchell! Stop all noise and lift your leg!"

"Mama, I can't! Please, Mommeee!"

"I heard you, Jake, but if you want to get better, you have to do this. Sweetie, I know it hurts, but you've got to try!"

Tears splashed onto the bright blue plastic mat as the small, red-haired boy struggled to lift his tiny bent leg. As soon as Jake got his leg three inches off the mat, Dyna's strong hands reached under the tiny ankle and leg. Slowly, steadily, she lifted the crooked leg a quarter, then a half, then finally, one full inch higher.

Jake sobbed.

Dyna closed her eyes to her young son's wet, flushed face. But she could not close her ears to his painful cries. As she held his leg in place and massaged it, she felt the warmth of tears filling her eyes.

Slowly, she eased his leg down to the mat and quickly wiped her tears away. She saw he hadn't noticed her holding back her tears and felt a little better. Someone had to be strong here and today, she just had to fake it.

"See Jake, you did it! You really did it! Mama is so proud of you!"

His hiccup-like sobs softened. "Mama, am I done yet? Do I have to do any more?"

"No Sweetie, you did it, you did all of your exercises just right this morning. Mama is so proud of you! You're getting better."

"Really, Mama, am I getting better?" The sobbing slowed, and then nearly stopped.

"Uh huh. Now lie flat so Mama can rub your legs." As she gently kneaded and massaged his soft pink skin, Dyna began humming.

Jake soon drifted off to sleep. Exercising his crippled leg exhausted him every single time, even after all these years. As Jake lay sleeping on the mat in the living room, Dyna closed her eyes and continued massaging his leg. Even with her eyes closed, her tears began to flow.

IN THE FIVE years since her husband, John's, death, Dyna's life had worsened in every way possible. All of the insurance money was gone. The social security payments weren't enough to meet the mortgage payment and their living expenses. So she and the boys lost their house.

After John's death, she began to distance herself from friends and from people at the small church she and John had attended. At church, while sitting in the pew, she linked the place and the songs to happier days with John. Each time she attended, Dyna found herself becoming increasingly depressed. In time, she stopped going at all.

It was at this low point she met and married a charmer named Donald Woods.

Her marriage to Don Woods less than a year ago had become

a disaster. An unemployed carpenter who drank and gambled, Don could barely hold a job when he had one, let alone a decent one with insurance. Knowing she was a young widow, he figured she would support him with her resources, for better or for worse. For him, taking her money would be better. And he didn't plan to stick around long if it got worse.

WHILE LOOKING AT her youngest son dozing on the mat, Dyna made up her mind to go back to work. She needed money desperately. But more importantly, Jacob needed surgery on his left leg and therapy for both legs and none of the services that he needed would be cheap. Her baby, Steven Jacob Mitchell, suffered serious injuries in the same accident in which her first husband, John, died. Now, years later, he still had trouble with his right leg. His left leg was visibly crooked. No amount of home therapy could straighten out his leg. Dyna applied to agency after agency, all of which rejected her. She tried to do everything legitimately possible to get help and failed.

The daylight faded as Dyna sat near her sleeping son. The pinkish light seemed to highlight his features, intensifying the red in his carrot-colored freckles and hair. He was oblivious to the sun but not to the pain, for his little legs twitched occasionally and his little face grimaced in turn. How unfair, Dyna thought, even asleep, he can't get any rest.

As she sat on the mat while Jake slept, Dyna thought about what she had gone through so far for her children. It wasn't supposed to be like this. Life was supposed to be fair and a mother was supposed to be able to get help for her children when she needed it. A husband was supposed to provide for his children. Still massaging Jake's leg, she remembered what Aunt Alicia had said to her during an earlier dark time in her life. "Get it straight, girl," Alicia Sarcesi Carselli told her. "You gotta be ready to take care of you and yours. You can't always depend on a man, even a good one. You gotta do for you."

With no insurance and no money, Dyna had to find work at a

place that would guarantee the greatest chance for help for Jake. The only place nearby for the specialized surgery and follow-up care Jake needed was the Tanner, Meyer and Smertz Clinic. While she lived in Cellis, she learned that Brian worked there.

Maybe through her employment at the clinic, Jake would qualify for free or reduced-cost surgery. Even if he didn't, she hoped Brian would feel pity or something for her. Desperate, Dyna believed Brian would remember their good times together and help her.

But she had to be sure. Who could tell her much about Brian? Dyna thought about it for a few minutes and came up with an answer. Fred Butler could tell her. He seemed nice enough and was always pleasant to her whenever she called years ago.

Dyna contacted directory assistance from Briggandale, hoping that Fred might still live there after all these years. He did.

"Fred, this is Dyna Palpietro. Do you remember me? Dyna Palpietro? How are you?"

"Why, Dyna, how are you? I've always wondered about you! Whatever happened to you? How are you?"

Dyna hesitated, knowing that her stories of bad luck could fill a book. "I'm okay, I've had my share of ups and downs over the years. But Fred, how are you?"

"Well, I've been well. I'm a doctor now and married. I always thought that Brian missed the mark with you. He should have married you, Dyna. Over and over, through the years, Brian always regretted not marrying you."

Dyna secretly rejoiced. Fred was going to the very topic she wanted to talk about. "Fred, I've always wanted to know, why did he marry someone else?"

"Well," Fred sniffed, "Sierra Gleason was her name then and she claimed that she was pregnant by him. Brian felt obligated to her and so he married her. But he didn't love her. He loved you." Fred paused, "I haven't talked to him about you in years, but I know he resents her now. He has a miserable life with her."

This news was overwhelming for Dyna. Would she have fared the same? Would Brian have resented her too? Quickly, she decided

that she couldn't dwell on those thoughts right now. Fred added,
"Sierra and Brian had one child, a girl."

Dyna forced herself to ask, "What's her name?"

"They named her Andrea Eva."

After chatting for a few minutes more, Fred and Dyna wrapped
up their conversation, promising to stay in touch. As Dyna hung
up, she felt more confident about approaching Brian for help.

The next morning, while the children were in school and Don
was at work, Dyna went to the Tanner, Meyer and Smertz Clinic.
She applied for a job in custodial services and was hired right away.
Dyna knew what she wanted for her son. The only question was
what would she have to do for her child. She had no doubt about
her willingness.

CHAPTER 27

GRAY HAIR AND dark circles were all she could see in the tiny flaking silver of the bathroom mirror. Gone was the sparkle that she once had in her brown, nearly black eyes. So many lines, so many wrinkles, so much of her hard life hung on her like a ragged, worn housecoat. So much had happened in her lifetime that her face, her shoulders, her entire body, bore the weight of the world she had carried for so long.

Slowly, she pulled the handle of the top drawer in the bathroom sink. Poking among the lipsticks, the children's toys, the dirty bits of cotton balls, she dug deeply into the clutter and found it. She took off the cracked cap of the camouflage stick and cranked up the pale makeup slowly.

Careful now, there's not a whole lot left and you can't afford to lose the last little bit down the sink, she thought to herself. She put two or three dots under each dark-ringed eye, wet her finger and tried to spread the covering cream across each baggy lid. Not satisfied, she added two or three more dots on each lid. The rings under her eyes stubbornly remained, faintly bluish gray. Finally, putting the cover stick to her right eye like a lipstick, Dyna gave a firm swipe with the cover stick. The cover stick left a pancake like a clump under her eye, contrasting sharply with the bluish-gray circle under her eye. The cover stick popped out of the tube and dropped straight down into the open drain of the white porcelain sink.

Dyna put her head against the mirror and cried, splashing cloudy, beige teardrops onto the sink.

And the rest of her first day at her first job outside the home in a decade and a half continued to go downhill.

Working on second shift that day, one of Dyna's first assigned tasks was to clean an exam room. Some child had messed on himself, then purposely spread the hideously foul-smelling brown feces over two chairs, the exam table and the floor because he didn't like coming to the clinic.

CHAPTER 28

LONG AFTER THE clinic had closed, Brian Tanner sat in the lower level of the clinic in the records room, making up another hit list. He had chosen three files already and had one last file to look at this time.

As Brian thumbed through the file, he began smiling broadly. It belonged to Dyna, now Dyna Palpietro Woods. Surprised to see she was a patient at the clinic, Brian was even more surprised to find out that she now worked in the clinic. How was she hired without him knowing about it? According to one entry, she had started in April 1970.

Intrigued, Brian pulled out her personnel records to see what else he could find out about her and her family. From reviewing her records, Brian learned she had four kids. "Mmmph," Brian mumbled, "Her kids are all Mitchells, but she's married to a guy named Woods. I wonder what happened to Mitchell."

Brian looked closer at the children's birth dates. The birth date of the eldest son seemed to jump out at him. Realizing what had happened, Brian couldn't control his outrage.

"Well, how do you like that! This kid was born right before Andrea! Dyna was two-timing me with that Mitchell guy! She had to be pregnant when she was with me. No wonder she didn't care when we broke up! She was just using me to get married! The kid wasn't mine, or she would have told me years ago. She must have been trying to get me to marry her because Mitchell hadn't. All this time, she led me to believe that I was the only one and that she really loved me!"

By the time he had finished going through her records, Brian figured that Mitchell was out of the picture now and she had married some bum who couldn't support them all. Plus her youngest, Steven Jacob Mitchell, needs reconstructive surgery on his left leg.

Brian was glad to see her file. He remembered the day he broke up with her with strange bitterness. When he told her they were through, she hadn't reacted like he had expected her to. She seemed as if she wouldn't lose any sleep over it like he had. To Brian, it seemed their breakup meant little to her. He always wondered how she could go on with her life so easily without him. Now, he finally knew why she could go on; she had another lover on the side.

His hurt pride rose up inside him like a serpent. This was his chance to strike at her and inflict as much pain as possible.

Brian had convinced himself long ago that Dyna never really loved him, but she used him. Now, he finally had proof. Dyna was a greedy, grasping witch, just like Sierra had turned out to be. Now, he had a chance to get even with Dyna and he didn't want to miss it. Her file went on the top of the "yes" pile.

LATER THAT WEEK, Brian called her into his executive office. He stood at the door long after she had come in, then slowly shut the door behind him. Brian crossed the room and slid into the overstuffed leather chair behind his desk. He said nothing.

Silent, Dyna was frightened about what he had in mind. She sat in one of the dark walnut chairs in front of his desk and looked around. On the desk sat a picture of a blond-haired woman and a little girl. Peering at the photograph carefully, Dyna figured that she must be Sierra and the girl was Andrea. For some reason, the woman's face seemed familiar to Dyna.

Brian's office was huge. It held an oversized, black-leather stuffed sofa, a matching executive chair, several hard-backed walnut chairs, a small refrigerator and a walnut-paneled, stainless steel built-in bar. The room seemed like it was much more than just an office. The lighting was low, making the room dark, as if cloaking many evil things that had happened there.

Brian leaned back and just stared at her. If she wanted anything from him, she would have to ask for him. No, he decided, Dyna would have to beg him for anything she wanted from him, and he would make her pay to get it.

Dyna stared at all of his diplomas and awards on the walls and purposely did not look at him. She said nothing to him—she couldn't. And despite all the planning she had done, hours of thinking about what she would say and how she would get her idea across to him, she couldn't say a single thing.

Does he know I need something from him? Does he know how much power he has over me? Dyna couldn't help but wonder. Should I tell him that Javier is his son? Would he help Jake if he knew about Javier? She decided against telling Brian about Javier right then. Since she had never told him about Javier before, he might not believe her, or if he did, he might feel like she was pressuring him.

Finally, she started slowly, her voice low, "Brian, I really need your help. My son, Jake, well, he needs surgery on his left leg. I'll do anything—just name it—if you could help him. Please Brian, please . . ." Her voice trailed off.

"Did you come to work here just to get help from me?"

"I, uh, I didn't know where else to go, Brian. My son really needs help."

Just as I thought, she's just trying to manipulate me one more time, Brian's thoughts toward her turned stone cold. Barely hiding his contempt, Brian smiled wickedly as he leaned forward in his chair and began, "Oh really? Anything? I think you know what I want from you, Dyna. I miss the good times we used to have."

She let him take the lead. After all, she needed him.

THE NEXT DAY, as Dyna walked into the brightly lit break room of the clinic, four or five women were gathered around a glossy magazine, chattering. Dyna quickly learned they were discussing the story of a divorced woman who had started an extremely lucrative prostitution ring. One of Dyna's co-workers pointed out that the woman began the business so she could take care of her three small children in a way she had become accustomed to while married.

"Can you believe it?" Disbelief, shock and criticism, the various comments were generally negative.

"Well, what would you do for your child?"

"Well, I wouldn't do that!"

"Come on—if your kids were hungry, you would steal bread or something, wouldn't you? You wouldn't let your kids go to bed starving, would you?"

"Well, it's not the same thing."

"Let's face it, we've all done things we aren't proud of, right?"

The women continued chattering around her. But Dyna didn't look up. She just stared at the magazine, pretending to read it. She just couldn't handle the eye contact at this point. What if her co-workers found out what she was doing now? She didn't want to answer any questions about what she would or wouldn't do. She was working at the clinic now specifically to do something she had sworn to her mother and to herself she would never do again.

But her baby meant everything to her. Dyna would do whatever she needed to for her child.

IN THE SMALL café on the edge of Briggandale, Merritt Hughes finished his sandwich, then checked his coffee cup. He slid his hand into his pocket to see if he could afford to eat anything. As he sat on a stool at the counter, a well-dressed man eased onto the stool beside him and pulled a menu out of the metal stand that sat on the counter.

Merritt glanced at the man, then looked back into the coffee cup. Melba, the waitress on duty at that end of the counter, came over. She pulled a note pad and pencil from her apron pocket and prepared to take the man's order.

"Mister, what can I get for you?"

The man looked up from the menu he had been studying. "I'd like a cup of coffee and the roast beef platter."

"Coleslaw or salad?"

"I'll skip those, thanks."

Melba looked over at Merritt's nearly empty cup. "Merritt, can I get you some more coffee?"

"Well . . . ."

"It's on the house today."

"Then sure."

As Melba walked away from that end of the counter, the man spoke to Merritt. "Did she call you Merritt?"

With his cup at his lips, Merritt swallowed, then answered. "Yeah, mainly because that's my name."

"Is that your last name?"

"No, my first." Merritt looked at the man now carefully. The voice and face were familiar, but he couldn't quite place them.

The man continued "Merritt, huh? Kind of unusual, isn't it?"

"Not really. I knew two other Merritts while I was in college."

"College? Did you go to Briggandale?"

"Yes, but I . . ." Merritt stopped. Did this guy know him? He looked familiar to Merritt, but Merritt didn't know why.

"Do you know Sierra Gleason?"

"Yes, I do." And with his answer, Merritt froze as he suddenly remembered who this guy was. This was the guy from Sierra's apartment. Quickly, Merritt realized that he had to pretend that he had never met this man before, or he might have some explaining to do. But Merritt just had to know how this guy had managed to get close to Sierra. "And who are you?"

"The name is Tony, Tony Agriniello. I've been looking for Sierra."

I'll just bet you were, Merritt thought to himself. "How do you know her?"

"I met her at Briggandale."

"Did you see her often?"

"No, only one time."

Merritt didn't know what to say. What he had seen through the vent—was it lust or an assault? Maybe he had come to the wrong conclusion years ago.

Just then, Melba came back with a coffee pot in one hand and a cup and saucer in the other. She set up the cup of coffee for Tony, then refilled Merritt's cup. "Sir, it'll be a few minutes longer for that platter. In the meantime, can I get anything else for you?"

"No thanks, miss." Tony flashed a smile at her and watched as she walked away. He turned back to Merritt. "Do you keep in touch with Sierra?"

"Not exactly. She's married now." Merritt paused briefly and looked into his cup. Here was a chance to hurt Brian and he decided not to let it pass. Maybe Tony could inject a little havoc into Brian Tanner's perfect life. "But I know where she lives."

The two men talked for a few minutes longer, while Merritt shared information about Sierra's life in Cellis. After finishing his coffee, Merritt got ready to leave. But as he said goodbye to Tony and to Melba, Merritt Hughes couldn't suppress a mischievous grin.

CHAPTER 29

STARING AT THE blackboard in front of him and totally unaware of his mother's efforts, Jake wondered when it all would end. Even as his fourth-grade teacher, Mrs. Morton, stood writing math problems with white chalk onto the black slate, Jake could hear them, whispering, tittering and chattering in the chairs behind him.

Mrs. Morton had seated her class alphabetically, but because of Jake's ongoing need to move and flex his left leg while sitting, Mrs. Morton seated him in the front row on the left side of the room. The only advantage to his position in the classroom was that he could see out of the window and most of his classmates could not.

Several seats behind him sat his tormenters, Russell Ammon Jr. and Eunice P. Driver. They had started it all. Even in class, their torture continued, although much quieter. Spit balls in the morning and rubber bands throughout the day—with his back to them, he was a perfect target. In a few minutes, it would be recess and another time he wished he could die.

No one in his class at school ever called him by his real name, except when Mrs. Morton was around. While sticks and stones may break bones, long ago, Jake had figured out it was a big fat lie that names will never hurt you. He hurt deeply because of the names children at school called him. They teased him mercilessly because of his stuttering and because of the heavy brace on his left leg. A small group of kids, Russell Ammon Jr., Eunice P. Driver, Tim Rausch and Roger Ederawski made it their mission to remind him daily of what was wrong with him and how much they hated him. Every chance they got, they called him names like Carrot Top, Crippled Carrot, Jerky Jake. Understandably, Jake hated those kids back. Worse, he hated his disabilities.

"One-one-one d-d-day, I'll show you. J-j-just you wait, I'm g-g-going to g-g-g-get you," he vowed.

"What can you do to us, Jerky Jake?" Russ asked.

"Yeah, what?" one of the other kids asked.

Pudgy old Russ weighed at least thirty pounds more than Jake. He had short, sandy-brown hair, freckles, and huge ears that drooped at the tips. Jake felt like making fun of those ears, but didn't. Russ could have easily knocked Jake down with one blow from his thick, fat fists. As a bully, Russ didn't worry about Jake what would do to him; he had terrorized Jake from his very first day at school.

"Wait! I know! Show us how you jerk when you walk!" Russ chimed in happily. Then he mimicked Jake's walk, but greatly exaggerated how the heavy brace on Jake's left leg made him drag his leg.

"Now you show us your jerky walk, Jerky Jake!" Russ repeated.

"No, show us how you talk, Jerky Jake!" Eunice teased, standing at his right side, her hands on her hips. Eunice was pretty, but only on the outside. She had sparkling blond hair, even pearly teeth and clear skin. Everyone said she was a little angel. But Jake knew better.

When Eunice and Russ started teasing Jake, other kids joined in.

"Yes, let's hear you say something, Jerky Jake!"

"S-s-s-stutter for us Jerky Jake!"

"Crip-pled Carrot! Crip-pled Carrot! Crip-pl-led Carrot!"

At times, Ms. Morton would step in and stop the children

from teasing Jake. But she couldn't be around him all the time. Today, she was in the nurse's office with some kid who had skinned his knee.

At night, in the safety of his home, Jake would tell his mother about the things that had happened in school. As she would massage his leg, Jake would pour out his heart to her and in doing so, he rarely stuttered. Often, he cried. But this time, he broke down and bawled.

"Jacob, I know you feel really bad about what they say to you. People may never stop teasing you. I'll tell you what my mama always told me when I had some bad times. She said whatever doesn't kill you will make you stronger."

"Mama, I'd just like to kill them, or at least make them hurt like they hurt me! See if that would make them stronger!"

"Jake! Just try to get stronger, remember!"

"I'm going to get stronger, all right!"

"Jake! Everybody has something inside of them that makes them stronger or makes them try harder when trouble comes. You can get past those kids."

Dyna noted that usually, Jake would get quiet then. When he made his intentions plain, Dyna felt more than a little uneasy. She wondered whether she should repeat her earlier lectures to him about self-control. If he didn't learn how to deal with his anger and bitterness at an early age, he was sure to have a miserable life. And their situation wasn't likely to change soon. With no extra money, she held little hope that he would receive the surgery that he desperately needed, that is, unless Brian came through for her. And after all these months, she was beginning to think that Brian wasn't going to help Jake.

She looked at her son and wondered what else she could do to ease his pain. She had contacted the school and a few of the parents to let them know about the teasing, but little had changed. This time, Dyna didn't lecture him, for she was sick of the problem too. She felt trapped in Cellis along with her son, Jake.

In time, Dyna didn't have to remind Jake to do his leg exercises. He finally understood what she meant. Facing his troubles could make him stronger. But with skills he had learned from his brothers, Alfred and Benjamin, Jake went just a little farther. He learned that even if he didn't improve himself, he could get revenge on his tormenters.

It was a Tuesday in early October. Russ had been up to his usual tactics. Eunice joined in too. Jake was sick of it. That day, something in Jake's heart began to take over.

He would get his revenge against Russ the next day while at school. Jake asked to go to the bathroom, but instead, slipped out of a side door. He went straight to the bicycle rack. With a pair of pliers he brought from home, Jake loosened the nuts on the front wheel of Russ' red bicycle. He made them not too loose as to be obvious, but loose enough so the wheel would come off if Russ tried to show off on his bike, or if he hit a bump.

Jake worked quickly and headed back to class. No one had noticed that Steven Jacob Mitchell had left the building.

Russ missed school on Thursday and Friday. When he came to school on Monday with a bright white cast on his newly broken right arm, Jake had something to smile about. And at least temporarily, the spit balls and rubber bands stopped.

It took a little longer to get back at Eunice.

After school, Jake often walked home alone, partially because of his leg but mainly due to fear. Usually, he took the same route by going three blocks north, then two blocks east and three blocks north again to get to their apartment on Chester Street. From hearing the talk at school, Jake knew that Eunice lived on Bodement Street. By walking one more block on the east portion of his route, Jake would pass by her house. If he walked half a block more, he would go through the alley behind her house. The evening after Russ broke his arm, Jake changed his route to go behind Eunice P. Driver's house.

She had a little blond, curly-haired dog that was friendly and trusting. Jake would make sure he was totally alone with the animal. After two weeks on his new route, with a rock in his hand, Jake coaxed the dog to come closer to the alley. After a few minutes of scratching and petting it, Jake pinned the dog so it could not move and used the rock to batter and break its leg. Now, he and the dog had something in common—a badly injured leg.

First, Russ, and now, the dog; and no one caught him when he hurt them. From that point on, Jake wouldn't let any tormenting go unpunished.

If the teasing at school would not stop, Jake at least took some pleasure each time he got revenge. At first, he was afraid, almost paralyzed with fear when he carried out his plans for revenge. But soon, he lost all fear. In almost no time, Steven Jacob Mitchell grew adept at exacting revenge in secret ways against his tormenters.

Even these moments of secret triumph didn't outweigh the misery he felt at the hands of the children at school. But his misery did help him to focus. He would be better than all of them in every way. In time, he would have the last laugh. And he would make sure they knew he had something to do with their pain, no matter how long it took.

LYING ON THE bed in his hotel room, Tony was tired. He'd covered nearly two hundred miles that day in making contacts, but most of those contacts were unfruitful. Tony unfolded a copy of the *Cellis Courier*. Tony flipped through the first two sections quickly and decided to skip the rest. He started to throw the newspaper away and as the paper dropped from his hand into the trash, Tony saw a familiar face on the society section. He pulled the paper from the trash; he had to make sure that it wasn't Sierra. But it was Sierra. Now, she was Sierra Tanner, the wife of Dr. Brian Tanner, who had hosted some charity event in Cellis. Seeing her picture brought back memories. After folding that part of the newspaper carefully and putting it into his briefcase, he pulled out the telephone directory from the nightstand. With any luck, her name and address would be listed there.

LIKE THE OTHER women who had agreed to Dr. Tanner's private sessions, Dyna wondered how long she would have to submit to Brian's desires. Over six months had passed since she first went to him in his office. Still, he stalled and delayed in giving her an answer about Jake's surgery.

At home in her kitchen, Dyna sat, thinking about her sessions with Brian when Jake interrupted her thoughts. "Ma, why don't we go anywhere anymore? I mean, you go to work and we go to school and that's all."

"What else is there?"

"Well, we could go to a movie or the park or church or something, couldn't we? We used to go to all those places before, remember?"

Jake's innocent questions pricked Dyna's heart. Compromising her morals carried a price much heavier than the cost of Jake's surgery. Since she had started her private sessions with Brian, Dyna had stopped sharing time with her sons. The guilt and shame of her activities made her reclusive and anxious. She wondered how much longer she could go on with her lying and adultery. She knew that her interaction with Brian was wrong when she first stepped into his office, but it had turned into something far worse than she had ever imagined it might become. And tomorrow, Brian would be looking for her again. Dyna sat silently, until a small voice broke through her thoughts again.

"Mama?"

She took him into her arms. "Jake, right now, just go to your room and play. Mama has a headache and doesn't want to talk now."

She had had enough. Dyna felt dirty; she was selling her body for the payoff of the surgery for Jake. In her mind, her actions had become inexcusable and unpardonable. It was time to end that relationship, free surgery or not.

On the following Monday evening in late October 1970, during her break, Dyna gathered her personal belongings from her locker and put them into her car. Brian would be looking for her sometime during that evening, and she was ready.

As usual, when she got to the hallway near his office, he motioned for her to come in for a private session. No one else was in that part of the building. After closing the door behind her, she asked him bluntly. "Brian, when are you going to fix Jake's leg?"

Standing behind his desk while he removed his tie, Brian stopped. To her surprise, he sat in his chair, then laughed at her.

"Well, what took you so long to figure me out? Did you really think I would help you Dyna? Ever? You stupid, stupid fool!" He leaned back casually and coolly and placed his hands behind his head.

"But Brian, you—you said you would help me! Jake, he really needs this surgery!" Dyna's voice trailed off in agony as she shrank back from him, withering inside.

Brian jumped up, shouting. "If you wanted help for your boy, why doesn't your husband pay for it? Because he can't, that why. He's a loser." As Brian shouted, he grew bright red from his neck to his scalp.

"You could have done a whole lot better in picking a man to support you and your brats. Then you come to me expecting me to help you. Just like before, all you want is someone to give, give, give to you." He slammed his hand down on his desk.

"Let's make this plain—I'm not going to help you! I'm never going to help you! And I never planned to help you! Ever!" He slammed his hand down again.

Though enraged by his ridicule, somehow, Dyna managed to control herself. Standing up now, she walked to the door, using superhuman restraint. From somewhere deep inside her soul, she drew the power to keep herself from giving him a black eye or a bloody nose or worse. With clenched teeth, she hissed an unmistakable threat. "Brian, you're an evil, sick man. I hope you'll get what's coming to you and really soon. You hurt people and use them and you just don't care. But you are not God and you are not in control in this. My son is going to get help whether you have anything to do with it or not. Just wait and see! But one day, somehow, some way, I'll get you for what you did to me and my family. I'll get you. Wait! Just wait!"

And with those words, she left and slammed the door so hard

that one of his sleek, black-framed diplomas on the wall came crashing down to the floor.

Dyna Woods left the clinic for good and abandoned all hope that the clinic would ever give her son, Steven Jacob Mitchell, the surgery he needed to regain full use of his leg. And Brian would never find out from her that Javier was his son.

CHAPTER 30

THREE DAYS AFTER Dyna quit the clinic, the first letter came. Addressed to Sierra, it had no return address and it had an Enid postmark. Sent in a dirty white envelope made from a cheap grade of paper, Sierra thought the envelope was junk mail and started to toss it, until curiosity got the best of her. Who in Enid knew her now that she lived in Cellis? Her obstetrician, Dr. Lerner? The hospital staff? It had been years since she'd been in Enid for Andrea's birth.

Sierra flopped down on the sofa in the basement den. Her glass of vodka on the rocks was already half gone. Running a long, red fingernail under the seal, she opened the white envelope. She pulled out the white sheet of paper. It had a short message typed on it.

> How are you doing, Boom-Boom? If you haven't exposed yourself recently, don't worry. I will!

Horrified, Sierra shrieked and began crying as she tore the sheet and envelope into a thousand pieces of white confetti. But she had to keep her fear to herself. And she could never tell Brian about the letter. For a short while, she sat, wondering who knew about her past and what she should do about the note. Could it be a disgruntled clinic employee? Or was it someone from her life in Enid who had tracked her down? Could it be Tony or Merritt? Who could have sent this horrid note?

When she gathered her wits, she threw the confetti into a small aluminum pot in the kitchen. With hands trembling, Sierra lit it. She watched the small pile burn until she was absolutely sure that nothing but ashes remained. Emptying her glass, she refilled it with vodka and gulped it down without taking a breath. She flushed the ashes down the toilet.

Hours later, when Brian walked into the house, he smelled faint traces of smoke. Something was burning, Brian thought as he looked for the source of the smoke. He checked the kitchen and most of the main floor of the house, but found nothing. He walked to the den, where Sierra had sprawled out on the sofa, snoring and drunk. The source of the smoke would remain a mystery for now—Sierra was in no condition to talk. He let her spend the night there.

TWO WEEKS AFTER leaving the clinic, Dyna got a job at a factory. While she worked on the assembly line, she tried to think pleasant thoughts, any thoughts to escape from the drudgery. Her children were fine, they had enough to eat and they had a roof over their heads. Apart from their poverty, her husband Donald was the only dark cloud in her life now. Don drank heavily, gambled and only worked sporadically. For a second husband, he could be a whole lot worse, but not much. She grew sad whenever she thought of Don. But with the work piling up in front of her, she figured she could not worry about him and get her work done that day. She made up her mind to be thankful for the areas of her life that were going well. And the best part of her life now was Javier.

FROM HIS SOPHOMORE year in high school when he made the varsity basketball team, Javier Mitchell was destined to be a great athlete. The local press had taken note of him, as had several college scouts looking for promising talent. As Javier continued in school, his playing skills improved. He could play several positions with ease. To the local coaches, he was the ideal player. Javier was easy to coach and willing to work for the team instead of for himself alone.

On Tuesday evenings, Javier stood at the kitchen sink, washing dishes. Big star basketball player or not, tonight was his turn to bust suds. Dyna sat at the table, peeling potatoes for the salad she would include in their lunches that week. The yellow bowl in front of her was half full of peeled and quartered spuds, and another ten pounds of potatoes lay in a bag on the floor beside her foot. The latest potato peel curled like a coarse ribbon from the sharp knife in her hand.

Javier had plenty to talk about that day and it wasn't just about basketball. "Ma, I've thought about it and here's my plan. If one of the scouts doesn't come through for me, I want to try out as a walk-on somewhere here in the Midwest. But just in case, I'm still studying hard. I want to major in business. I know I can make it, Mama, I really can. Just wait, you'll see."

Each time the local newspaper or broadcast mentioned him, Javier had made the winning score or had set a record, or had done something else exceptionally well. In everyone's mind, he was professional basketball material even at age sixteen.

At night, in the privacy of their small, stuffy bedroom, Dyna and Don talked about Javier's successes. "Few things ever turn out like we've planned," Dyna confided in Don. "When I couldn't see my own future, my son's was being laid out for him just like a road map. All I can say now is I'm really glad how Javier is turning out."

Don grunted and agreed with her quickly. But his reason for joy was different from hers. Don could see that if Javier were a success, the kid would take the family out of this pitiful apartment. Don planned to drink, gamble and party seriously if his wife got money flowing in from her son. And he was more than willing to stick around to enjoy some of Javier's success.

THE SECOND LETTER came in a plain envelope from Enid to the Tanner home in September 1971, addressed to Sierra. Alone at the house when it arrived, Sierra opened it, her hands shaking. It had been a year since she had gotten the first letter and with this one, Sierra relived all of her old fears. Would the writer ask for money or would he just drive her crazy from worrying? The letter was similar to the first one.

> I found you, Boom-Boom, and I'll keep in touch. In the meantime, if you haven't exposed yourself recently, don't worry—I will!

Sierra held onto this letter for two days as she tried to figure out what to do with it. As she considered her options, Sierra began to relax a bit, figuring the writer hadn't asked for anything or even that she do anything. Since the first letter, nothing had happened anyway. She would wait and see what would happen. But Sierra tore the letter and envelope into tiny pieces, just in case. She poured vodka on the rocks. While sipping her drink, she watched as she burned the pieces of paper in the recreation room fireplace.

EVERETT SEARS SAT on a table in one of the clinic's examination room. Growing cold, he wished that Brian would finish the exam soon.

Since they had met, Everett made sure he had some contact with Brian at least every two or three weeks. He dropped by for lunch, hit the links many times with Brian and even sent him a custom putter bearing the autograph of one of the Chicago professionals Everett had associated with in the past. Everett even had dinner with the Tanners several times. These contacts were necessary. They allowed him to gather basic information about them and their lives. Early in his relationship with Brian, Everett learned that Brian was from Cellis and Sierra was from Starp, Florida, and that they met at Briggandale. He also learned that their daughter, Andrea, was born in Enid. With this information, Everett did some checking on his own. Everett had to know the backgrounds of the people that he might be working with or for. Everett also wanted to know whether they had any close connections who could send him to prison.

On that day in the clinic, Everett decided he had been poked and prodded and peeked at enough for one day. He wanted to get down to his real reason for coming to see Dr. Tanner.

Peering at an old scar on Everett's left side, Brian decided to include a note on it in Everett's records. He measured it and then started an entry in the chart. "That looks pretty nasty. How did you get it?"

"I was knifed."

Brian looked up from his writing. "Oh, was someone trying to rob you?"

"No, one of my friends was trying to make a point."

"You have got to be kidding!" Brian looked at Everett. Everett wasn't laughing.

"Doc, do you remember the New Libertyville murders?"

Silence, then an uneasy laughter followed. Brian answered, "What you did you do, clean the suits afterwards? You couldn't have had anything to do with those."

His humor wasn't appreciated. Everett continued.

"I wasn't involved in the killings. But one of those dead guys, Mike Hoffer, well, he was my boss. He gave me this scar. Lucky we were friends, I guess, or he would have really hurt me."

Dumbfounded, Brian just stared at the chart in front of him. He felt as if a bowling ball had hit him in the gut. With a voice that sounded as if it were coming from someone else, Brian asked quietly, "Are you a mobster or a gangster or something?"

Everett stared at him and Brian could feel the icy-cold look. Brian cringed. Maybe he had just asked one question too many. He pulled together enough courage to turn and to look into Everett's face.

Could he trust him? Everett wasn't sure, but he decided he had little choice if he wanted to get help for his son. He had gotten to know Brian intimately. If he needed to, Everett would use a trump card.

Everett pulled two snapshots from the hip pocket of his slacks. He handed one to Brian. "Here. Take a look at some of my handiwork."

Brian gasped at the blood-soaked victim in the first photograph.

Everett explained, "Doc, I used to do some collection work, all kinds, if you get my drift. Let's leave it at that. But Brian, I need a favor. I need help for my little boy. He's not my wife's son; he's my girlfriend's. You know I can pay you. But I can't let my wife find out about him. Ever. And I know you don't really need the money. But I think I can give you something more valuable." Everett told him about his wife, his mistress, his son, and his proposal.

Although the prospect of working with someone like Everett scared Brian, the thought of associating with the raw, dark power of the underworld tantalized him. But he wasn't willing enough. Brian hesitated. "Let me think about it."

"I don't want you to think about it too long." He would have to use his trump card. Everett handed Brian the second photograph. "Here. I think that you'll recognize this."

The photo of Brian and one of his female patients was explicit. The look on Brian's face told Everett that his trump card had worked. Brian exclaimed, "How did you get this photo of me?"

Everett didn't answer that question. "Look Brian, I'm not out to hurt you. I just want help for my boy. If I wanted to cause you any trouble, I could have done it a long time ago. Plus, I'm not asking you to do it for nothing. What do you say?"

Brian realized that he had been outwitted. He had underestimated this dry cleaner and his oversight would cost him something. He would do the surgery or risk the end of his professional career, or worse. Brian decided to make the best out of this bad situation. Anticipating that he too might need special help one day, Brian agreed to perform the corrective surgery. In exchange, Everett would perform a favor for him.

If Brian needed special services, he didn't want to have to look for them. He might even use Everett's help to get rid of his philandering wife, Sierra.

CHAPTER 31

A T AGE SEVENTEEN, Javier looked like Dyna's father, only taller and just a little bit more good-looking. Javier had turned out to be a very handsome young man and well mannered. He was protective of his mother and younger brothers. Even Don, Dyna's second husband, seemed to genuinely like Javier.

Outside of their home, it seemed like most of Cellis liked Javier too. As a junior, he made the high school basketball team. Javier made good grades in school and his teachers liked him. And of course, the girls followed him like flies. Not that he seemed to notice the girls. His career was more important. Javier Mitchell planned to go to college, play pro basketball and help his mama to leave her life in Cellis. He would have plenty of time for girls later.

Sitting in the kitchen as they drank hot chocolate, Dyna and Javier frequently talked about his future in big terms. Professional basketball, a big-league team, product endorsements, all of these came with his dreams of a great future.

"Mama, I'm going to do it all. Then I'm going to buy a house for you like the one we used to have." Javier looked around the kitchen. "No, I'll get a better house than that one for you. I'm tired of this apartment—and you deserve a nice house. I'll even get a brand new car for you. Then you won't have to drive the raggedy one we have now." He took another big sip.

Dyna defended the vehicle, "Our car isn't raggedy, it's just a little used up, that's all."

"Raggedy! Raggedy! Raggedy! Mama, you see the same car I do. How can you say it isn't raggedy?"

"Young man, you should be grateful that we have a car at all."

"I'm grateful, but it's still raggedy!"

They both laughed and continued dreaming about the day he would make money beyond their wildest dreams.

Dyna marveled at how well her oldest boy had turned out. Occasionally, she wanted to tell Brian, Javier's father, about their son, but she always stopped herself. After all these years, Brian Tanner would have nothing to use against her anymore. Brian did not deserve a son as good as Javier. As far as she was concerned, Brian Tanner being Javier's father would be one of those secrets she would carry to her grave. She would never share with Brian the only true joy he had given her.

The next evening, Dyna stirred the soup that simmered in the large cast-iron pot on the stove, then tasted it. It needed to cook only a few minutes more, she decided. Tomatoes, carrots, peas, corn and a little bit of pork, her sons and her husband would really like this pot of tasty soup. With six mouths to feed, she was sure there would be no leftovers, even if they didn't like it. Dyna could hear three of her sons coming up the steps in the hall outside their apartment, yelling and roughhousing. The fourth, Jake, played sleepily in the living room.

While the soup simmered, she opened the letter that came that day. It was from Aunt Vernice. Aunt Vernice Mitchell was the only sister of John's father and had no other relatives closer than John. Independent and headstrong, long ago, she had planned to be an attorney or doctor. But with the financial constraints of taking care of her own parents, she never completed her degree.

Like John, Aunt Vernice once had red hair and an impish sense of humor. Thoroughly gray-haired in her old age, Vernice still carried her own luggage, walked five miles a day and still maintained her own home at age seventy. From the pictures she sent and the way she talked, she reminded Dyna of a spry old lady leprechaun.

Every year, she and Dyna exchanged Christmas cards and talked on the phone once or twice a year. She rarely wrote at any other time. Whenever Dyna tried to visit her or get her to come for a visit, Aunt Vernice had plans already made to be someplace else in the world. Today's letter was very unusual in that Aunt Vernice had written to her for no special reason. Dyna finished reading the letter, looked at the enclosed pictures and placed the letter and pictures on top of the refrigerator.

In the bathroom, Don finished washing his face and called out, "Boys, time to clean up for supper!" He stepped out to let Benjamin and Alfred in, but stood in the hall to supervise. "Be sure to wash your hands. That means putting them into water and using soap, you two." The twins usually tried to avoid any extended contact with water. And for them, using soap generally was out of the question.

When Don was certain the boys were clean enough for their mother, he sent them into the kitchen. He peeked in at Jake, who by now was fast asleep. Deciding the little fellow needed his rest, Don left him alone.

Most of the time during dinner, the boys laughed and talked about sports, school, the neighborhood, or something else of interest to them. This evening over soup, the discussion was especially lively as the boys shared details of their day with Don, laughing uproariously. Dyna went to check on Jake.

The twins had been in a fight on their way home from school. "Don, he shouldn't have said it," Benjamin laughed, "That's when Alfred hit him."

"Well, you hit him first."

"Yeah, but you hit him second and tore his jacket."

Don interrupted, "Well what did you do next?"

"We got him down on the ground—"

"And you know what? We got both of the pockets off the back of his pants." Each held up a pocket like a trophy. Dyna walked back into the kitchen as the twins waived the blue jean pieces. Aghast, she stopped at the door.

Don didn't realize Dyna was there and continued, "What did you do next?"

Excited, the twins told their story in unison, with Alfred taking the lead. "Well, he was crying then——"

"And he said he was going to tell his mother."

"We told him that since he was going to tell—"

"That we would give him more to tell her about."

"That's when Benj pulled off his jacket—"

"And you pulled off his shirt—"

"And we tore them up!"

"And all he could do was cry like a baby!"

"Yeah, a big raggedy baby!"

The boys and Don laughed until they cried.

Some kid had made a smart-aleck remark about Alfred's patched blue jeans. When the twins got finished with him, his mother would have to throw away his jeans, his jacket and his shirt. The twins didn't leave enough to patch them.

While Don and the boys laughed, Dyna felt sick. She didn't need some mother calling her about her kid's injuries or torn clothing. She scolded the twins for fighting. To herself, she prayed that her sons would not be expelled from school.

"Ma, don't worry about it," Benjamin said as he pulled off a piece of bread and chewed slowly on it. "He won't tell his mother or anyone else. We let him know he'd better not tell anyone about it, or we would fix him good."

Dyna's heart sank. While secretly she was glad her sons had stood up for themselves, she wondered how far these two would go. At this rate, reform school or jail were distinctly foreseeable possibilities for their futures. She scolded them for a few minutes more. Now, she had to wait and see what would come of the torn clothing incident.

Her boys surprised her with the things they would tell her. She appreciated their openness. She had always wanted it this way. Her relationship with them included almost anything they wanted to tell her or wanted to talk about.

After the boys and Don finished their dinner, Dyna put up a small bowl of soup for Jake and sat down with a bowl for herself. Don sat in the living room, watching television, and the twins went to their room to do homework. Javier stayed in the kitchen with Dyna. It was his turn to do dishes. Routinely, he used this time to talk to her privately.

"Ma, I met a girl today."

"Mmmh." Even cold, this soup is delicious, Dyna thought as she dipped a thick piece of bread into her bowl. Javier sometimes talked about girls, but he wasn't seriously involved with any.

"Her name is Andrea."

When Dyna heard Andrea's name, she stopped eating. She didn't hear anything else Javier said for some time. Dyna wondered silently. Could this be Brian's daughter? She didn't even want to think of the two of them together.

At first, Javier didn't notice his mother's sudden lack of appetite. He washed dishes as he described the girl. There for a non-conference basketball tournament, Andrea had been visiting his school along with a group from Pye Academy, one of the private high schools in town. He went on and told his mother about the rest of his day. As he rinsed the last dish, he looked over at his mother.

"Ma, aren't you hungry? If you aren't, can I finish your bread and soup for you?"

As her son wolfed down the rest of her meal, Dyna stood by the refrigerator with her arms crossed, silent. She hoped he wouldn't mention Andrea again—not in any dating or similar context. If Andrea were Brian's daughter, how could she tell her son Andrea was his half-sister? All of his life, she had led him to believe that John Mitchell was his father.

Dyna stayed in the kitchen that evening long after everyone else had gone to bed. The secret she had kept to herself for so many years now was at risk of being revealed.

CHAPTER 32

B RIAN CAME HOME unannounced in the middle of the
day with a banker friend, L. James Norman, which he
hoped to influence for a loan. While L. James stood in the foyer
taking off his coat, Brian opened the door to the living room and
saw them. Sierra had Javier pinned against a table as she kissed
him passionately. Shaken, Brian backed out of the living room
doorway as the banker slammed the closet door.

Somehow, Brian managed to regroup quickly as he faced L.
James. Acting as if nothing had happened, he escorted the man
into the living room. Sierra was sitting on the sofa while Javier
stood next to the table. Sierra smiled graciously, as if nothing had
happened. Javier looked away, his skin pale and his hand ice cold,
as Brian introduced L. James Norman to them. Within seconds,
Javier excused himself and disappeared.

While L. James chatted about the loan, the interest rates and
other topics, Sierra smiled and played the role of the devoted wife.
All the while, Brian sat quietly, his stomach in knots. He wondered
whether he could maintain his composure much longer. With the
loan, Brian had planned to buy a bigger share in the clinic. He
steadied himself, for Brian decided he wanted the loan more than
he wanted to hurt his wife right then. He had business with L.

James now. He could deal with his wife later. When they completed their meeting, Brian left with L. James, but he didn't return to the clinic.

BY SEVEN THAT evening, Brian returned to the house, but it was empty. After changing his office outfit for a pair of navy sweat pants and a tee shirt, Brian went straight to their exercise room.

Hours later, the wheels of the exercise bike spun faster and faster as Brian thought about the two of them together. He had seen them kissing in the living room earlier that day and he still could not believe it. His wife and that . . . that . . . that boy! His daughter's new boyfriend, Javier, and Sierra, his wife! The very thought of those two together made Brian gag. The sweat ran down Brian's face as rage burned within him. Brian was angry—he had done so much for that woman. He felt betrayed—he could not believe she was willing to risk her reputation, his reputation, and their marriage over some teenager.

He felt even more anger for his daughter's sake. Brian could never tell her that her own mother had a thing for her boyfriend—it would kill Andie. His heart ached from that thought. Brian loved his little girl so much. That this no-name lowlife came into his own home and seduced his wife, and his little girl made Brian Tanner furious. And what was he doing at the house during the daytime anyway? He should have been in school.

Now, even several hours later, Brian still fumed. He wanted to beat that boy up, along with Sierra. Could he fight like some common hoodlum? Brian knew he couldn't; he had to maintain some respectability. Brian struggled to put those thoughts out of his head.

But he could not let that punk run over him. Should he confront the boy and Sierra? Brian stopped riding the bike suddenly. What if his wife chose the boy over him? The shame would be intolerable and the whispering would never end. The heartbreak for his daughter, well, he could not imagine it. Would Sierra want a divorce? She might even want a good portion of the clinic and other assets he had worked so hard to build up over the years. Brian's thoughts raced.

For hours, Brian struggled between reason and rage. He had to do something. He could not let Javier Mitchell get away with seeing Sierra. But if he put his hands on the kid, or if he went too far, it might cost him his career, his home or more. Brian's thoughts grew more and more irrational until he couldn't contain them any longer.

"Dyna has to be behind all of this. She couldn't get to me so she's using her son to get back at me. Well, I'm not going to let him ruin my life or my daughter's life like she ruined mine. I'm going to end her interference once and for all." As he pedaled harder, Brian noticed three ladybugs on the floor inside the room. Looking up at the window, he saw two more. And the very existence of those little creatures in his home infuriated him. Should he call an exterminator? And what would he do about Sierra and that kid?

That night, Brian Tanner slept in his easy chair in the den.

The next morning, he skipped breakfast and announced he was going to work early. On his way out, he told Hilda, their housekeeper, to arrange for an exterminator to take care of the ladybugs in the house.

When he got to the clinic, Dr. Tanner called Everett Sears. They agreed to meet at the dry cleaner's nearest store.

THE THIRD LETTER to Sierra came four days after Brian had brought the banker to their home. She looked at the envelope and at first started to burn it up without reading it. But after opening it, she found this letter was different.

> Boom-Boom,
>   You've been busy! You've had another man this month,
> Boom-Boom. It's time to expose you!

She had dismissed the other letters as the acts of a pervert. But now, someone was watching her! Her tormentor knew she had an encounter with another man that month. Still, with no demand for money, she wondered what the sick jerk wanted. Was the pervert trying to make her afraid? She decided to curtail her extramarital activities, at least for a while. If the pervert could count her affairs, then Brian could too. And she didn't want to lose what she had.

During the last month in particular, Sierra thought she was being watched, as if someone were peeking right into the window of the recreation room at times. Once, as she entered the recreation room after dark, she thought she saw a light, maybe a flashlight right outside the window that went out quickly as she stood there in the darkened room. Was it her imagination? Or was someone watching her from right outside the window? Sierra was too afraid to try to find out right then.

BRIAN EXPLAINED TO Everett what he wanted done, and to whom. He didn't tell Everett why.

"Yes, I can do that job for you. To make sure it goes off without a hitch, I'll need your help." Everett Sears outlined his plan with Brian.

"Doctor, trust me. You'll be glad you got a professional to do this job. Even the best amateur forgets or overlooks some detail. That detail usually results in jail time for someone. But the way I deal with problems, well, I deal with them. Period. There won't be any mistakes."

Brian planned a five-day vacation for himself and his family. The vacation would start on Tuesday, March 14, 1972. Hilda normally took Wednesdays as her day off. Brian gave her Tuesday, Thursday and Friday off as well and canceled the mail and paper deliveries for that week.

On Monday, after slipping on some latex gloves, Brian pulled several of Andrea's old homework assignments and one of her old notebooks and stuck them into his briefcase, along with a small pink envelope he had taken from her room. The notebooks contained Andrea's attempts at farewell phrases to friends who had graduated in 1971. He would have to get her handwriting down

pat that day. Within an hour, he had finished the letter but left it
unsigned. Somehow, as he worked on the letter, he cut his left
arm, just above the glove and left a tiny, almost imperceptible
drop of blood on the letter. He finished the letter and sealed the
envelope, aware of the cut, but unaware of the drop of blood on
the letter.

Early on Tuesday morning, just before leaving for the airport,
Brian called Javier Mitchell. He got lucky—Javier answered the
phone. "Hello? May I speak to Javier Mitchell? Oh, this is Javier?
This is Dr. Tanner, Andrea's father. I wondered whether you could
stop by today. Will five thirty work for you? Six thirty is better?
Okay, six thirty it is then. I wanted to talk you and two of Andrea's
friend from Pye Academy privately about something. Oh, and uh,
could you keep your visit a secret? I'm planning something special,
a party for Andie, and I don't want anyone else to know about it. I
really need your help. Why don't you plan to meet us here at six
thirty? Oh, and if we're running a little late, just have a seat on the
rear deck near the pool. I have one other stop to make this evening
but I don't think it will take too long. Great. See you then."

Brian made another call, this time to Everett. "It's all set. He'll
be here at six thirty. I'll call you when I get back."

As his family sat waiting in the car in the garage, Brian put the
pink envelope down under the edge of the doormat. He had done
his part. The rest was up to Everett Sears.

NEAR DUSK, EVERETT hid behind an overgrown fir bush
on the left side of the Tanner home. Javier Mitchell was late. As he
crouched, Everett wondered if the kid would come at all, and if he
did, whether he would come alone. If he did not, what Everett
had planned for the kid could not take place, not at least on that
night. As he waited, he tried to think up other plans for getting
the job done while Dr. Tanner and his family were out of town.

More than an hour earlier, Everett had walked the two miles
from a local fast food restaurant to where Dr. Tanner and his family
lived. The restaurant sat in a small strip mall on the way out of

town. Everett wore a plain dark-gray overcoat, a matching felt hat, glasses and a fake black mustache as he walked briskly to his hideout. He gave the appearance of a businessman taking an evening walk. When he got close to the edge of the Tanner property, he looked about, then skirted along the dark hedges that separated that estate from the next. In time, he made his way to the dark green bushes on the left-hand side of the house.

Now in place, he waited. The sun wouldn't set until almost seven. And with the new moon, it would be dark.

It had been partly sunny that day, with temperatures in the low fifties. Now it drizzled. The only good thing was the rain wasn't constant and it wasn't too cold.

Huddling in the drizzle, Everett wondered what had the boy done to deserve death. Had he stolen money from the good doctor? Hurt the girl? Did he deliver a bad pizza? Everett stopped himself. He could not afford the luxury of unnecessary thinking—it might cloud his judgment and cause some error. He had to stay focused on his mission.

Everett had done this kind of job before. He anticipated it would take him less than five minutes. He wasn't worried, but the chance of being caught was always there, even in this remote area of town. Neighbors were far enough away, but anyone jogging or walking by might see him.

Startled by some unknown noise, Everett looked up. Someone in a car had slowed down and turned into the Tanner driveway. He waited. An old compact car pulled up to the Tanner garage door, and then stopped. The car looked ragged and sounded worse. It stood out like a sore thumb in contrast to the obvious luxury of the Tanner home.

Everett relaxed. The car would be easy. That model had brake lines that probably should be weak because of old age. They would be easy to snap. But he could not crawl under this model very easily. He hoped the doors were unlocked.

The boy went to the front porch, picked up the pink envelope from the doormat where Brian had left it, rang the doorbell and waited. While standing there, he opened the envelope, gasped and walked quickly to the rear of the house. As he headed to the back of the house, he stuck the letter into the pocket of his jacket.

As soon as the boy walked to the right side of the house, Everett emerged from the bushes. He went straight to the car and found it unlocked. He eased open the hood, reached down into the wheel well with a pair of wire cutters and went to work. But the job was not as easy as he had anticipated. The first brake line was solid— not weak at all. Everett struggled and then squeezed the cutters harder. With a snap, he broke through the line close to the wheel. The first line had taken too long.

Startled, he hesitated. Was the boy coming back to the front of the house? Looking anxiously about, Everett went to the second line. Fortunately, it was not as difficult. He yanked that one from the wheel.

Having completed the job in less than seven minutes, he closed the hood of the car. Quickly, he headed on his way back to his hiding place. He hid just in time, because a car passed by on the street. The open car hood might have been noticeable from the street.

In the meantime, the boy paced on the deck, then walked back and forth from the rear of the house to the front drive several times. Eventually, he sat on the covered rear porch and covered his face with his hands.

While waiting, Everett pulled a plastic bag from his shirt pocket. Laying the plastic bag on the ground to catch any debris that might fall, Everett peeled off the mustache. He took care to slip it into the bag. For several minutes, Everett kneeled over the bag, carefully rubbing the area under his nose and on his cheeks to remove any rubber cement and stray hairs that might remain. He rolled up the bag and placed it back into his pocket. Everett stuffed the hat in the same pocket. From an inner pocket in the overcoat he pulled out a folding cane, a tattered navy scarf and an equally tattered matching cap. He was ready.

CHAPTER 33

AFTER WAITING MORE than an hour at the empty Tanner home, Javier returned to the car. After pulling the letter and envelope out of his pocket, he read the letter once more, and left both on the seat beside him to let the damp letter dry. Within minutes, he pulled out of the driveway and headed toward the stop sign. About a quarter mile down the road at the stop sign, the boy applied his brakes for the last time, waited at the stop and then took off.

The puddle of brake fluid left at the stop sign and trailing behind the car indicated that the brake lines would be empty before he would need them again. Heading back toward town, he would have to go through two hilly areas on the road with speed limits of fifty-five miles per hour and several sharp hairpin turns. And he would face all of those without any brakes.

WHY WOULD ANDREA break up with me? I don't understand it. Did her mother have anything to do with it? Did her dad? Was this a trap, like the one that her crazy mother set up? And why in the world did her father invite me out to his house and not show up? He didn't act like he saw his wife kissing me, or he wouldn't have ever invited me out here. Javier struggled with his tears and his thoughts as he rode in the darkness out on old Indiana Road.

Puzzled about what had happened, Javier Mitchell paid little attention to his surroundings or the road until he saw the posted fifty-five miles per hour speed limit sign just before the first hairpin turn. He glanced at the speedometer—he was doing sixty-five already. He tapped on the brakes—going downhill now, the car sped up. He floored the brakes—they didn't work at all. Doing seventy by now, he gripped the wheel—the compact car was too close to the guardrail on the right and the shoulder of the road was too narrow. He scraped the right side of the car along the rail as he struggled for control. He pulled the wheel to the left, over-compensated, and crossed the median strip into the opposite lane. Now out of control, he hit the left lane guardrail head-on at the curve. After hitting the guardrail, Javier helplessly watched as the last few seconds of his life went by in very slow motion.

From the impact, the car flipped over the guardrail and landed upside down in the gully almost thirty feet from the road. It slid upside down for another twenty or more feet until it hit a tree and started smoldering.

WALKING IN THE opposite direction, Everett Sears reached his car more than an hour later. Using the cane to walk like an old man had slowed him down significantly.

Once in his car, Everett pulled off the tattered cap and scarf. After waiting another half hour, he began the drive from the outskirts of town toward downtown Cellis. To make sure he had completed the job, he had to see the wrecked compact car.

Everett Sears quickly reached the first hairpin turn on the way to Cellis. He drove slowly through that turn. Emergency personnel had narrowed the road down to one lane with flares and barriers. As he inched through the area, Everett could see the crumpled highway barrier. Below, with the illumination from the flares, vehicle headlights and directed spotlights, he could see several police cars, an ambulance and a fire truck. The boy's small car had hit the rail, flipped and lay upside down on the ground. The emergency personnel were trying to free the boy from the wreckage.

FOR HOURS THAT evening, when Javier did not come home, his mother anxiously paced. Something was wrong, terribly wrong and Dyna knew it. Could this be the fulfillment of the old woman's prophecy Dyna received more seventeen years ago in New Jersey? With fear and anxiety immobilizing her, Dyna could remember some, but not everything the woman had said. She had never completely figured out what the old woman had meant. But Dyna knew Javier was seventeen now. If the old woman's words were true, Dyna had plenty to worry about.

By 11 P.M., she called the hospitals and the police. She got no news about Javier from them.

At 1 A.M., the doorbell rang. Dyna forced herself to answer the door. Two officers, Danny Sledge and Dean Forsythe, had come to bring the news.

Her worst fears had come true. Javier was dead. Dyna's anguished screams could be heard through out the entire building. As she moaned and cried, she was aware of nothing except the grief that reached down into her soul and squeezed it flat.

The two police officers waited patiently as Don tried to calm a near hysterical Dyna. With disheveled hair, her eyes puffed shut from crying, her face red from her inability to take deep breaths, she looked terrible. In time, when Dyna could respond, Officer Sledge asked Dyna a puzzling question.

"Did your son have a girlfriend?"

"Did someone else die too?" Dyna sobbed.

"No, nothing like that. We found a partially burned note in the car, but it wasn't signed." Dyna did not answer right away. This was her decisive moment. Would she tell them about her son and Andrea Tanner? Would she risk the further disclosures that might result? What if somehow, some way, Javier was identified as

Dr. Brian Tanner's illegitimate son? What would happen to her son's reputation if his relationship with Andrea came out?

She had suffered long enough. She did not want and could not handle any more pain. Her son was a basketball hero now in everyone's eyes. What good would it do to bring up dirt now?

She whispered quietly through her tears. "Javier didn't have a girlfriend. He dated around. He wasn't serious about any particular girl."

The older officer, Danny Sledge, spoke up. "Mrs. Woods, we'll need the names of some of his friends and their telephone numbers, if you have them. Did your son go to Cellis High?"

"I, uh, sure, I think I can give you those. And yes, my son went to Cellis High." She stood up, unsure whether her legs would carry her into her dead son's room.

The younger blond-haired officer, Dean Forsythe, touched her arm as she passed and said, "One last thing then, ma'am. Could I get a sample or two of your son's handwriting?"

As she went toward the boys' room to get some of Javier's homework assignments and the other information that the officers requested, Dyna saw them and stopped. In the hallway, just outside the living room, the twins knelt, immobilized. Both pairs of eyes were full of tears. Benjamin had cupped his hand over Alfred's mouth and had bitten his own lips to keep from crying out. They had heard everything.

Once outside in the squad car, the officers waited. "You okay, Danny?"

He cleaned his face with a single wipe of his oversized hand. He cleared his throat. "Yeah, Dean. I'm okay. I really had to hold back when she started crying. But then, I saw those two boys in the hallway! I couldn't help it, I almost lost it right then."

OFFICER SLEDGE CAME in early for his next shift to follow up with a few of Javier's friends from school. From them, he learned about Javier's recent involvement with Andrea Tanner. But they didn't know her very well. She didn't go to their school—she went to Pye Academy, a private school. Meanwhile, Forsythe stopped by the morgue. Fortunately, the body hadn't been released to the family yet. He would make sure that fingerprints and a blood sample were taken.

Entering the precinct, Sledge and Forsythe said hello to the counter clerk, Callie, with the same generic greeting, "Hey Callie." Busy with a telephone call, she waved as they passed. The other officers who weren't involved with perpetrators, telephone calls or victims acknowledged the pair by gestures, waves and quick hellos.

But Chief Gardener ignored them. He stood at the door of his office, reading the newspaper. He waved the newspaper in their faces without saying a word. His favorite candidate, George C. Wallace, had won by a landslide in the Florida primary. He left the newspaper on the table outside his office and shut the door.

Sledge picked it up, skimmed through the front-page articles regarding the 1972 Florida primary and saw the article about the plane crash that killed a hundred and twelve. The article that mattered to him that day was that a local basketball star, Javier Mitchell, had died in a car crash on Tuesday evening.

AS PART OF his investigation, Sledge contacted the Tanner home on Saturday. But based upon his call, he decided substantial contact with the Tanners might be unnecessary. From Hilda, the housekeeper, Sledge learned the Tanners had left on Tuesday morning for a five-day vacation. To her knowledge, on Monday evening, when she last saw the family, everything in the household seemed fine. He left his name and telephone number with her and asked that Dr. Tanner give him a call upon his return.

When the Tanners got back from vacation, Hilda pulled Brian aside and whispered an urgent message. Then in front of Hilda, Brian took his daughter into his arms and broke the news to her. Amidst Andrea's sobs, Brian called Officer Sledge. Brian confirmed his daughter knew Javier, but she did not know anything more about the boy's death. They had been on vacation out of state when the boy had died.

The officer asked the questions Everett had anticipated and warned Brian about. "So at the time of the accident, was your daughter dating Javier Mitchell?"

"Yes."

"And they hadn't broken up?"

"They were still dating."

Officer Sledge continued, "Do you know how he was doing before you left? I mean, was he sad, depressed, suicidal, anything?"

Brian took the telephone from his ear and spoke to his daughter while Sledge waited on the telephone line. Sledge could hear a girl's voice, still sobbing, but clear. After a few moments, Brian came back on the line. "Javier was fine the last time my daughter saw him. He wasn't sad or anything."

"How old is your daughter? May I speak to her please?"

"Under eighteen. And you may not talk to her. And if you'll excuse me, she really needs me now." Brian hung up.

As Brian put the telephone handset into the receiver, he thought about Everett's request that he write the note to Javier. He had been right. The note seemed to be working. The police were investigating Javier's death as suicide or something other than murder.

Hanging up the telephone, Sledge commented, "He didn't sound too sad or too cooperative!"

"Don't make too much of it. Dr. Tanner just sounded like a father who wanted to help his daughter through a hard time," Forsythe replied.

"Well, somebody was breaking up with somebody, and that could have been the reason for the crash."

CHAPTER 34

OFFICERS SLEDGE AND Forsythe had been partners on the force for seven years by this point. As a team, they were the Old Man and Baby Face—and each looked the part. Sledge's salt-and-pepper hair and his dark-framed glasses made him look much older than thirty-eight. Dean Forsythe, who had joined the Cellis Police Department two full years before Danny Sledge, was the older of the two. Dean had short, curly blond hair, hazel eyes and a round face. At age forty and in excellent shape, he looked like he was almost half that age. Put together when their first partners retired, the pair was a perfect match.

Considered mavericks, often, Sledge and Forsythe were at odds with Police Chief Nathan Gardener and others in the police department. While they would never make detective grade under Gardener—he didn't want to pay them for the higher rank—they could investigate cases just like the other detectives on the force. Sledge and Forsythe just wanted to solve their cases, but their approach to casework at times was unconventional by the standards of the Cellis Police Department. Under Chief Gardener, the department operated as if it were still in the 1950s, even though it was 1972. Plus, both Forsythe and Sledge hated office politics. Within the department, they had made a reputation for pursuing matters long after others had given up and for stepping on toes to get results. They didn't cross the line in obtaining evidence; Sledge and Forsythe just didn't give up until they were completely satisfied.

They figured out quickly that the chief had put them together as a team so he could keep his eye on both of them easier.

WITH A PAIR of tweezers, Sledge held the scorched note while he and Forsythe considered the next steps to take in the investigation. With no fingerprints to go on, Sledge read the words aloud. Maybe they held some clues. "'I don't love you any more and I never want to see you again. I'm going with someone else. Forget me. Goodbye.' Okay, Dean, what do you think?"

"What strikes me is that it's not signed. You know how kids are. They write their names in these swirling patterns, add stars, you know, the works. So for something this important, why didn't the girl sign it?" He peered at the note closely. "Say, what's the dark spot?"

"I can't tell, but it looks like paint or something." Sledge removed his glasses and pulled out a magnifying glass to look closer.

"Maybe, maybe blood too, but we can't tell. If we would figure out who wrote the note, we could ask."

"Dean, do you have all of the samples—handwriting samples, I mean?" Sledge opened the envelope containing Javier's handwriting.

"Well, I've looked at samples of Javier's handwriting. His writing doesn't look like the note at all. I've got to get a handwriting sample from the girl, no question about it. Plus we've got some clear prints from the boy on at least three of the documents. Let's go to the next item. What did you learn about the car, Dean?"

"Well, Charles in the shop said one of the brake lines didn't appear to be cut, but the second had some inconclusive marks on it."

"Well, that's consistent with the scene—no skid marks and all, Dean."

"What gets me is this. The kid had made it from downtown to

the outskirts of town. He had to go through at least a dozen lights or stop signs between his home and the spot where we found him. He had to go through that same hairpin turn while going out of town. Everything we have now suggests Javier was coming back toward town when the accident happened. He made it through all those stops before. But why not on the way back? Plus, no one we've talked to so far knows exactly why Javier was in that area on that day and at that time."

"No one knows or no one wants to tell us, Dean. What about the parents?"

"The man we saw—he wasn't Javier's father. I learned that from the kids at school. Could he have set it up, say, for the insurance?"

"No, they didn't have any insurance, not even to bury him."

"Boy, that's really tough, Danny."

"Yeah, tell me about it. They lose a boy and don't even have the money to bury him."

"I hate this—this part of the job."

"Me too."

They sat silently for a long time. Dean spoke first. "Well, let's include that in our notes, at least. They didn't do it, at least, not for the money. From what I can tell, they lost out big when that boy died. He had a golden future, that's for sure. Will you talk to Callie?"

"Yeah, Dean. I'll take care of it."

Danny Sledge left the squad room and went back out to where Callie sat. She was the one who stepped in, made public appeals for the family, took donations and set up trust fund accounts. She had done it before. It wasn't officially a part of her job, but she just did it.

In the meantime, Dean Forsythe went back to Sergeant Stanley Link's office. Link was sitting at his desk, looking at papers and plotting how he could escape.

Link didn't care much about his job, except for doing the bare minimum to keep it. With his obvious lack of enthusiasm, his subordinates tried to work around him. So when Forsythe came into his office, Link didn't wait for him to say why he was there; Link just needed to vent.

"Baby Face, I'm chained to this job. You know that I'm sixty and ready to retire. But I've got to keep working. With two kids in college, a large mortgage and a wife—I've got to work, that's all there is to it."

While he wanted a less responsible position, Stanley Link's wife wouldn't let him take a demotion or pay cut. Depressed, he could barely do his job, let alone be an effective leader for the cowboy crew of the Cellis Police Department. His hairline gave some indication of his emotional state. He was bald on the top and tried to cover his head with a long comb over that started almost at ear level. He had lost his hair in his early thirties, primarily due to stress.

His wife had two habits—credit card abuse and a weakness for shopping.

Stan was afraid that if he stopped working, his creditors would be at his door the next day. Earlier, he had considered having an arsonist to relieve him and his wife from all the things she had accumulated, until he figured out that he was woefully underinsured. That revelation started a new round of worrying.

"Dean, my only solution now is to die. Even with my pension, insurance and other income, my wife won't have enough to pay off all the bills. Then, she'll have to find some other way to support her habits."

And thankfully, Stanley Link couldn't take any of the stuff with him. He looked forward to a clutter-free existence in heaven. With her, he figured he'd already served time in hell.

Recognizing the sergeant wasn't at his best and would likely say no, Forsythe decided he would try someone else. The telephone rang and Forsythe slipped out of Link's office as quickly as he could.

Outside Sergeant Link's office, Danny waited. As Dean stepped out and closed the door behind him, Danny started in right away. "Well, Baby Face, this leads us back to the Tanner girl. The girl is under eighteen, but I don't know how old. We need to talk to her, even if her parents don't consent to this. We just don't have any other leads to check on."

"Which one? The chief or the captain?"

"Why not the sergeant? You were just in there with him, Baby Face."

"He's in one of his classic moods today—not very receptive. You know he always says 'no, don't push it.' So why bother with him, Old Man?"

They laughed.

"Let's talk to the chief. Maybe that glory hound can find some way he can look like a hero for figuring out how the boyfriend died."

IN POLICE CHIEF Nathan Gardener's office, Forsythe stood at the door while Sledge stood in front of the chief's desk. Sledge gave details about their progress in the case, to which the chief nodded approvingly. Then Sledge started to explain why he and Forsythe had come to the chief's office. "Chief, I want to get a handwriting sample from Andrea Tanner, Dr. Tanner's daughter. I believe the Mitchell boy had gone out to the Tanner home and was on his way back when he had the wreck."

The heavyset man pushed his chair back from his desk, revealing the two rolls of flab above his tight belt. His thick fingers tapped on the desk. The puffy areas around his eyes seemed to stand out even more. Sledge looked at Nathan Gardener's eyes carefully. They were good indicators of the chief's irritation level.

SLEDGE NOTICED THE puffy areas around Chief Gardener's eyes stand out for the first time when he questioned why a burglary case was closed without any serious investigation. The chief had ordered it closed without any explanation. As the chief yelled and berated him, Sledge noticed his eyes then.

The second time, the chief stopped for a photo shoot and interview following the breakup of a major robbery ring that had operated for years in Cellis and the neighboring communities. Some impertinent wag in the crowd asked Chief Gardener if he was glad to send his competitors to jail.

The local newspapers and two television stations carried pictures and shots emphasizing the breakup of the ring. Media outside of Cellis showed unflattering pictures of the enraged chief, thrashing through the sea of reporters as he tried to figure out who had made such a smart remark.

The third time, a perpetrator jumped over a table, handcuffs and all and tried to strangle the chief. The fellow made Nathan Gardener's long, skinny tongue hang out as he tried to permanently relieve the chief of his last breath.

Sitting in front of Chief Gardener today with Forsythe standing at the door, Sledge figured the chief was plenty hot. His blood pressure was visibly rising. The two officers knew they had struck a major nerve.

"Do you know for certain that the boy was at the Tanner house, Sledge?"

"Well, no, but —"

"Now, you're just assuming too much then. You can't prove he was at the Tanner house before the accident. And you said you've already called them twice. You've got better things to do with your time than to bother the good doctor. Leave that family alone, mister."

"But —"

"The first rule around here is you don't accuse without proof. Remember that in the future. Dr. Tanner does not need any bad press—especially unsubstantiated rumors linking him or his family to a death. He is a good man—a fine, upstanding member of our community. He runs that clinic, you know, where needy children sometimes get free surgery. Let me spell this out to you. I don't want you to contact them again. Ever. Be sure to put the note you found back into the file in case you ever come up with some real leads. Get out. I've got work to do." Now bright red in the face and on the top of his bald head, Chief Gardener looked down at the paperwork before him.

Outside, in their squad car, both officers expressed surprise about their chief's reaction. Slamming both hands on the steering wheel, Forsythe started first, "What a pure-dee unadulterated jerk!"

"In case you ever come up with some real leads." Sledge repeated, mocking the chief. "How can we get any leads with our hands tied?"

"I expected him to be cautious but I never thought he would limit the investigation!"

"He must have something going on with the doctor. But what?"

"Who knows? Even if he doesn't now, it's only because he hasn't figured out how to use the doctor yet." The officers chuckled, their tension subsiding.

"Being a rich doctor probably helps. I thought the first rule was 'Protect and Serve.' For Chief Gardener, that must mean we protect the rich and don't serve the poor!"

"What did you expect—that the chief would let us investigate this case in the right way? That's what we get for playing it safe."

"What's next, Dean?"

"Let's see what we can find out without attracting too much attention. Let's keep this to ourselves."

The two officers knew most of the rumors about Chief Gardener. Supposedly, he had been involved with a prostitution ring, the disappearance of key evidence and loose ties to one of the local crime bosses. The rumors persisted, yet nothing ever came of it.

For the next three weeks, Forsythe and Sledge tried to figure out Dr. Tanner's routine. Individually and as a team, they sat out near the Tanner home. They drove by the clinic. Dr. Tanner followed the same routine every weekday, except one. On that day, he drove to the Gilmer Motel in West End. Dean figured it out first. "Well! Well! The good doctor isn't as good as he holds himself out to be!"

The blond-haired woman sitting in the station wagon caught Forsythe's eye.

"So it's true! Blonds do have more . . . will you look at that!" Shocked, Dean interrupted his own cliché as the woman got out of the car and walked the short distance to the same hotel room Dr. Tanner went into only minutes before.

The woman wasn't Mrs. Tanner and neither officer recognized her. The officers waited. Finally, the doctor left the motel after an hour. With his custom-made front license plate, RICHDOC, and expensive car, Dr. Tanner was easy to spot.

In time, Sledge tailed Andrea Tanner too. Each day, her mother drove her to school and picked her up. The girl stayed at home during the weekends and rarely ventured outside.

The officers didn't note anything unusual during their surveillance of the Tanner home. They did notice two red-haired teenagers who rode bicycles back and forth near the clinic and the Tanner home. And they noticed the nosy neighbor to the north, who watched them and tried to edge closer and closer to get a clear view of the officers.

Discreetly, Sledge checked on Andrea Tanner. He wasn't able to get any handwriting samples from his sources. He confirmed she was a junior at the private high school and she was seventeen. As for getting any teacher to release one of Andrea's homework assignments to him, he ruled that out quickly. The gray-haired lady in the school office asked him to leave as soon as he told her he was an officer. Andrea didn't belong to any clubs within the school or outside. She didn't drive and she appeared to have no visible ties to any church. Andrea Tanner didn't even have a library card. Pye Academy had its own extensive library. Sledge made a few more inquiries, but nothing more came out.

INSTEAD OF OFFICERS Sledge and Forsythe, Police Chief Gardener personally handled the contact on the Mitchell case with the coroner, Hiram Graf. He and Graf were old friends and teammates on the same local high school basketball team. The two were extremely proud of their local basketball team even though they had graduated many years before. Javier Mitchell had been a star player. He would be remembered as a star and not as a suicide if they had anything to do with it. Before leaving the police station for the coroner's office, the chief pulled the scorched note out of the file and dropped it into the trash can on his way out of the office.

Old friend or not, the chief never told the coroner about the note.

Weeks after Javier Mitchell's death, the coroner ruled Javier Mitchell's death as an accident. With a copy of that report in the file, Police Chief Gardener could now officially close the police file on Javier Mitchell.

THE FOURTH LETTER came in April 1972. Like the others, it had no return address, it was postmarked from Enid and it was addressed to her.

Sierra ran a butter knife under the seal and opened the white envelope. She pulled out a white sheet of paper with a short message typed on it.

> Boom-Boom,
>   I'm still here. Look at today's newspaper on page 2.

No demand for money—no overt threat—just the short message. She grabbed the newspaper and read page two over and over until her eyes watered and her head hurt.

Sierra didn't see anything that pertained to her or anyone she knew. Frustrated, she threw the newspaper on the coffee table and pushed the table over with her foot, sending the newspaper cascading to the floor. She burst into tears.

This letter came so soon after Javier Mitchell's death. Who would so cruelly threaten her peace of mind? Like before, she tore the letter and envelope into a thousand pieces of white confetti before burning it. Trembling now, she went to the recreation room bar and poured herself a drink. She drank vodka heavily that day and the following three days.

CHAPTER 35

THE LADYBUGS WERE taking over his garden. As he stood in his garden that afternoon in mid-August 1972, spraying them, the bugs reminded Brian of Javier and Everett.

Months had passed since Javier's death. Everett had not been in contact since the surgery was done on his son, less than two weeks after Everett had done the brake job. While they spent time playing golf and socializing before Javier's death, since that time, Everett had not called or stopped by. It wasn't a coincidence that Everett had stopped coming around, but Brian didn't see him anymore, even at the dry cleaners.

Glad Everett had not called him, Brian still worried. Would Everett try to blackmail him? So far, there had been nothing. Could he trust Everett to keep his mouth shut forever? And there were questions about the envelope he had used to hold the break-up note. Shortly after the call from the police, Brian realized that he hadn't been as careful with the envelope as he thought he had been. He didn't know whether Andrea had handled the envelope.

Unfortunately, only time would tell. In the meantime, Brian still ate antacids whenever he thought very long about his involvement in the Mitchell boy's death.

"SLEDGE, WHERE IN the world did you get that note?" Openly astonished, Dean Forsythe yelled loudly. "Chief Gardener said it was lost months ago."

The two men sat in Sledge's den, drinking beers on their day off. Sledge's wife was ironing in the next room. Sledge held up the sandwich bag that held the scorched note and envelope.

"It was lost all right. The day the chief took the file to the coroner for a ruling on the Mitchell kid's death, I came back to the station after our shift. When Ernie dumped the trash from the chief's office, I spotted the pink envelope on top of his cart. How many pink envelopes do you think we use here? I saw it in the trash. In the trash! Can you believe it? Chief Gardener had it last, remember?"

"Why, you old scrounge! Good work!"

"I just had a hunch, that's all. It bothers me that the chief would do something like this."

"What would motivate him to take this kind of risk? I mean, throwing evidence away? There must be more to this than just an accident. Danny, it just doesn't make sense otherwise."

"It makes sense if the chief is trying to protect someone."

"Well, we still don't have a lead, but who knows what will come up in the future? But I sure won't keep this note at the station, that's for sure."

TWO YEARS AFTER Javier's death, on a Saturday morning, the rain drizzled down onto the dirty, grayish-brown snow, melting the ice but making mush. The mush outside the apartment window looked like the mush oatmeal she had given to her three boys just minutes before. And she was sick of them both.

As Dyna looked out of the dirty window, the dreary look of Cellis and bad memories of the difficulties she had had there dragged down her spirits like suffocating smoke.

For Dyna, every day of living after Javier's death was a struggle, still hard to get used to. Today, she relived some of her lowest moments, focusing on Brian. That morning, when she opened the newspaper, his face was the first Dyna saw. Some group had given Brian an award for his civic work.

Brian Tanner and his daughter, Andrea, had been the source of grief in her life repeatedly. Dyna shuddered as she remembered some of the things Brian had done to her. She had tried hard to put him out of her life over and again, but today, for some strange reason, memories of him and the pain he and his daughter brought Dyna pierced her senses. How she wished she could get even with them and make them hurt, like they hurt her. They deserved the same misery she was suffering now. But they were rich and happy and doing very well. The tears started flowing and Dyna did little to stop them. Her boys, sitting at the table, hadn't noticed her suffering or pretended not to notice. Today, as she stood at the window looking out into the gray, gray sky, Dyna just felt like having a good, long, slow cry.

She could see no end to her troubles, her desperation and her miserable life. The weather outside, her past in Cellis, and the letter on top of the refrigerator made the day almost impossible to handle.

The letter was from some law firm in Todda, Ohio. With the thick, white fancy envelope—it must have weighed at least three ounces. Maybe it wasn't for her, maybe it was for someone whose name sounded like hers. But the only way to find out would be to open it and Dyna just didn't have the nerve so far. So she waited, but she wanted it out of sight. Too afraid to open it, she had left it on top of the refrigerator, next to the bananas. She hadn't had any business in Todda and hadn't been there in some time. So why were they bothering her? She didn't need any more trouble. By Saturday, she had waited three days already and still had not opened it. It had to be trouble, for she wasn't getting anything else lately but trouble.

As the boys sat eating oatmeal, Dyna pulled the letter off the top of the refrigerator and ran a butter knife along one of the short ends of the envelope. If it were trash, it could be added to the full paper bag in the kitchen and taken out.

But the letter was treasure.

Benjamin noticed the surprise on her face. "Mom, where in the world is Todda, Ohio?" Benjamin asked. He dipped his spoon in his oatmeal, lifted a huge, grayish-brown clump and stuffed it into his mouth.

Benjamin had seen the letter on top of the refrigerator. Had he read the letter? Dyna examined it and wondered whether he had actually opened it. She figured he had and had done a really good job in resealing it. This child was heading toward a life of crime, she thought. But today, even he could not ruin the good news.

"Benjamin, take smaller bites! Your food isn't going anywhere. That's better. Well, Benjamin, it's not too far from Bubbock's Bay. Todda is about an hour away on the other side of Bubbock's Bay. The next big city is Toledo, just off Interstate 80-90. It's about a hundred and fifty miles from here. Todda is where we're going to live."

After skimming through the letter again, Dyna explained to her children that the lawyers had written to tell her about a house their great-aunt, Vernice, had left to her. She read the letter for a third time, this time more carefully. She didn't understand it all, but she knew that she was getting a house. Just as Dyna finished, she noticed her youngest son sitting with his mouth hanging open. "Jake, finish your breakfast."

Jake couldn't help his surprise. "Why are we going to live there?"

She explained again. "Well, Auntie Vernice Mitchell died and left us a house. Remember her from the photo album? Auntie Vernice was the one with the fat, black-and-white old dog. We're going to move into her house. We've got a chance to start a new life there."

"Why can't we stay here? We really like it here," Alfred added. He had good reason to like it in Cellis. He and Benjamin were regulars at Waterman's Grocery Store. There, the twins routinely filled their pockets with anything they could steal.

"Honey, I know you like it here. But we can't stay here anymore. You'll like it there. Just wait and see. Now finish your breakfast."

Dyna had suspected the twins of thievery for some time. She

taught them stealing was wrong, but she could barely give them
the basics of life, let alone anything nice. She could hardly blame
them—the family had been poor for so long. Too tired of being
broke, Dyna just couldn't fight them all the time.

From the grin on his face, Dyna knew at least Jake was happy
with her decision. She hoped the move would be good for all of
her children, but especially for Jake.

It was time to stop looking at the rain.

VERNICE MITCHELL WAS John Mitchell's aunt. Never
married and with no children, she worked as a legal secretary for
many years. After retiring, she spent time traveling. But to
everyone's surprise, Vernice Mitchell had also amassed a small
fortune.

After John's death, Vernice had contacted Dyna once or twice
a year. But she had never really been involved in the lives of Dyna
or the boys.

She traveled all over the world, yet Vernice Mitchell never
made it to Indiana. She would tell her friends and neighbors she
never wanted to cause any trouble for anyone, even for a few days.
In reality, she didn't want routine contact with her closest living
relatives because she feared she would fall in love with them and
would become lonely when they were not around. And she feared
that someday, she might be a burden to them.

Her sudden death let Aunt Vernice avoid nursing home care
or dependence upon her closest friends. She died at home in the
way she wanted, not more than three months after the death of
her dog, Noodle.

Surprised that Vernice had left the big house to her, Dyna
welcomed the chance for such a major change. It would take some
time to settle the estate, but the house would go to her.

While it was true Dyna wanted to move because she had
inherited the house, Dyna wanted to move away from Cellis for
other reasons. With the death of her oldest son Javier two years
ago, Jake's problems at school and because of her encounters with

Brian Tanner over the years, Dyna felt she had to get away from Cellis. Period. She was sick and tired of the shame and the sadness that had been in her life so long. She wasn't going to miss this chance, especially for Jake and for herself.

WHEN TWO YEARS had passed since Javier's death, Brian Tanner finally began to relax consistently. As far as he knew, Everett Sears had kept his word. No news is good news, Brian kept reminding himself.

His daughter Andie had been dating other boys for more than a year now. She seemed to have gotten over Javier Mitchell.

ZACHARY MINEAR WAS doing well since having the surgery on his leg. He could walk with his father now and had even started to run like other little boys. That is, until what seemed to be a simple cold got progressively worse. After being hospitalized for pneumonia, the boy died within a week. His mother, Gina, was inconsolable.

Gina never understood why it had taken so long for Everett to agree to pay for surgery for Zach. And she couldn't understand why he wasn't more supportive to her during her grieving. All she knew was that she no longer wanted to be Everett's mistress. Within a week after burying Zachary, in the middle of the night, Gina moved back to her hometown in Gillette, Utah.

Within five months after Zachary's death, Ellen Sears finally died too.

Now, after juggling his relationships with Gina, Ellen and Zachary for so long, Everett Sears was alone.

CHAPTER 36

WHILE WAITING FOR dinner, the twins sat in the kitchen of the small apartment in Indiana. Excited by the upcoming move to Ohio, they talked about what things they would do there. Their younger brother Jake sat alone outside on the stoop of the apartment building.

While Dyna busied herself making dinner, the twins also talked about things they had hated about living in Cellis. One of those things was the teasing that Jake had suffered at school. They were in high school now and he was in middle school. Abruptly, they changed the topic.

"Ma, why didn't Jake get his legs fixed?" Alfred asked.

"Yeah, you worked for some doctors." Benjamin added, "Why didn't those doctors fix Jake's leg?"

"We didn't have the money and they never picked him for the free help." She stirred the pot of stew.

"Ma, you worked there. They owed you that, at least." Alfred pointed out.

Bending over the hot oven door, she peered in at the baking bread. Dyna couldn't help thinking about what she had done with Brian. She knew she had done more than enough to earn the surgery for Jake.

"So they had to pick him, huh?" Benjamin continued.

"Well, it was a little bit more than that. They put all the names into a hat, pull a name and talk about the child they choose."

"So it's just the name of the kid?" Benjamin persisted.

"No, from what I know, they have the names of some kids and they have letters and cards about some of the others."

"Letters and cards?" Alfred repeated innocently.

"Yes. Sometimes, people write these letters and cards saying how nice the child or the family is and how the boy or girl really deserves or needs to have surgery."

"Is that all the time? I mean, do they use the letters and cards all the time?" Alfred continued.

"No. They don't always get letters and cards. I found that out while I worked there. And they don't always look at the stuff people send in, I don't know why."

"Well, who decides which kid will get the surgery?" Benjamin asked in his usual direct way.

"Uh, the head doctors, you know, Dr. Meyer, Dr. Smertz and Dr. Tanner."

"Just those three?" Alfred demanded.

"Far as I know." She stirred the stew again. "Usually, they don't let the employees watch, except for Rosalie. And they don't let her watch all the time either, Rosalie told me."

"Who has the final say, Ma? Which one of them?" Benjamin persisted.

"Just be quiet. They could have picked your brother at anytime while I worked there. It's probably too late now." The bread was done so she pulled it out and placed it on top of the oven.

"But Ma!" the twins exclaimed. Slamming the oven door, she whirled around yelling. "Boys, the clinic people didn't pick Jake! That's it! No more questions!"

Dyna went to bed early. Dinner that evening was unusually quiet.

THAT EVENING, WHILE they were in their bedroom supposedly hard at work on their homework, the twins plotted. It wasn't their first illegal activity, but it was the first in which someone other than them would directly benefit from their skills.

"Boy, she got really mad!" Alfred stood at the end of their bunk bed, balancing a dart in his hand. He wanted to hit the bull's eye, but so far, he had hit only the outer rings of the dart board on the wall.

Stretched out on his back on the upper bunk, Benjamin looked at the ceiling. His mother's outburst was unusual, but the twins needed all the information they could get to set up their plans.

"Well, what would you expect? She went there and worked hard for them. I remember she used to be so tired when she got home after work. She did all that work for them and when it was time to pick a kid, she didn't get help from them. They just ignored her."

Hearing the thwack sound the dart made as it pierced the board, Benjamin rolled over onto his stomach and looked down onto his brother. "What's the matter with you, Alfred? Stop that noise before Ma comes in here. She's mad enough already."

"Oh, yeah, I didn't think about it." Alfred came closer to the bull's eye, but he need more practice. He pulled the dart out and threw it into the top drawer of the dresser. "Well, what did you have in mind, Benj?"

"It'll be simple, but it's going to take some work. First, for the volunteers." Benjamin swung his legs down over the edge and dropped to the floor.

"Volunteers?"

"Yep—the very best kind. They'll say what we want. Get the telephone book, Alf."

"And the phone?"

"We won't need it. If any of these people call, it'll really be long distance."

While Alfred went to the dining room to get the telephone book, Benjamin sat at the desk in their bedroom. He pulled out his school notebook and from the back of the black binder, he pulled out several pages of newsprint. He'd collected them over the last week, but needed to talk to his mother before using the newspapers.

"What do you have there?" Alfred was back and looking over Benjamin's shoulder.

"Go back and shut the door. Lock it too. We have work to do. Alf, I got this idea about a week or so ago, so I started saving the obituary sections from the newspaper."

"The *Courier*?"

"Yes, and the *West End Gazette* too."

"And what will you do with all these notable stiffs, oh wise brother?" Alf asked sarcastically, "Send letters to them?"

"Nope, they'll be the ones sending letters."

Alfred caught on then. "I like it!"

"They might have ignored Ma, but they won't be able to ignore all these people asking for help for Jake, that's for sure. I learned this trick from good old Don, 'Stack that deck,' he would always say."

Alfred chortled, "And that might have been the only useful advice Don ever gave."

Alfred and Benjamin started with the telephone book and the obituary columns from the newspaper. They agreed forty letters would be plenty and the dead people would not mind lending their names for such a worthwhile project. In a few of the letters, the twins would include copies of old sports articles about Javier, in hopes those articles might persuade the doctors to look at the public relations value in choosing Jake for the free surgery. "Which doctors should we send them to, Benjamin?"

"Let's send some to each of them."

"No, wait a minute. Did you ever hear Mama talk about Dr. Smertz?" Alfred asked.

"Yeah and Dr. Meyer too."

"What about Dr. Tanner?"

Benjamin thought for a few moments. "Uh no, wait—no. I can't ever remember her talking about him. Why?"

"Well, maybe Dr. Tanner doesn't know her. Why should we waste time on him?"

"Good point, Alfred. What do you think?"

"Let's send only a couple to him."

"Good thinking. That means more for the other two. What about the sportswriter?"

Alfred smiled. "Let's have him call Dr. Meyer and send his letter to Dr. Smertz."

It took the twins almost the whole weekend to finish the letters. Over the next week, they rode their bikes, walked or took the bus all over Cellis to put the letters in various mailboxes.

While carrying out one of their planned mail drops, the boys contacted the *Cellis Courier's* lead sportswriter, Ray Turabian. Surprised and delighted to hear what the two youngsters wanted, he agreed to call the clinic and to write a letter in support of their younger brother Jake. Ray covered many of the high school sporting events and remembered Javier very well. Proud to be able to help these two fine, upstanding boys in getting the special help their younger brother needed, he prepared his letter that same day and called that week. And at their request, he agreed to keep quiet about the twins being the source for such a noble idea.

WITHIN THE MONTH, Brian Tanner, Herve Meyer and Bill Smertz met to select their next charity surgery case. When Brian put the brown paper bag containing the children's names on the table, Bill didn't reach for it, as he usually did. Herve Meyer started talking immediately, "Brian, Bill and I think Steven Jacob Mitchell should be a candidate for free surgery." Smertz quickly agreed.

Brian was stunned. He had thrown away the three letters requesting help for Steven that he had received. They must have planned this already, Brian guessed. And for that reason alone, Brian wasn't going to cave in so easily. He protested, "We've always done this by blind draw. Why change now?"

Herve replied immediately. "We're not asking for a change. We think this one should be done in addition to the child chosen in the normal way."

"What? Why?"

"Well, the boy's mother used to work here. Remember Dyna

Woods? She was on the cleaning staff. According to her supervisor and Rosalie, the woman was really nice, hardworking and prompt. We should have had more like her."

This was Dyna's kid! Brian now had a second reason to oppose the surgery. Brian protested, "I don't think it's a good idea!"

"Plus, Ray Turabian from the *Courier* contacted us about this kid," Bill interrupted.

They had newspaper support already! Brian was surprised, his partners had never undermined him before that he was aware of. Then he thought about it. "Wait a minute! Isn't Turabian a sportswriter? Why in the world should he care? That Mitchell kid couldn't possibly make the news based upon his athletic abilities."

Herve countered quickly, "You're right, Steven can't. But his older brother did. Remember Javier Mitchell? He was that local basketball hero who died a couple of years ago in a bad accident."

"Yes, but . . . ."

"We can get double coverage on this one, Brian. The family of a dead sports hero and the usual charity coverage, just think about it! We couldn't buy this kind of publicity, Brian, and you know it. We started this surgery thing years ago as a public relations move, remember?"

"Yes, but I . . ." Brian interrupted.

"Let me finish. Now, when his mother worked here, it might have been a little sticky to pick her son. But she doesn't work here anymore. So what's the problem?" Herve was growing impatient.

Bill Smertz interjected, "Javier Mitchell had national exposure for basketball. Think about it. We could get kids from across the entire country to come here for needed care if we play this one right."

"Well . . ." Brian started.

"Plus, you did some free surgical work for some kid named Zachary two years ago that you counted as a special case. Remember him? And it wasn't cheap! You had three doctors from the clinic plus a specialist that you brought in, all at the clinic's expense," Smertz added, then gave a few more details. He knew about the Zachary Minear matter intimately, which surprised Brian.

At the clinic, Alma Hormiga or Trina Kent processed routine insurance claims. Occasionally, the office manager, Rosalie Franson, reviewed those claims. On rare occasions, Brian or another one of the partners would look over the claims too. All large or unusual claims were submitted to one of the partners without exception.

Brian had directed Trina that bills for the Minear surgery would be absorbed by the clinic. Behind Brian's back, Trina went to Bill Smertz, just to cover herself in case any questions would arise. Bill figured that the information might be useful someday.

"Brian, is there any personal reason why you don't want to pick Steven Mitchell?" Herve Meyer sat back in his chair, tapping the pen he held. He narrowed his eyes into little slits. He did that only when he wanted something really badly.

Brian hesitated. He couldn't have the partners asking too many questions about Everett Sears' son or about Dyna. He couldn't risk irritating Herve over this issue. Herve might contact Everett or Dyna, or both of them. And the whole messy truth might come out.

"Do what you want! It looks like you're going to do it whether I agree or not."

Herve smirked. Bill reached for the paper bag and drew out a name. The charity child would be Sophia Allegro. Summarily, they accepted her. The partners had little else to say to each other right then.

While Herve contacted Dyna to set up the surgery for Steve, Brian got on another telephone line and called his travel agent. Brian had made up his mind. Steven Jacob Mitchell could get the free surgery at the clinic. But Dyna wasn't going to get a chance to rub this in his face. No matter what it took, he was going to be out of town or somewhere else when the surgery on Steven Jacob Mitchell took place.

CHAPTER 37

AUNT VERNICE'S OLD green shingled Victorian house sat upon a hill. As they pulled up in front in Attorney Grant Gilroy's car, Dyna thought the place looked like a museum. Two stories, plus a full attic and a deep basement, the place was huge.

Dyna had visited only twice with John years ago when the children were very small. But she didn't remember that the home had so many steps.

Looking up at the concrete rising well above their heads, Dyna worried that Jake couldn't make it up the steps. She wondered whether the house would be wrong for them. Maybe she had made a huge mistake in considering a move from Indiana.

The twins bounded up the steps. Jake took his time, still stiff from surgery and rehabilitation. As he reached the twelfth step, he turned and gleefully looked at his mother. Still standing next to the attorney's car, discussing final details, Dyna looked up when she heard her youngest cry out. "Mama! Look! I can do this! I can get up these steps! Aunt Vernice is helping to make me strong." Right then, Dyna got a strong sense of peace about her decision to come to Ohio. Everything would be fine.

AT THE BOTTOM of the long flight of steps to the house, Attorney Gilroy asked her several questions about her trip and then directed her attention back to the house.

"You understand the house includes contents and furnishings, right?"

"Yes." She understood it now; she didn't know it before. This was good news to Dyna; she didn't own a whole lot of furniture.

"When was the last time you were here?"

"Maybe 1960, no, 1961."

"You know Miss Mitchell was a collector, right?"

"Well, Aunt Vernice mentioned she picked up some things in her travels." This guy made Dyna edgy. What was in the house, a collection of shrunken heads?

He licked his lips and hesitated. "I, uh, we haven't completed the inventory yet. I was her attorney, but I've only been here once."

So this was why he was nervous, he just hadn't done all of his work yet, Dyna thought. Relieved, she chirped back, "Oh, that's all right, we'll be happy to help." The attorney gave Dyna a strange look and said nothing.

Dyna and Attorney Gilroy made it up the steps at a much slower pace than the twins. He flipped through a ring of keys; some were skeleton keys, others just looked odd. When Attorney Gilroy opened the door for them, Dyna and her boys stood there, frozen in place. From the front entry, they could see only a narrow pathway to walk through, for starting at the entry, the house was jammed full of stuff.

Aunt Vernice's home was full from cellar to attic with the treasures and trash she had accumulated over fifty years. In her travels, she collected artifacts of all different kinds, plus any other items that caught her eye. Knick-knack racks, hooks, holders, display boxes, cases, sconces, plate racks, tapestries, wall shelves, cases, baker's racks, easels, curio cabinets, collections, accumulations and stock piles, almost every available surface space was full. And the house was musty, as if Aunt Vernice hadn't opened the windows in years.

Dyna was speechless. The boys were too, but only shortly. They went into the house.

"Ma, maybe this is why she never let us visit," Benjamin commented.

"Yeah," Alfred added, fascinated with the sight of so much treasure. "We would have had to sleep with old Noodle—he had the only bed that wasn't covered with stuff."

IN THE UPSTAIRS bathroom, the old house had an old ball-and-clawfoot tub, deep enough to allow long and luxurious neck-deep soaking. She had spotted it during the walk-through with Attorney Gilroy. Exploring the rest of their castle could wait until the next morning. Dyna knew where she would spend most of her night.

At the drugstore two blocks from the house, she carefully selected the things she would need for that evening. While the boys wandered in the magazine section and near the toys, she stopped in the gift section. She located pale vanilla candles, her favorite kind, and a large box of cherry cordials, candy that she wouldn't share with the boys. Moving on, she found thick, pink, rose-scented bubble bath and a cigarette lighter.

Later than evening, when the boys were settled in the bedrooms on the second floor, Dyna made her move. At first, when she turned on the water, it ran rusty; she feared this would end her escape. But after a few minutes, the water ran clear. With the yellowed stopper now in the drain, Dyna poured a lavish amount of the thick liquid into the tub.

The fragrant scent of the vanilla candles wafted though the bathroom as Dyna swirled the mounds of fluffy white bubbles around with her. Dyna dried her hands on one of the thick, soft, white towels Aunt Vernice had in the hallway closet and thinking ahead, she placed a second one over the large, hot air grate in the floor. Then she looked carefully at the strange item in the corner. Made out of iron or steel, it stood several feet high and consisted of three main sections, a painted pedestal base, a polished midsection that looked like some sort of dispenser, topped by a round, ball-like silver basin. Lifting the handle on the basin, Dyna opened it up. To her utter delight, Dyna found Aunt Vernice had installed an old towel steamer in the bathroom, probably picked up from a barber's shop.

While looking through the first floor of the house earlier in the day, Dyna found a small radio. Now in the bathroom, she located a classical music radio station. As she waited for the deep tub to fill, enjoying the peaceful music and fragrance, she unwrapped her treasure. She pulled one of the dark confections out, took a bite and let the delicious liquid seep into her mouth. With her senses heightened, Dyna turned out the light and got ready for the bath of her dreams.

In their first night in their new home, Dyna soaked in the tub until all the bubbles were long gone, the water was cold and her children knocked on the door to make sure she hadn't drowned.

EARLY THE NEXT morning, with the twins in front of her armed with brooms and a flashlight and Jake moving slowly behind, Dyna opened the door to the basement. She turned the round knob on the wall just inside the door; it controlled the lights to the basement stairs. The light of the single dim bulb that hung at the bottom of the stairs cast a yellow tint and created eerie shadows from the items in the basement. Like the rest of the house, Aunt Vernice had stored knick-knacks, furniture and collectibles in her basement too. But what else was down there, waiting for them? Dyna almost didn't want to know.

Dyna and her boys ventured down the stairs slowly, one step at a time, afraid of what was there, what they might find in the darkness, or what might find them. The old house creaked as if to warn them. Upstairs, something moved, sending echoes from behind them. Dyna and the boys stopped. They paused for a few seconds and again started down into the bowels of the huge old house.

Now at the bottom of the steps and unsure which direction to go, Dyna felt something cold touch her right elbow. A bone-chilling scream escaped from her throat. The twins, unsure of the source of danger, dropped their brooms and the flashlight. Somehow, in the jumble of legs and arms, the twins managed to climb over Dyna and Jake. As they raced back up the steps, with Dyna and Jake close behind, the twins screamed shrilly, like little girls frightened out of their minds.

Back in the kitchen now, the family tried to sort out what had happened, the twins yelling at each other, blaming each other for being scared, for dropping the brooms and leaving the flashlight down in that pit. Dyna sat in a straight-backed chair, trying to catch her breath from the fright.

Then Jake spotted it. Covered with wallpaper, the three-pole light switch plate blended into the wall, almost invisible, except to someone who knew its location. He eased over to it, flipped the three switches on and turned to see light streaming from the basement door.

"Ma, look!"

Dyna looked up and started laughing uncontrollably. The twins, still arguing fiercely over who was a big chicken and who had ran up the stairs first, didn't hear their mother or see the light.

"Alfred, Benjamin, look, look!" Dyna pointed at the basement door, still laughing hard.

Aunt Vernice had paid good money to have the basement well lit. Eight-foot-long fluorescent lights ran across the basement from front to back. The lights weren't the only update. The best treasure of all for Dyna was hidden in a small room next to the chimney. Sometime just before her death, Aunt Vernice had a fifty-gallon model hot water heater installed.

AFTER MOVING TO Todda, Ohio, Jake Mitchell worked hard to change from his past. Just before moving to Todda, he had the surgery on his leg and completed physical therapy. But there were other limitations to overcome.

Long after surgery was done, Jake kept doing his leg exercises. Eventually, Jake was able to buy size-eight shoes off the shelves, instead of the specially fitted shoes he wore as a youngster.

As a sophomore, after overcoming his stuttering, Jake went out for the debate team. By the time he was a senior, he had several ribbons and a small silver trophy on display in their home, based on his efforts in speech and debate.

As a junior, Jake even found a job working as an intern for a real estate development firm, the Westwood Group. With his quick wits, he got a chance to participate in activities of the firm that few interns had access to. Jake worked in the accounting, plan development and legal departments, and with the site managers. In each area, Jake developed contacts that would serve him well later.

The day he graduated from high school, Jake looked over the crowd to see how many faces he recognized. Nothing would have pleased Jake more than if Russell Ammon Jr., Eunice P. Driver and Tim Rausch were there. They weren't really welcome, but Jake sent each of them a graduation announcement anyway out of spite. He doubted that they would come, but he wanted to see those three for one reason. He wanted to rub in their faces that he had made something out of his life. Despite all their efforts to tear him down, they didn't succeed. They would have to sit in the audience and see him receive recognition for his accomplishments on the speech and debate team. And as he walked across the stage, he could do so without the heavy brace that he wore for so long. Today, if they were in the audience, they could eat dirt.

He was proud of his awards and his physical accomplishments. But at times, especially at his graduation, Jake regretted that some of his tormenters from Cellis couldn't see how far he had come. Jake felt he had never quite repaid Russ, Eunice and Tim for the damage they had done. He felt that he owed them something, preferably some misery.

"SO WHY THE dye job, Jake?" Benjamin was the first to see his younger brother's handiwork after graduation. Jake was now Steven J. Mitchell and had dyed his bright-red hair brown.

"I need a change, bro. With what we went through in Indiana,

I don't want to go back to that kind of life again!"

"It wasn't that bad."

"Being broke wasn't bad? Being teased about having red hair wasn't that bad? Having people treat us like trash because we were poor and couldn't do anything major back to them wasn't that bad?" Steve sneered at his brother. "Maybe that life was okay for you, but I don't intend to be poor again. And by the way, don't call me Jake anymore. I'm sick of Jake. Now that I'm done with high school, there's no reason for me to keep that name anymore."

"And you think that changing your name and hair color will change all of that?"

"No, I'm making other changes too. I enrolled in a hotel management course right after graduation. I've got my own life to make, and I figure money, power and real estate will be good tools for success and to even a few scores as well."

Benjamin laughed scornfully. "There are easier ways to make money!"

Steve retorted, "Like burglary and petty theft? You can keep those, brother! You and Alfred are going to be caught, and you'll do time for stealing peanuts."

Benjamin laughed again. "We'll see, Jake, we'll see."

While Steve took courses in real estate, business and hotel management at the local college, he worked full-time at the Westwood Group's plan development department located in the firm's Todda headquarters. In five short years, he would become a minor partner in the real estate development group. He progressed from position to position, in part because of his managerial skills. But his promotions occurred in part because of his dirty tactics.

AT FIRST, ALMA didn't have much experience working with Brian. In her first six months or so at the clinic, she met with him individually only four or five times for medical claims reviews. During those times, he believed he was being warm and friendly; she thought he was aloof and cold. She preferred meeting with the office manager, Rosalie, or one of the other partners for approvals, if she needed any. But Alma Hormiga noticed Brian seemed to be most happy when he had pushed for and gotten additional payments.

Occasionally, when an especially large check came in, Brian complained to her. His complaint was not about the work he and Alma had done in collecting it, but that he had to share it with the other partners. Those complaints were rare, but they stuck in Alma's mind.

In her second year at the clinic, Alma purposely sought out Brian's approval on claims. While she didn't neglect contacts with the other partners and Rosalie, she sought out Brian whenever she had large claims to submit or when a claim might allow for wiggle room. In claims review sessions she had with Brian, Alma noticed Brian looked at the forms differently from the other partners. Aggressively, he tried to bill, picking up expenses that had been omitted from the forms, looking for the exceptions, the loopholes and the obscure. Alma Hormiga worked closely with him to try to detect how far he would go to get money.

Those sessions convinced Alma of several things, mainly that Brian liked money and he wanted to submit claims for the maximum allowable under each plan. She was certain that if given half a chance, he would cut corners to get benefit payments. He might go even further if the motivations were right.

CHAPTER 38

DYNA CRIED AS she finished reading the letters from the twins. Both let her know they were all right but needed a little money to buy things prisoners sometimes need. At age twenty-two, this was the first time they had to do hard time. They had been involved with the theft of a semitruck-load of electronic equipment—mainly radios and stereos. Despite her anguish about her twins' imprisonment, Dyna knew in her heart they had done worse things in their lives.

They just hadn't been caught before.

SHE HAD PRAYED for those two for years. When she had moved her family to Todda, Ohio, she had hoped her sons would take advantage of their new home and begin new lives. Don and his bad habits were long gone. He left within two weeks after Javier's death. Steve had graduated and was now reaping his rewards, working for a resort chain. But the twins had not changed. Now, they were receiving the consequences.

When the twins were sentenced, she grieved. But she also hoped they would learn something and straighten out their lives. Why the twins had turned out so poorly, Dyna just could not understand.

They were so unlike her baby boy, Steven Jacob. And they were nothing like her dead son, Javier.

Still clutching the twins' letters in front of her, Dyna cried harder as she thought about the twins and Javier.

Throughout the years following Javier's death, she struggled with her grief and what the old woman had said. She repeated to herself the old woman's words, "Seventeen but not eighteen. Seventeen but not eighteen. Seventeen but not eighteen. Beware of the healer and the one of blood and cloth." What could these words possibly mean?

Dyna never told her children about the old woman or what she had said. She always thought it best to shield them. Sitting in the big, old rocking chair in Aunt Vernice's dining room, Dyna held the twins' letters and rocked slowly, reflecting back on the day in New Jersey when she encountered the old woman and the events that had happened since. But for the first time, Dyna considered that a different interpretation might apply to the old woman's saying. Could it be that the twins were also included in this prophecy? Were they "the healer" and "the one of blood and cloth" the old woman had spoken of? Dyna wondered. Alfred seemed to be the more violent of the two. And Benjamin always came behind Alfred to patch things up or cover things up. Could this be the meaning behind the saying?

Dyna wrapped the quilt around her legs a little tighter. Maybe she needed a shield to protect herself from those two. They had caused her enough pain over the years. And she was certain that unless they totally changed, they would cause her even more pain as time went on. She had tried to raise them to be responsible young men and felt she had done all she could do. Any change in them now had to come because of forces well beyond her. In the meantime, she continued to pray for them as only a desperate mother could.

"HERVE AND BILL, can we get this session over with?" Brian Tanner asked. "We have only one more employee to discuss, and

that's Alma. I think that we should give her six percent." Brian
wanted to finish the meeting soon.

The question of employee pay was one of the few areas of
responsibility that Meyer and Smertz had not turned over
completely to Brian Tanner. In most aspects of managing the clinic,
Brian had free reign. Unlike Brian, the other partners were more
interested in receiving a share of the profits than in the mechanics
of the clinic's operation. But in this one area of the practice, they
insisted upon having input, even for those employees they had
little or no direct contact with.

Herve Meyer agreed quickly with Brian's pay recommendation
for Alma, but Bill Smertz hesitated. "Brian, why should she get a
greater increase than the other salaried employees? We're only giving
four percent or less to the rest. Why should she get more?"

Brian pulled out a sheet of paper. "Well, for starters, she's
brought fantastic organizational skills to the clinic. She made
effective recommendations to cut down employee absences. She
cut the time it took to receive payments from the insurance
companies. Plus, she set up a brilliant procedural system with
cross-checks so staff error rates have gone down significantly. She's
smart and well liked by the clinic patients and staff alike. I think
we should pay her more in recognition of her good work. Plus, she
would be hard to replace. She's been with us for two years now
and should be making more."

"Brian, I'd like to pay her more, but before we do, I want to
know whether she had any involvement in the Hasty-Greenly
billing matter. If she didn't, then I'll go along with the increase for
her."

Brian objected, "Hasty-Greenly Clinic? Why, she left there
over two years ago, Bill. What are you talking about?"

Herve explained. "Alma's supervisor at the Hasty-Greenly Clinic
was just charged for her part in fraudulently billing insurance
companies. It was on the news yesterday as part of some medical
exposé. Some reporter had investigated and found that the woman
had pulled off the same scam in three different states. The woman
had been doing it for years."

"So?"

"Why should we give a pay increase to Alma if she were a part of that and is about to go to jail?" Bill asked.

Brian found the logic compelling and agreed to check on Alma Hormiga.

While the partners were in their meeting, Alma Hormiga got a telephone call from Tammy Hanson, a friend at Hasty-Greenly Clinic.

"Hello, Alma, this is Tammy. Did you see us on television yesterday?"

Alma thought back over the last twenty-four hours. Normally, on a Monday, she would watch the news, chat on the telephone with friends and relax. In her one-bedroom apartment, she didn't have space to do much else and yesterday, she really didn't want to do anything else.

Yesterday, she went straight home after work with a headache. Massage, pain killers, resting in a darkened room, even some chocolate, nothing seemed to stop the band of pain that started just behind her eyes and wrapped around her head like a vise. That evening, she turned off the ringer on her telephone and went straight to bed.

No, Alma thought, she hadn't seen anything, nor had she cared to.

"No, what happened?" Alma asked.

"The clinic was on the news yesterday!"

"You're kidding! Why?" The pause was appropriately dramatic. Had her prediction come true? Alma had been waiting for this telephone call for two years.

"They charged Mrs. Sherschainger with multiple counts of fraud."

"Details! Give me some details, Tammy!"

"I don't have much. Yesterday morning, Mrs. Sherschainger came in as usual. At ten, maybe ten thirty, two police officers came to the clinic. They met with Dr. Hasty, then took Mrs. Sherschainger with them."

Tammy put away the papers that she had in front of her and put her purse on the desk. "By noon, we had two camera crews out here, poking around and asking questions. With our patients still coming in and out, Dr. Hasty made sure the camera crews got off the property."

"Did he give an official statement?"

"No. He hasn't told us employees yet either. He said he would have a meeting sometime to fill us in, but he didn't know when." Tammy pulled a small mirror out of her purse to check her makeup.

"How do you know all of this, Tammy?"

"I was sitting in the front desk yesterday. One of the receptionists called in sick, so they put me out front. I had front row seats for this."

"Did you have any idea that something was going to happen?" Alma put her head down and lowered her voice. Someone had passed too close to her desk.

"Yes and no. For the last three weeks, we've had some guy here, poking through the records. But last Thursday and Friday, he didn't come in. No one ever told us he was investigating her."

"Who was he? Who did he work for? Was he a cop?"

"Who knows? I thought he was an attorney and then figured he might be a claims adjuster. Dr. Hasty brought him through, but didn't tell us why he was here. His name was Porter, John Porter. Whatever he was, when he didn't come back on Thursday and Friday, I figured we were in the clear."

Tammy pulled a nail file out of her purse and began working on her left hand. "Now they've arrested her, I figure they must have been investigating Mrs. Sherschainger for some time."

"Well, what did Dr. Greenly have to say about all this?"

"You know," Tammy paused, nail file in mid-air, "I don't really know. Come to think of it, he didn't come in yesterday at all." She shrugged and started on her right hand.

"Even though Dr. Hasty didn't make a statement, someone must have leaked something. On the five o'clock news, they gave details about the arrest and stuff about the clinic they couldn't have known without talking to somebody here." Tammy lowered her voice, "Ooh! I have to go. One of the doctors is looking for me. Bye Alma."

"Goodbye Tammy, and thanks for the news." As she hung up the telephone, Alma wondered if Brian knew about her former supervisor's arrest. She didn't have to wait long to find out. Within minutes, Brian stopped by her desk and asked her to stay after work to meet with him.

For the rest of that day, Alma worried about her job at the clinic. Did Brian believe she had been a part of the fraud? Would she have to defend her actions at the prior clinic? Did Brian believe she had been padding billings at the Hasty-Greenly Clinic? In the hours before her meeting with Brian, Alma had plenty of time to think and plenty of things to think about. She decided to deny any knowledge of the swindle and pretend to know nothing about it.

That is, unless Brian Tanner could make it really worthwhile for her.

BUBBOCK'S BAY RESORT was Steve's first development with the Westwood Group. He had been with the Westwood Group since 1975, working his way up with them since he was in high school. Somehow, he had managed to endear himself to one of the senior partners. That senior partner made Steve his assistant and second-in-charge of the Bubbock's Bay project. After overseeing the initial stages of the project, the senior partner turned the project over to Steve, retaining very loose supervisory control.

Having lived in nearby Todda, Ohio, a little less than an hour away from Bubbock's Bay, Steve knew the area well. He had the pleasure of hiring two of his high school friends as assistant managers. Many acquaintances of Steve's from Todda became staff members at the resort.

As a manager, Steve created a tight-knit organization. Promptness, service orientation and attention to details were keys for Steve. To back up his commitment to running a top-notch resort, Steve structured bonuses, raises and benefits around customer satisfaction.

Bubbock's Bay was an enormous success.

Some Westwood Group partners grumbled about the costs initially. But with the unquestioned success of the resort, both financially and based upon customer acclaim, even the most critical partners gave Steve plenty of leeway to run the resort as he saw fit. Besides, those partners had other issues to deal with. Despite the success of Bubbock's Bay, some things were clearly beyond the control of the Westwood Group. While Steve promoted Bubbock's Bay, the Westwood Group's efforts to develop other resorts fell short repeatedly. As Steve Mitchell made progress in completing Bubbock's Bay, he made careful plans toward his next goal. Long before the other Westwood Group partners knew the location of the next resort, Steve knew exactly where that resort should be, and he would be running it.

BRIAN STARTED THE meeting by asking about her past. "Alma, I need to talk to you about the Hasty-Greenly Clinic. Have you heard any recent news about it?"

"Yes." She said no more, but sat stiffly in the hard-backed chair.

Brian figured she wasn't about to volunteer much information unnecessarily. To him, her reluctance meant Alma not only knew about the fraud, but she also may have participated in it. "Well, have you heard about the big fraud case involving a woman named Sherschainger who used to work there?"

"Yes, I heard about it. I used to work in her unit."

"We were discussing pay increases and the topic kind of came up. Were you involved in that?" He studied her body language for she sat back slightly at his question.

Alma leaned forward slightly, wondering if Brian was looking for information or for an opportunity.

"Brian, I worked with the woman, but I kept clear of any padded transactions. I didn't want to be part of that. She was so greedy."

"Alma, I don't want to sound funny about this, but how did the woman do it? We need to know, in case we need to make some security changes here."

From his questions, Alma figured Brian wasn't just interested in her involvement with Mrs. Sherschainger. She wondered whether Brian Tanner was really interested in how the scam operated for his own use. Alma explained briefly but added, "She might not have been caught if she had been consistent in her billing and a lot less obvious."

"Thanks for being so honest. By the way, I'm going to recommend that you get the maximum possible raise, six percent. But keep it to yourself; almost everyone else will get four."

But if he wanted her help in setting up the scam for this clinic, he would have to be willing to work with her, and do it her way.

"Brian, I'll take the four. Six might create some unnecessary problems."

Within the next several months, Brian Tanner and Alma Hormiga came to a clear understanding of what each needed from the other and what had to be done.

CHAPTER 39

RIGHT AFTER HIGH school in 1978, Steven J. Mitchell visited Cellis to look over the area he had in mind. He had no money to buy any land and no authorization from the Westwood Group to buy anything for the partners. Still, if he ever got the chance to suggest a site, he wanted to make sure Cellis was considered.

The area Steve chose sat between a state highway and a couple of county highways. It was only ten miles from an interstate highway and travel to the area from the interstate wasn't too difficult. Woodland, multiple streams and several small lakes naturally occurred in that area. Lots of cleared land with few structures on it was an added benefit. In some areas, the resort soil base had to be built up first, to elevate it well above the surface water. Landscaping to create the right conditions for an eighteen-hole golf course, hiking paths and riding trails would take place after the infrastructure was complete.

Cellis had lots of farmland, much of it held in the same families for generations. With the increased number of recreation vehicles factories opened during the last thirty years, the younger generations began choosing jobs in the city over working on the farm. Clearly, in the recreation vehicle industry, the wages and benefits were better and the hours were shorter.

With the changes in the work force, farms held by families for many generations were sold to neighboring farmers or to corporations. Steve Mitchell and the big agribusinesses could see the market shifting and the availability of abundant cheap land in the region. As Bubbock's Bay neared completion, Steve noted a trend that would change the labor situation in Cellis. That trend was exactly what Steve needed to move ahead with his plans for his next resort, Elkora Hills in Cellis, Indiana.

Between 1979 and 1980, gas prices jumped astronomically. Higher gas prices continued throughout the following two years as well. In response, sales of recreational vehicles slumped, as factories and supporting industries in and around Cellis slowed down and began massive layoffs. By the spring of 1980, the employment situation in the Cellis area was bleak. Of the nearly twenty thousand persons employed in the recreation vehicle industry in the Cellis area, almost half of those persons were unemployed or worked only three days or so each week. With a population of only about fifty thousand, the entire community suffered. Cellis had to diversify its economic base to survive.

The gas problem would not last forever. Steve reasoned that in time, either gas prices would drop or people would get used to the higher prices and begin spending again. In Steve's mind, four things usually made resorts successful: cheap land, cheap labor, high unemployment, and most important of all, politicians afraid of joining their unemployed constituents. Steve knew that in Cellis, Indiana, all four were available. Besides, he had a few scores to settle there.

STEVE FOUND RENE DEZZA in 1980 in the typing pool at Westwood Group, while working on the development of Bubbock's Bay. Uncharacteristically, he had put together a rough draft of a report he needed at the last minute. Rushing it to the typing pool at the Westwood Group headquarters, left it on the desk of the lead worker named Bob, and prayed.

When Bob found the envelope on his desk, he turned it over to Rene Dezza. Under her skillful fingers, Steve's last-minute scribbling on envelopes, napkins and notepaper was magically transformed into a decent, legible, well-formatted report.

When he got it back, Steve was impressed and extremely grateful for her work. When he emptied out the envelope containing the report, he knew he had to meet this woman.

She had taken the time to include notes on additional sources of information. Steve followed up on those sources and found them extremely useful.

In checking with Frieda, the Westwood Group's personnel manager, Steve learned more about Rene. Frieda gave him the details he wanted to know.

"Steve, from what we have on file, Rene Dezza has substantial experience in several work areas. Her experience includes mortgage brokerage and insurance before her employment with the Westwood Group. And from what I remember from her interview, Rene had grown tired of big-office politics. She just wants to do her job and go home."

Frieda looked over Rene's last three performance evaluations. "She's meticulous in her work and very, very sharp. You can tell she has got a lot going on upstairs. She keeps to herself. She doesn't waste time chit-chatting with the others in the pool."

Rene must be married, Steve thought. He was surprised to learn she wasn't. Frieda set him straight on that right away.

"You've seen that red convertible in the employees' parking lot, haven't you?"

"You mean the one with the black roof?"

"Yes. From what I've been told, her ex has been going to a lot of trouble to get her to go back with him. That sports car is just one of his efforts. My brother works at the dealership, and he said that her ex came in and paid cash for that thing."

Steve whistled. "She must be something! Has she gone back with him?"

"Not that I know of. But it isn't because he isn't trying. He sends flowers and candy all the time, but she never keeps them.

The candy goes straight to the break room and the flowers go into the lobby or to the trash."

"Is she seeing anyone?"

"I don't think so. I know she isn't seeing any of the guys here, or the girls would have let me know. But she may be burned out. That may be the reason why she keeps so much to herself. She's overqualified for the typing pool, but she seems content, and so we've left her alone."

Steve planned to change that.

As he stepped into the typing pool wearing a dark gray suit, he tried to figure out which one she was among the many females concentrating on the work before them. Bob, the lead worker, a short, thin guy, dressed in a cheap white shirt and blue pants, stopped him from going farther into the room. Steve couldn't help but notice Bob's hair. Bob's brown hair was badly cut in a bowl shape. It looked as if the guy had cut his hair himself while drunk and in the dark.

"What can I do for you?" he asked.

"I'm Steven J. Mitchell and I'm looking for Rene Dezza. I'd like to thank her for some work she did for me. Is she available? I'd like to talk to her for just a few minutes."

"Oh . . . pleased to meet you, Mr. Mitchell. I met you some time ago. I'm Robert Wuiese. Rene's here. She's almost due for a break, anyway."

The lead worker walked past four desks where employees were busily typing. He stopped beside a woman, who kept on typing and didn't look up until he spoke. After talking quietly to her for a few minutes, Bob waited while she gathered a cigarette case and a cup. When she stood up, she was at least a foot taller than him.

Rene was tall, well over six feet, slender, freckled, and had a cute, upturned nose. Her most distinguishing feature was her bright red hair. It didn't look as if it was dyed. It had gold and orange highlights that could not come from a bottle, and it was very curly. Steve had hated his own red hair, but admired how red hair looked on her.

Steve and Rene walked quickly through the office corridors

and headed for the break room. As they walked, he expressed his gratitude for her work—especially the extra details she had provided. As soon as they stepped into the inner courtyard of the Westwood Group's headquarters, she lit a cigarette and took a long drag. Steve waited. She let the smoke roll out over her pink lips.

"Well? What do you really want?" she asked.

She surprised him. She was a bit more direct than he had expected. He deduced she wasn't much for socializing and decided to try a little humor. "What would it take to steal you away from old bowl head back there?"

Rene laughed for a few seconds. Her nose wrinkled and her bright blue eyes sparkled. "Not much. He's really quite nice, though. But how did you know that's what they call him?"

After a few minutes more of discussion, they agreed she would start working for Steve by the end of the month. She had no children, no husband, and she was ready for a change.

DESPITE HIS ATTRACTION to her, Steve kept his relationship with Rene strictly professional. He needed her to do her job without the influences romance sometimes bring. In a moment of jealousy or if a lover's spat separated them, if she ever got wind of his actions, she could easily expose him and his dirty schemes.

Steve rewarded Rene well for her loyalty to him and she reciprocated by giving him exceptional services. He helped her in some personal matters and otherwise took very good care of her.

In so many ways, she was his better half, and they both knew it.

For Steve, it was logical to send Rene out first to begin exploring the political and zoning environment and requirements in Cellis and the surrounding counties. He knew he could count on her to get him the information, if it existed.

RENE PULLED OFF the heavy, black, high-top boots with green tags and put them at the end of the bed in the hotel room.

She sat on the bed, rubbing her feet through the thick white socks she wore. The red-and-black work shirt and the coarse blue jeans she wore were not part of her regular office attire. Checking the time, she found she could still reach Steve if he hadn't left the office early. He was still there.

Rene reported to Steve precisely the news he and the Westwood Group needed to hear. "Steve, this site looks good, really good. Zoning and planning approval for the development look like a sure thing. They've got a good-sized labor pool here, lots of unemployment."

"With all those factories?"

"The gas prices have really hurts sales of the recreation vehicles here. They've had an economic depression here, lots of layoffs. People need work, even if they get lower wages than they're used to."

"I met with the area alderperson, common council leader and one of the zoning commissioners. They could see the need to attract businesses other than recreation vehicle factories. A resort or another tourist attraction would be welcome here."

"Rene, that's great! Uh, did you tell them you were from the Westwood Group?"

"No."

"You didn't drive your car, did you? I mean, it's kind of expensive, you know. It might have been hard to overlook."

"No Steve, I picked up a company car yesterday." She laughed. "I went there as a concerned citizen, a farmer's wife."

"In a suit?"

"No, in heavy boots, flannel shirt and jeans and all. The alderperson must have thought I had just left the milking barn. He looked at my boots and asked me three times whether I wiped my feet at the door."

CHECK AFTER CHECK came into their dummy corporation from their version of the insurance swindle. Brian and Alma had built up a nice reserve by now. But they couldn't take any money out, not at least until the next step. In communities around Cellis, Alma rented the twelve post office boxes, paying in cash for each. For all outward purposes, the owners of those boxes were businesses with employees. In reality, there were no businesses, no employees, and only she and Brian had the keys.

It was finally time to reap the rewards of their labor from the entity. They agreed to take a small amount to begin with. Four months after they started the scam, the first two checks were issued to service providers of the dummy corporation. The stolen identities were the secret to the success of the scam. The people were real and the social security numbers were real. Most were unemployed and not actively looking for work, and whose annual incomes were below the level required to file tax returns. Alma chose the victims carefully, using their identities for only brief periods. And of course, no portion of the money would ever go to them.

Fanatical in how she ran the company, Alma made the corporation look legitimate in every way. And the swindle worked effectively now. Brian and Alma could wait and take their rewards when the real money would come in.

RENE PUT TOGETHER initial marketing research reports about the recreational vehicle industry as well. The reports showed that throughout the nation, middle-aged couples, many of which owned their own homes and had reached their peak earning potential, bought the bulk of the low to mid-priced recreation vehicles. But younger couples still wanted and needed to spend time away from home. Most were unwilling to make a commitment to a long-term purchase agreement. Furthermore, few had the big cash outlay needed to buy the recreation vehicles. Both groups would be interested in going to a resort in their region and other Westwood Group resorts as well.

Rene also noted that sales of the high-priced recreation vehicles had continued despite the gas prices. The persons who could afford the high-end vehicles weren't influenced by higher gas prices. But some of those persons would be interested in coming to a new resort for the novelty of it. More would come if the resort could reach arrangements with the recreation vehicle clubs and associations many of those persons belonged to.

ARMED WITH INFORMATION from Rene and information he had gathered on his own, Steve convinced the Westwood Group to begin purchasing and taking options on real estate in the Cellis area. To keep prices down, Steve used agents, shell corporations and other means to purchase and to secure options on land without attracting attention. Early in his employment with the Westwood Group, Steve had witnessed the impact on land prices when the public found out that a resort was being considered for their area. Land prices would skyrocket as speculators, area residents and even a few politicians scrambled for the targeted sites. Steve knew there had to be a better way. When he had the power and influence to do so in the Westwood Group, he tried a different approach.

To fight the impacts of land speculation, Steve set up one company, Mortgage Salvage, specifically to gather information, provide financing and even buy properties in distress. He needed an entity licensed to do business in multiple states and where professionals could gather financial and real estate information without raising too many eyebrows. He bought into a small mortgage company licensed to do business in Ohio and Indiana, then pushed for licenses in other states as well. Mortgage Salvage fit his needs perfectly.

BASED ON STUDIES of the region and the recreation vehicle industry, Steve focused on attracting recreation vehicles to the resort. He planned for two separate areas just for those vehicles. One site would serve owners of low to mid-priced vehicles. A second, more exclusive site near the golf course on the other side of the resort would cater to the owners of high-end vehicles. Clusters of condominiums and cabins would be built throughout the site.

Just beyond the main area, campsites would be established also. Steve placed emphasis on developing the high-end site and the main area first, planning to develop the campsites only as the high-end part of the resort reached full capacity.

Steve knew attracting the high-end recreation vehicles to the resort would take plenty of advance leg work. He assigned Rene to work with Westwood Group's marketing department to start gathering information about the clubs and associations that owners of high-priced recreation vehicles might belong to. An open house or a party for those owners would attract them. Scheduling the resort's events around the annual meetings or gatherings of those clubs would help to draw prospects from the groups too. Steve decided Rene would handle the public relations necessary to get these groups and individual owners to come to the development.

After Rene had completed her initial investigative work concerning Cellis in mid-1982, Steve arranged for Rene to spend some of her time at Mortgage Salvage as his personal liaison. With that arrangement in place, Steve knew he could cover his legal activities quite easily. He would perform his illegal activities on his own.

CHAPTER 40

WHILE MORTGAGE SALVAGE had other businesses it conducted, Steve's key involvement in that company was limited to purchases for the Westwood Group. But Steve had other interests that he hid from the Westwood Group, and even from Rene.

Many farmers were willing to sell their land, but not all of them. Behind the scenes, Steve Mitchell did whatever it took to get the land, sometimes even if some of the owners were not interested in selling.

In developing Elkora Hills in Cellis, one deal in particular gave Steve Mitchell special pleasure. For months, Mortgage Salvage had gathered for him critical information, including probate notices and property transactions in the targeted area near Cellis. In Mortgage Salvage's October 1982 report, one entry seemed to jump out at Steve—the probate notice for Russell Ammon Sr.

Steve carefully checked the real estate history for the Ammon property. For the last ten years or so, while the senior Ammon had it, the property was free of any mortgage. Steve made a special note on his planner and waited.

Within months, the property passed to Russell Sr.'s only son, Russell Ammon Jr.

During the few months or so after Russ Jr. got the farm, Steve checked the real estate reports from Mortgage Salvage for any changes involving the farm's legal status. His diligence paid off. According to one real estate report, in February 1983, Russell Ammon Jr. gave a mortgage to Maxion Mortgage Company for three-quarters of the full value of the farm. With the mortgage, Steve saw his chance to get the property for the Westwood Group. And he would get it while getting something else for himself.

Starting in April, Steve drove past the Ammon farm occasionally. On his third visit, Steve noted some improvements made on the exterior of the house and a new shed replaced a dilapidated one. A new, bright, shiny red truck sat on the gravel driveway in front of the shed. What caught Steve's attention was that Russ had cleared more acreage that his father had in years. Also, cows now grazed in the field near the front.

Steve continued to watch the progress of the Ammon farm and considered how he would get that farm. An offer to purchase the land then would be quite expensive, if Russ accepted an offer at all. Further, Steve noted the corn Russ had planted was nearly four feet high and looked great. But Steve could wait and pursue other purchases. He still had his reports from Mortgage Salvage and knew they would call if something new came up.

One Friday afternoon in June, Steve got a call from Rene.

"Steve, I don't have much news at this point. Nothing new has come up since last month. We've made some progress on buying the Mulcahy and the Lewis parcels though."

"That's great Rene. Anything else?"

"We've had a record heat wave here, Steve. There hasn't been anything like this for years. I drove past the Doll farm, the Ammon farm and the Blake place and the crops look really withered there. Some of the other farmers must be using some sort of irrigation systems, or something. But those three places really look dry."

Steve drove to Cellis that evening.

Early the next morning, Steve drove past the Ammon farm. Instead of what should have been bright green field after bright green field, cracked, dried, brown dirt with wilting green stalks sticking up appeared instead. Sometimes, one man's problem is another man's goldmine, he reasoned. He moved the Ammon farm to the top of his list of purchases. During the rest of the summer, Steve kept up his progress in picking up properties. He worked on the easier purchases first, which became more frequent as the heat wave continued.

That fall, whenever he came to Cellis, Steve checked on the condition of the Ammon farm.

Russ must have rigged up some sort of watering system at the last minute, Steve concluded. Some stalks were still standing, but not nearly as much as on neighboring farms. And the herd of cows he had noticed before was gone.

At the beginning of November, using his childhood name of Jake Mitchell, Steve set up a mailbox in Cellis to receive mail and a contract with an answering service.

Later that month, Steve traveled back to Cellis and from a hotel, contacted Russell Ammon Jr.

"Hello, is this Russell Ammon?"

"Yeah."

"Russ, I don't know if you remember me, but this is Jake Mitchell."

Russ hesitated, "Uh, no. I don't think so."

"Come on, you know me—Jerky Jake, remember?"

After a few seconds of silence, Russ answered, "Yeah, I remember you. What do you want?" The contempt in his voice was still clear, even after all these years.

"I want to buy your farm and all your implements."

"They're not for sale." The irritation in his voice was obvious. This must be a prank call, a joke, Russ thought. He hoped Jerky Jake was serious, but he couldn't count on it. The Mitchells were as poor as church mice when they were children. Where would Jake come up with any money?

As for his unwillingness to sell, Russ lied. If the price were right, he would take the money and run, leaving the miserable existence he and his wife had suffered through there. The gasoline crisis in the prior years and the drought in 1983 had left him strapped. During the last two years before his father's death, Russ had run the farm, knowing it would be his eventually. By 1982, his wife joined Russ in running the farm after losing her job at one of the local RV factories.

But his old man had refused to mortgage the property to help pay for some of the expenses. The heat wave in 1983 was the second worse that the area had in almost fifty years. Russ was in the hole financially and the loss of the 1983 corn crop meant that he had no foreseeable way out.

"I'll give you whatever your mortgage balance is, plus $20,000."

"Why, the equipment alone is worth more than ten times that, you piker!"

"Well, my telephone number is 555-1515, in case you change your mind."

"Jerky Jake, I ain't selling you nothing!" After thoroughly cussing Steve out, Russ banged down the telephone.

As he hung up the telephone, Steve laughed hard. He tilted back in his chair and put his hands behind his head. For the first time in his life, Steve enjoyed being cursed out. He had gotten under Russ' skin. His next steps would hurt Russ even more.

In checking with the answering service over the next few months, he noted that he, as Jake Mitchell, had gotten no messages.

THE FIFTH LETTER in late 1983 made Sierra Tanner sick. It had been years since the last letter and she figured the creep had finally given up on torturing her. Like before, the letter came in a plain envelope postmarked from Enid. And when she saw the envelope, she immediately recognized the typing.

> Boom-Boom,
>
> I missed you. Glad to see you haven't moved or contacted the police about my letters. Follow these directions and you'll never hear from me again. Send this letter and envelope back with $1,000 in a package not larger than 9 x 12 inches to P.O. Box 9883813 in Enid. Wrap it in brown

paper so it looks like a book. When you do, I'll lose your name and address. Don't tell anyone. No marked bills and no police and I'll forget your dirty past forever.

P.S. If you don't follow these instructions to the letter, I'll make sure your husband and all of Cellis finds out about your past and what you're doing now.

At first, she started to do exactly what the blackmailer had asked. But she thought about the letter carefully. The creep had finally given her something she could use, a post office box number. Maybe she could deal with this person in another way.

On the telephone in the kitchen, Sierra called directory assistance for Enid and asked for the telephone number for the Enid Post Office. Next, she called the Enid Post Office. A man with a gruff voice answered.

"Hello, Post Office."

"Yes, I want to know the name of the owner of box 9883813?"

"We don't give out that information over the telephone."

Sierra hesitated, unsure of what to say next. Apparently, she waited too long. The gruff man hung up. As she put the handset back into the telephone receiver, Sierra considered other alternatives. Should she hire a private investigator to find out who rents the post office box? Try the post office again and hope for a different clerk to answer? Drive to Enid and check out the post office box herself?

After a few minutes, she decided to make the drive. Maybe she could learn who the blackmailer was on her own, and then figure out what her next steps would be.

Early on Tuesday, Sierra made the four-hour drive to Enid. Located on Main Street, the post office was easy to find. Through the double doors to her right, she could see the counter area. Two women were in line when she walked through the doors. The first bought stamps and left quickly. The second didn't leave so quickly. That's when she recognized him. The clerk at the counter was the same person Sierra had talked to the day before. She could tell he was the same guy based on his comments to the lady in front of her.

Now it was her turn. Sierra asked in her most sugary-sweet voice, "Sir, could you tell me who rents box 9883813? Please?"

"We have rules on that. You know, privacy and all. Why do you need to know?"

Sierra cringed and tried to come up with an answer. But she wasn't going to tell him about the demand letter. "Well, I was just curious."

"No. I can't tell you who rented any box, lady," he growled and turned away. He started organizing the flat of letters beside him as if she wasn't even there. He looked back at her, "Anything else?"

Sierra looked both ways. Desperate now, she wanted to talk to someone other than Mr. Unhelpful, but no other workers were at the front counter. What would she do now?

She walked back through the double doors out of the counter area, back to the area where silver box after silver box lined the walls. One by one, she checked the numbers on them until her eyes watered. She could use a drink right now, but she had too much work to do. When she reached the last box on the last row of the very last column in the furthermost aisle from Mr. Unhelpful, she felt as if she would faint. But there was no box 9883813.

Sierra leaned against the silver wall and put her head back. Her only option again was Mr. Unhelpful behind the counter. He saw her coming back, gave her an evil scowl and put up the closed sign for his window.

In the next aisle, a woman straightened up and removed the closed sign from the counter. She had been stocking supplies under her aisle. The lady had silver curly hair and silver-framed glasses. Her dimpled cheeks showed that at least she knew how to smile. From the next aisle, Mr. Unhelpful growled, "Going on break, Sylvia, I think I'm going to have a cigarette."

When he was out of earshot, Sierra asked, "Is he always that cheerful?"

Sylvia laughed, "Gordon? No, he's trying to quit smoking. He's such a bear when he doesn't get his nicotine that I almost wished he would just smoke." They chuckled.

"But seriously, he's trying hard and I hope he can make it. But as for you, may I help you?" she asked.

"Sylvia, could you tell me who rented a specific box, number 9883813? Please?"

"Well miss, that number isn't one we have here."

Not knowing what to think at first, Sierra froze. But she thought quickly. "What happens if mail is sent to a nonexistent box?"

"If a piece has a return address, we return it. If not, it goes to the dead letter center. It can be claimed there after the sender can show he or she sent it."

ONCE OUTSIDE, SHE sat in the car, but only for a few minutes. Sierra headed back in the direction she came from. She found a telephone booth at a local gas station, the telephone book hung down by the cable attached to the booth. She turned to the category "Investigators," finding six names listed there. Unsure of how much progress she might make, Sierra copied the names and telephone numbers onto an envelope. Sierra went back to her car without calling any of them.

In the privacy of her car, Sierra tried to decide which one to call and what she would say. Should she pick the one with the largest ad? What about the one with the address on Main Street? Fear, uncertainty, tension and indecision, her feelings made her head pound.

She decided she would have a drink. As she drove along Main Street, she turned off onto one of the side streets, heading back to the neighborhoods she knew years ago. She stopped at an intersection and decided right there. She wasn't going to have a drink. And she wasn't going to call an investigator; the investigator might be another person who might try to blackmail her later. She didn't really want anyone else to know about her interest in the post office box.

Sierra decided to mail the package. Maybe this was just a test. If the blackmailer could see her meeting with other men, the person might be watching to see what she would do. And if Sylvia were correct, her package should come back to her anyway. She headed back to Cellis. Once there, she dropped off the package at the post office.

The creep had finally asked for something Sierra could finally understand. The letters sent before left her upset and afraid, but she never could figure out why this person was writing to her, torturing her and frightening her.

But maybe this payment would end it all.

CHAPTER 41

ALMOST THREE WEEKS after Sierra mailed the package to the post office box in Enid, it came back to her. Hand-canceled and marked "Return to sender—no such post office box," the package was unopened. Sierra was distraught, she didn't know what to do next except wait.

Each day for the next three weeks, she opened the *Cellis Courier*, expecting to see her life story laid out like a feature in a cheap, sleazy tabloid. During those three weeks, she rarely got out of bed, stopped taking care of herself and was rarely sober.

THE NEXT YEAR, Steve took things into his own hands. In making trips to Cellis, he started watching the Ammon property again. Driving by was as close as Steve got. In his surveillance, he avoided getting too close or slowing down as he made his rounds. Steve waited until Russ had gotten his crop into the ground and the corn stalks were at least six feet high. It looked like Russ would have a bumper crop if the good weather continued.

In the middle of July 1984, at twelve thirty on a Wednesday night, Steve made his move. He had slept all of that day. Steve knew he needed all the rest that he could get to do this job. It might take all night. Once he was half a mile west of the Ammon property, Steve pulled his car off the road. He would walk around the property first to see how he might carry out his plan. As he walked up the gravel driveway, he discovered he should have looked at the property a little bit more carefully. Somewhere on the Ammon farm, a large dog detected him and started barking. Steve froze in his tracks. Steve could hear the dog but couldn't see him. A dog bite wasn't part of the plan. He needed to figure out where the dog was, and quickly.

Steve waited to see if the barking would grow louder, but it didn't. The dog probably is chained up nearby, Steve thought. He prayed that he was right.

He knew he could not carry out his plan without dealing with that animal. But killing the dog outright would arouse Russ Ammon's suspicions. Postponing his plans for that night, Steve retreated.

The next night, he returned. In the dew-dampened ground beside the gravel drive, Steve walked slowly, his weapons in a bag slung over his left shoulder. At the point where the dog had begun barking the night before, Steve hesitated briefly, then forced himself to go on. As he crept along the grass beside the driveway, Steve looked carefully in the area under the spotlight near the barn. If he had guessed correctly, the dog was between the barn and the house. Almost as soon as he saw the dog, the dog saw him and began barking, straining at the thick chain. Steve was glad he brought his arsenal this time.

He dropped down behind bushes near the drive and waited. Would anyone come out to check on the barking dog? With the bag clutched tightly, Steve waited a few minutes while the dog kept barking. To Steve's surprise, no one came outside to see what the ruckus was about.

Reaching into the sack he had carried, Steve got ready, aimed and fired. His first shot hit the mark—the barking dog stopped in its tracks.

The cold hot dog had landed within a few inches of the dog. The animal stopped barking long enough to wolf down the hot dog in a single gulp. Steve's second shot missed the dog completely. After three more hot dogs, the animal stopped barking altogether. Instead, it began wagging its tail expectantly. Five hot dogs later, Steve completed that night's mission and left quickly.

The next night, Steve returned with another pack of hot dogs. He stayed just long enough to shoot the ten hot dogs, like rubbery arrows, at the animal.

By the third night, the dog had stopped barking at him completely. But from all appearances, no one in the house paid any attention at all to the barking. Steve would go ahead with his plans the following night, with the dog as his newly found friend.

It took Steve seven packs of hot dogs and an additional four full nights to cover all of the Ammon fields, but he got it done.

Four weeks later, he checked and found that the Ammon fields had very few plants standing. Wilted, dying corn stalks covered acre after acre. The herbicide he had pumped out onto the fields had done the job.

Within a week after Steve's inspection of the Ammon farm, the answering service reported that a gentleman had called three times for Jake Mitchell, but left no messages.

IN AUGUST OF 1984, Mortgage Salvage contacted Maxion Mortgage Company and bought the mortgage and note for the Ammon farm. With payments more than six months in arrears, Maxion Mortgage moved quickly to accept the chance to avoid the foreclosure. Mortgage Salvage began the foreclosure process almost immediately.

Once it began, Steve contacted the answering service for a status report on the proceedings. During the week following the date that Russ Ammon Jr. got the foreclosure notice, Jake Mitchell got more than seventy telephone messages from him.

By the end of that same month, Steve Mitchell ended his arrangement with the answering service. Purposely, he left no forwarding number. He closed his post office box soon after that. He never returned a single call to Russ Ammon Jr.

MONTHS LATER, RENE called from Mortgage Salvage to give Steve an update on the Ammon farm. "Steve, this is Rene. We got the foreclosure done on the Ammon place. This one had a few complications. Russ didn't want to leave without a fight. The sheriff and two deputies escorted Russ away from the farm in his beat-up old brown pickup. He's gone now, but I'm sure this isn't the last we'll see of him."

Only an hour later, someone set a small fire in the farmhouse. The house and other buildings would have been razed anyway. The Ammon farm was among the last properties needed for the Elkora Hills site.

CHAPTER 42

IN EARLY 1985, when his brother, Benjamin, called him from Todda, Steve just knew he was looking for money. Benjamin had finished his prison term and parole and found a job working for a construction firm in Todda. Since he had just started the job, Benjamin hadn't made much money that Steve was aware of. Over the years since Steve had left home, Benjamin hadn't contacted Steve more than once or twice. So Steve never expected Benjamin would call about something like this. Steve left the volume up on the jazz selection he had playing in the background. He didn't expect to talk long.

"Well, did he do it or not?"

"Who did what? Benjamin, what in the world are you talking about?"

"I mean Javier. Did he kill himself or not?" Benjamin lit a cigarette.

"Where did that thought come from?"

"I spent a lot of time thinking about him when I was in prison, and now, just lately. Did he kill himself or not?" Benjamin inhaled deeply and blew out a thin stream of smoke.

"Why would you even think he had killed himself?"

"I don't." Benjamin flicked an ash onto the floor and coughed.

"They said it just might have been an accident." Steve looked for another jazz cassette in his tape collection.

"Alfred and I have been talking about Javier. We don't think he died in an accident. We don't think he killed himself. We're certain someone killed him."

"Don't be ridiculous," Steve replied. At that remark, Benjamin left the cigarette in the ashtray and stood at the window.

"Don't be so smart, Steve. Look at the facts—the bare naked truth here, Steve. First, I don't think Javier had an accident. He wasn't lost or anything. He knew that road well. Javier drove that car all over northern Indiana and lower Michigan. And it wasn't very late. So he had to be awake." Benjamin leaned against the window frame and looked at the muscles in his arms. Developing a strong physique was one of the few good things about prison.

"Okay Benjamin. Go on."

"Javier kept that raggedy car going, but not with tape or rubber bands. He worked on that car all the time, remember?"

"Yeah, yeah, go on." Steve turned down the music and sat behind his desk.

"He changed the brake pads on that car a month before the accident, remember?"

"I don't remember that."

"What do you mean, you don't remember?" Irritated, Benjamin pounded on the window frame so loud Steve could hear it on the other end of the telephone.

"Well, I was pretty little then."

"True, true, you were a squirt. But Alfred and I remember. We sat right out on the stoop and watched him do it." Benjamin picked up his cigarette again.

"So how is it Javier missed any problems with the brakes then? He would have looked, Steve, I know he would have." Benjamin coughed again.

"How could you remember that?"

"Remember the neighbor on the first floor, Mrs. Bird? She went crazy when she saw Javier taking that car apart to work on the brakes in front of her window. She threatened to call the landlord and get us all kicked out. Mrs. Bird was screaming and yelling."

"Wait, wait, I remember her now! Her eyes bugged out and she got really, really red!"

They laughed for some time about that memory.

"No, seriously now, let's forget about that for a second and concentrate Steve. There were no skid marks right?"

"Okay."

"The way the car was all scraped up on the side and smashed in the front, he must have been trying to swerve so he wouldn't hit the guard rail head on. He wasn't trying to hit the rail. He was trying to avoid it. With no skid marks, it had to be suicide or murder."

"Well, I'm not convinced . . ." Steve started.

Benjamin cut him off angrily and pounded on the frame again. "Why in the world would Javier kill himself? I've thought and thought about it over the years and I can't see any reason why he would! None! He had everything going for him. Basketball star, good grades in school, girls chasing him—what else did he need?"

"Didn't he have a girlfriend?"

"You mean Andrea? Well, he liked her a lot, but I can't say she was the only girlfriend he had when he died. But I do know he never did it with any of them. He always said he was saving himself, you know. So I know no father killed Javier because of a pregnant daughter, that's for sure. I remember Andrea called here a few times after she got back, crying and all. She wasn't here when Javier died and didn't come to the funeral because she was out of town." Benjamin picked up the cigarette, inhaled and coughed.

"What was her last name? And by the way, those things will kill you man."

"Tanner, Andrea Tanner. Yeah, I know they will. I picked up the habit in prison."

"Okay, what else Benjamin?"

"Even on the day he died, we had breakfast together and he was fine. I remember the telephone call he got just before we had to leave for school."

"Who called him?"

"Steve, I don't know. But it couldn't have been too important or Javier would have mentioned it. He didn't seem to be sad or mad or anything. So, do you see what I mean? Javier couldn't have committed suicide then, could he?" Benjamin ground out the cigarette. It didn't taste good with his little brother nagging him.

"Come on Benjamin, I'm sure they looked at all this stuff back then."

"Maybe they did, but they never asked any of us about Javier. We could have told them about his working on the car, having a girlfriend and feeling fine that morning. We were just kids, but we did know our brother pretty well."

"I know you pretty well too—so, Benjamin, where are you going with this?"

But he didn't answer Steve's question. Benjamin asked a question of his own. "Steve, did you ever take a look at the death certificate?"

"No, did you? I don't hear you puffing any more over there."

"I put out the cigarette already, so lay off. Yeah, well, Ma had one at the house. The certificate was dated almost three weeks after Javier's death."

"Really? Maybe the coroner was on vacation or something."

"Maybe he wasn't sure either."

"Benjamin, we can speculate all we want. But what does it prove?"

"Steve, I just want to know, that's all. When it first happened, I tried talking to Ma, but she just clammed up."

"Well, go on then. Got any theories?" As Benjamin talked, Steve started the gold, black and silver pendulum device. Rene had given it to him. It had seven balls of silver, gold and black, suspended by wires. He started the first ball swinging. As it hit the stationary balls, the last ball on the other side swung out due to the transmitted force. Steve stared intently as the suspended globes moved back and forth from momentum. One ball had started a chain reaction that took a long time to end.

"Well at first, I thought Don could have had something to do with it."

"No way Benjamin! Don betted on some of Javier's games. Plus, you know he would have his hand out if Javier went pro."

"Well, what about a bookie or something?"

"What bookie would kill over a fifty-cent bet, Benjamin? You know Don never had any money. That no-good bum was always after Ma to get some money from her. Let's look at something else. Where was Javier going that evening?"

"He was coming toward town, you know, out on old Indiana Road."

"Okay, so where was Javier coming from?"

"Steve, the only people I know that live out there are rich doctors, lawyers and stuff."

"No real people?"

"Not like us, no."

"Benj, who did Javier know out there?"

"What about Andrea?"

"Why her?"

"Wasn't she Dr. Tanner's kid?"

"What? You mean the clinic doctor?"

"Yeah Steve, him."

"Well, I'll be! Is she his daughter? She sure doesn't look like him. But realistically, what would they have to do with this? You just said they were on vacation, remember?"

"But why would Javier go out to their house if they weren't there? Now that doesn't make sense."

"It bothers me too."

Suddenly, with the pendulum device still swinging in front of him, Steve remembered Eunice P. Driver's little dog. As a child, he had enticed the dog to come to him and then broke its leg with a rock. "Benjamin, what if somebody invited Javier to come there and set him up? Some rival boyfriend or something?"

"I've thought about that too, but I thought I was just being paranoid."

"Benjamin, you know that leads to three questions—who did it, how and why?"

"I've got at least two more. First, how can we prove it and what will we do to get even? Steve, I've got to get going now and check on a few things. I'll get back to you as soon as I can."

Benjamin hung up at that point. He desperately wanted another cigarette, but he didn't want to hear any more of his little brother's comments.

•

OFFICER DANNY SLEDGE only had a few years to go until his retirement. He had been a good officer over the years. And he had survived corrupt Police Chief Nathan Gardener for more than twenty years. He figured he didn't owe Gardener a single second of his life, but he didn't know what else to do.

Sledge had solved a high percentage of his cases, but not all of them. Three unsolved cases over the years had stuck in his craw. Of those three, the death of the Mitchell kid still bothered Danny Sledge the most.

In the Mitchell case, Sledge never found out who wrote the break-up note, or why. The kid had been at the home of Dr. Brian Tanner, Sledge was almost certain of that. And he was convinced the brakes were tampered with at that home or nearby. But without more information or even a motive, Sledge faced a roadblock. To make it worse, Chief Gardener had been absolutely clear about his ban on further contacts with the Tanner family on the matter. With Gardener still in place, Danny Sledge knew the Mitchell case was not going anywhere. In the meantime, he could hardly wait for Chief Gardener to be indicted or fired, or to retire.

STEVE WANTED TO offer his help to Benjamin when he called. But Steve was busy with work on Elkora Hills.

The Westwood Group acted as general contractor on most of its projects. It worked with a local general contractor, but still kept some control over the bidding process. Bids would be solicited for certain aspects of the projects to encourage citizen participation in the communities where the resorts would be located. Those bids also kept the local politicians happy.

Steve monitored the local bids. It allowed him an easy way to reward friends and hurt enemies.

Steve learned about Tim Rausch's company almost as soon as he arrived in Cellis. Another opportunity for revenge could present itself and Steve wanted to take advantage of it if he could.

On the construction site, Steve called out from his temporary office in the trailer. "Rene, have you heard anything from the GC about the bids on the cabinet work?"

Only one room away, Rene opened the file cabinet in her area and pulled out a thick manila folder. With it in hand, she walked back into his office. "I've done better than that, Steve. I went by and picked them up already. Here they are, they haven't been awarded yet. The GC wanted your approval first."

Steve glanced through the papers while he listened to Rene's report.

"Ten companies submitted bids on time. Krodder Construction had the lowest bid, followed by Rausch Improvements, then AA-Plus Builders. Four others were way too high and two others don't have enough help for a job this size. The last company is out already—can you believe it? They're in bankruptcy now."

"What else is there?"

"Well, I got the background info on the companies and the principals, you know, the usual details, like company histories, other jobs, insurance information, credit reports, and so on. Krodder and AA-Plus seem to have their ducks in order. Rausch is a little shaky. They don't have a stable enough history."

"What else is there?"

"Rausch's wife has called three times already about their bid. I learned from her they're going to build a new home. She said her name is Eunice and her husband's name is Tim. She seemed so anxious about getting the bid, Steve. I think they would even go down on their price if they could get paid quickly on this project."

"Excellent work, Rene. Anything else?"

"Not now. I'll let you know if I pick up on anything else." As soon as she left his office, Steve pulled out the materials on Rausch. His hunch had been right.

Sometime after high school, two of Steve's childhood enemies, Tim Rausch and Eunice P. Driver, married and started a construction business. Rausch Improvements specialized in carpentry. The company had struggled initially, but finally seemed to be stable enough for the couple to purchase land for their new home on the outskirts of Cellis, but not to begin building yet. And except for some small jobs, they couldn't see any chance for any change in their situation soon.

On a whim, Tim and Eunice submitted their bid for providing and installing cabinets for the first two hundred units at Elkora Hills. But they really didn't expect to get the job. They knew how shaky they were, in comparison to Krodder Construction and others in the area. Still, getting this contract would give Tim and Eunice the cash they needed to start building their home. It would be like a dream come true.

For Steve, their names meant one thing, that he had a chance for another payback. He wanted to strike them hard, but he had to play it safe. Steve still had to get Elkora Hills done on time. After thinking for a few minutes, he called Rene back into his office and asked, "What was the name of those cabinets the company used on the San Diego project?"

"You mean the ones that they had such a hard time getting?"

"Yes, those."

"I don't know. I'm glad we weren't involved in that mess!"

"Well, please contact San Diego directly for that information, Rene. Don't call headquarters."

"Steve, why would you . . . ."

His sharp glance told her plenty—no more questions, just answers. "I'll get on it right away."

Later that day, she got back to him with the information.

"Here's what I want. Let Rausch know we'll give him the contract with one change, change the cabinets to the ones used on the San Diego project."

"Won't Rausch question the change?"

"Good point. Increase the contract amount by ten percent, with a bonus for completion within thirty-five days after the contract award date. We want a copy of the purchase order for the cabinets within two days after the award. Oh, and include this in the termination clause, they have to have the cabinets on site in twenty-five days after the award date."

"Steve, uh, isn't this schedule a little tight? I mean, do we really need the absolute dates?"

"I do. By the way, do not let Krodder or AA-Plus know about these changes. But Rene, please keep in contact with Krodder throughout this. Unofficially, of course."

Tim and Eunice celebrated the bid award with champagne and by contacting their lender. They would have the down payment and revenues to build their new home. They placed the cabinet order and dropped off a copy of the purchase order with Rene.

•

CHAPTER 43

WITH THE SIXTH letter in the beginning of 1985, Sierra considered contacting the police. The stress associated with getting the letters was causing her to drink almost constantly. In tears and shaking uncontrollably, she opened the plain envelope, expecting the writer would threaten her or demand more for her failure to get the money to the right post office box. She steadied herself and read the typed letter.

> Boom-Boom,
>
> You follow directions very well! I just wanted to see if you would get back to me without involving the police. That letter was just a test. This is the real thing. Send this letter and envelope back with $5,000 to P.O. Box 3997813 in Enid. When you do, I'll lose your name and address. Don't tell anyone. No marked bills and no police and I'll forget your dirty past forever.
>
> P.S. If you don't follow these instructions to the letter, I'll make sure your husband finds out about your past, along with all of Cellis. You would make front-page news there and the doctor would dump you like yesterday's trash.

As she read the letter again, Sierra tried to figure who could have written it. Who was it, a postal worker at Enid or at Cellis? Who else knew that her response to the last letter was returned to her?

But $5,000 wasn't too much to get rid of this person. In all the years she had gotten the letters, she had figured she might have to pay some day to stop the harassment. If $5,000 was all the writer wanted, it was a small price to pay to end these sick letters. She would do what she was told.

She went to the bank and withdrew another $4,000 from her private account. Back at home, she took out the $1,000 that she had on hand from the first package and began putting the second package together.

As Sierra sealed the package, Andrea startled her. "Mom, what are you doing?"

Instinctively, Sierra put her hand over the mailing address. She needed a good lie, and quickly. "I'm returning a book to one of my friends. I borrowed it a long time ago and I just found it."

"Oh," Andrea said, "Someone I know?"

"I don't think so dear. No, I'm sure you don't know this friend." Andrea was asking too many questions and still hanging around. All Sierra wanted to do was to get the package to the post office as soon as she could.

"Well Ma, I'm going downtown now, I'll drop it off for you." Andrea reached for the package. Reacting immediately, Sierra slid forward to lean on the package with her forearm. What could she do now to stall? Sierra anxiously tried to think of another lie. "No, no, that's all right dear, I'll take care of it myself."

With a puzzled look, Andrea peered at her mother carefully. Sierra seemed nervous about something. And she wasn't drunk.

"Mom, is everything all right?"

"Everything is fine, honey, just fine."

But Andrea was reading her like a book, and she knew it. Sierra forced herself to relax. "I'm just nervous about your father, that's all. I wanted to get him a little gift or something and I haven't found anything so far. I wanted to get downtown before he got home and I'm running so far behind on things I wanted to do today." Sierra looked down, then up. "What time is it dear?"

"It's almost four."

"Well, I'd better get going." She stood up, tucked the package under her right arm, the mailing information pressed tightly against her body. Andrea stared inquisitively. Her mother had just told her a pack of lies and they both knew it.

While troubled by what her mother said, Andrea was more troubled by what she observed. Her mother was in some trouble, something so serious that she was afraid to drink. Here it was in the late afternoon and from what she could see, her mother didn't have her glass or bottle out. Nothing had slowed her drinking down like this in years. Her father's yells and threats and even Andrea's own pleading over the years didn't seem to bother her mother this much. Could the package have something to do with it? Andrea wondered as she watched her mother get into her car and drive away.

CALCULATING THE TIME it would take for Sierra's last package to return to her, the blackmailer watched her mail carefully.

Finally, the blackmailer saw her returned package and was ready to strike. Using a plastic bag to grip the package, the blackmailer pulled the package out of the Tanner mailbox and enclosed it in the bag.

DRIVING A TRUCK was not in his career plans while he attended Briggandale. But since it paid much better than the last factory job he had, he would make it work for now. By driving a truck, he could take extra assignments to pick up extra cash if he needed it, and he could work in relative quiet. Often, Merritt Hughes used the longer rides to think and make plans.

"Merritt, John called in sick. Can you take his delivery route today? It will be an overnighter."

He had been on the job for less than a year when a chance to take a route that passed through Cellis came up. He didn't keep the dispatcher waiting. "Sure," Merritt said, "I've got something I want to take care of there."

The next day, after dropping his semi-load, Merritt found a motel nearby. Now, in the room, he pulled the yellow slip with the telephone number on it from his wallet and made his call.

"Hello, is this the Tanner residence?"

"Yes," a female voice answered.

"May I speak to Brian please?"

"I'm sorry, he's not here."

Should he ask for Sierra? The voice on the line wasn't hers. Merritt decided to take a chance. "Is Sierra available?"

"She's not at home now. May I take a message please?"

"Tell Brian that Merritt Hughes called. He and Sierra know me from college. I live in Enid now. I'll try calling Brian later."

FROM THE FRONT entry of their home, Andrea called to her mother in the dining room. "Mom, I've got to get going to class. Oh, can you let Daddy know that Merritt Hughes called? He said he lives in Enid and that he knew you and Dad from college. He said he would call back this evening." Andrea closed the door, then reopened it. "I forgot. Some guy called and asked for you, but he said he would call back. I asked, but he didn't want to leave his name or number. I didn't recognize his voice."

Andrea closed the door and headed for her car. She was glad to get out of the house, even if only for a short while. In the two weeks since she had found her mother working on that brown package for mailing, her mother had gotten significantly worse. If she wasn't drunk, Sierra was extremely edgy, and nearly unbearable to be around.

Sierra looked up. Sitting at the dining room table, she had been looking at a magazine, but she was thinking about the package she had mailed. Andrea's message about Merritt Hughes surprised her and gave her something new to think about. If Merritt Hughes lived in Enid, could he be the one? Sierra walked into the kitchen to look at the telephone notepad. The pad was blank; Andrea didn't write down anything. Hands shaking now, Sierra walked to their recreation room and poured herself a drink.

With Merritt Hughes, the pieces of who had been tormenting her fit together, starting with the post office box in Enid. He was with Brian when she first saw Brian in June 1953, in Enid. In late 1953, when she moved into the apartment building where he lived in Briggandale, she was almost certain that Merritt had recognized her from her days as a stripper. Merritt paid too much attention to her when she was his neighbor; he gave her the creeps, as if he were spying on her. But he never said anything to her to confirm her suspicions.

After she married, Sierra pressured Brian to move to a different apartment building. Later, Merritt had gotten into some trouble about a girl, although Sierra never found out from Brian exactly what had happened.

Maybe it was time to tell Brian about Merritt. But afraid of the consequences of this disclosure, Sierra emptied her glass and filled it over and over until she passed out.

CHAPTER 44

THE DAY AFTER Sierra's package was removed from the Tanner mailbox, Andrea got ready to leave before eight to head to the college. She couldn't study at home that morning, her parents had been fighting. Although the battle had ended and her mother had gone to the rec room, for Andrea, the remaining tension interfered with the studying she needed to do to prepare for a test.

AFTER HIGH SCHOOL, Andrea worked in a number of low-paying, low-skill jobs. Unsure of what to do, she didn't want to go to college and she didn't want a lot of responsibility. So for years, Andrea had no definite plans for what she would be when she finally grew up.

She watched her friends get married one by one, go to college or pursue some career, or have children and work at home. Some got divorced. One went insane. And one died of an overdose when she found her husband with a lover. Andrea watched certain ones most carefully, especially those who seemed to rebound after tragedy.

Andrea moved out of her parents' home in her twenties, only

to move back home at age thirty. She eloped with a loser named Earl and within three weeks, filed for divorce. Now enrolled in college, Andrea planned to be a social worker.

AS SHE GOT ready to leave, Andrea walked through the kitchen, where her father sat with the morning paper and his breakfast. She felt sorry for her father that morning, for during the fight, her mother had been particularly abusive.

"Dad, I couldn't help hearing you and Mom. Are you okay?"

But Brian didn't seem upset at all and even joked with her as she headed out to school. He assured her, "Andie, honey, don't worry about us. We've had worse fights over the years. Your mother is just nervous, that's all. Besides, I'm leaving soon to go to the clinic. The quiet house will really help your mother."

HOURS LATER, ANDREA came home from school. Certain she had done poorly on the test she just took, she didn't want to think or feel anything. If she could curl up on the sofa and watch a little television in the recreation room, maybe, just maybe, she would feel human again. It had been a rough day.

But at the door of the rec room, she could see her mother stretched out on the sofa. With the half-empty glass, a condensation ring on the table, no ice cubes left in the glass and the tipped-over, empty liquor bottle, Andrea could easily guess what had happened. Her mother was drunk again. Disgusted, Andrea left her in their recreation room. She went to her own room and shut the door.

At the clinic, Brian checked his watch carefully. At two in the afternoon, Andrea was sure to be home. He called, letting the telephone ring four, five, six, seven times. He was about to hang up when she finally picked up the telephone.

"Uh, hello?" Andrea said.

"Hi baby! Did you just get in?"

"Oh, hi Daddy. No, I, uh, I've been here for a little while."

"What's the matter? You don't sound right, Andie."

"I just woke up Daddy. I, uh, just took a nap. I was feeling kind of down."

"Tell me about it, please."

"I think I failed my test today, Daddy, Psych 101. I bombed on it—I just know I did."

"Oh honey, I'm so sorry!"

"Think about it Daddy. Psych 101 is basic human behavior, you know, what makes us think, what makes us tick. How hard could it be Daddy? I should be able to figure out what people do and why!"

"Sweetheart, don't be so hard on yourself. First of all, you probably didn't fail it, as bad as you may think you did on it. And there will be more tests to come, right?" The long pause on the other end of the telephone let him know he had gotten through to her.

"Yes, Daddy, I know what you're saying. And thanks for understanding. I feel better now."

After talking to Andrea for a few more moments, Brian asked, "May I speak to your mother? Is she at home?"

"Daddy, she's in the rec room on the sofa."

"Is she asleep?"

Andrea hesitated. "Daddy, she's drunk."

"Go get your mother. I want to talk with her. We've got that dinner tonight with some people at the clinic, remember?"

"Thanks for the reminder. I'll go get her, Daddy."

Andrea left the telephone on the counter while Brian waited. In time, he could hear Andrea's distraught cries in the distance, "Mom, wake up! Mom! Oh no! No! Mom!"

She ran back to the telephone. "Daddy, Mom is dead! Daddy! Daddy!"

Hearing his daughter's wails made Brian cry too. "Sweetheart, I'll get the hospital ambulance out there right away. I'm on my way. Andrea, baby, please listen. Clean up your mother if you think she needs it. Don't let them see anything bad about her. She was a good woman. You know what to do."

While Brian and the ambulance headed toward his home,

Andrea went back to the recreation room. She took the liquor bottle and glass to the kitchen and returned to finish cleaning up. Recognizing her mother's handwriting on the unopened package, she picked up the brown package and slowly opened it. The money fell from her fingers as she read the enclosed letter from Enid.

When the doorbell rang, Andrea slipped the money, her mother's package and the letter from Enid into her book bag. Still crying, she answered the door and let the paramedics in. Brian came in shortly after.

Within minutes after the ambulance arrived at the Tanner home, neighbors had gathered in the drive. The neighbor to the north, Mrs. Talley, pulled off her gardening gloves, dusted off her clothing and adjusted her gardening hat. She sauntered over to the Tanners' front yard. Standing on her tiptoes, Mrs. Talley peeked through the recreation room window and watched as the paramedics tried unsuccessfully to revive Sierra.

Mrs. Talley was first on the scene after the ambulance and supplied all the juicy tidbits that the other neighbors wanted to hear. The neighbor with the white toy poodle yanked at the leash to get the dog to cross the street. The poor animal just wanted to do his business. Another neighbor just happened to jog by after seeing the commotion. The questions that they asked of Mrs. Talley were predictable, like "What happened?" and "Who was hurt?"

The answers were not.

"Mrs. Tanner is dead."

"What? How do you know? What happened?"

When she had a small audience in front of her, Mrs. Talley cleared her throat. "Mrs. Tanner is dead," she repeated. "It's a wonder that she was alone today." She barely concealed her cattiness.

"What do you mean? Does she have a lot of family or company?"

"Yes, male company, if you get my drift. But if someone was here, he must have left while I was away."

The group got quiet as the paramedics wheeled out Sierra's body. Andrea followed closely behind, crying hard and oblivious to the onlookers. Mrs. Talley immediately followed, making noises of pity as she slid an arm around Andrea. She would go to the hospital with Andrea. And of course, she would fill the neighbors in later.

Within moments, Dr. Tanner came out of the home, obviously distraught. With an ashen face, he cried openly before his neighbors. He followed the ambulance to the hospital alone in his luxury car.

Later, back at her home, Mrs. Talley held court again to give the latest juicy update on the Tanners. "At the hospital, Andrea told the admitting nurse she found her mother at home alone. She thought her mother was drunk and just left her mother sprawled out on the sofa in their recreation room. Then, Dr. Tanner called home and asked to talk to Sierra. That's when Andrea went to check on her and found she was dead. Stone-cold dead, can you imagine that?"

As Mrs. Talley finished, the neighbors started questioning her. "What was the cause of death?"

"Yeah, why did she die?"

"I don't know."

"But do you think she died of natural causes?"

"Sure, if drinking herself to death counts as a natural cause," Mrs. Talley remarked.

LATE THAT EVENING, when they were alone, Andrea pulled the letter, package and money from her book bag. "Daddy, look at this. I think I know what happened to Mom."

Shocked, Brian just looked at her. Did she really know? He took the letter and the cash from her. He put the cash down, opened the letter and read it. Trembling by now, Brian stared at the letter and didn't look at Andrea.

After pausing for nearly a minute, Andrea continued. "Daddy, I was there when she was working on that package. She was really upset and didn't want me to know what she was doing. Maybe I should have said something then."

The tears began rolling down Andrea's face. "I didn't tell anyone about this. Should we tell the police now?"

"No, Andie," Brian folded the letter slowly, "Your mother was a good woman. We should let her rest in peace. If anyone finds out that she was being blackmailed, they'll want to know why. Your mother was a good woman, we need to protect her memory, even now."

"But Daddy, who do you think was behind this? Who could have done this to Mom?"

"I don't really know, but . . . ."

"But what? Tell me, tell me please!"

"I think it was a woman who has caused trouble for me in the past. Her name is Dyna. But Andie, I don't really know if she was involved. I'm just guessing at this point. I don't have anything concrete, just a gut feeling. I'm probably wrong, so just drop it."

"Daddy?"

"Andrea, look at the letter. While your mother was alive, I put up with a lot. Even with all of the drinking and fighting, she was still my wife and your mother. Please, for my sake, let's keep this to ourselves. Let your mother rest in peace."

The news of the sudden death of Sierra Tanner made the society headlines in the *Cellis Courier*. She was relatively young, outwardly healthy and the wife of the very rich Dr. Brian Tanner. The *Courier* did a decent job of describing her contributions and activities among the elite socialites in Cellis County, along with many details about the substantial contributions made by the Tanner, Meyer and Smertz Clinic.

Within that same social group, rumors flew about the real cause of her death. Many knew she drank like a fish. A few doubted she died due to natural causes. And none of those socialites who knew them were willing to swear publicly that the good Doctor Brian would miss her.

But his immediate and hefty contribution to one of their favorite charities, in the name of his late wife, quickly quieted some of the most vocal among them. As a group, they had an image to maintain, and he was one of their own.

CHAPTER 45

A MONTH AFTER his first call, Benjamin called again to give Steve an update. He had gathered all the records he could get his hands on—copies of the death certificate and the police report.

"Okay, Steve, what else would there be?"

"Did the officer look at the car?"

"There were two officers involved in this case—Danny Sledge and Dean Forsythe. The report had both names on it."

"I meant, did you contact either of them?"

Benjamin laughed.

Steve understood. "Thanks for the answer—I take that as a definite 'no.'"

"Now, little brother, I didn't contact them because I don't like contact with the law. I didn't contact them in case we have some dirty work to do. Besides, there's nothing here we don't already know about. I wanted to take a look at the note."

"What note?"

"The break-up note."

"What are you talking about?"

"One of the officers, the older one, asked Ma whether Javier had a girlfriend. Then he told her about a note they found in the car."

"How did you know that? Did Ma tell you?"

"Alfred and I were in the hallway when the police came. We heard everything."

"I didn't know that."

"But check this out, the note they talked to Ma about is missing from their evidence records."

TWO WEEKS HAD passed since the cabinet contract award to Rausch Improvements. Steve figured he had waited long enough. Using the purchase order provided by the Rauschs and pretending to be Tim Rausch, Steve canceled the contract for the cabinet construction.

On the twenty-third day after the bid award, Eunice checked on their cabinet order.

"Mrs. Rausch, we don't have a record of a pending order for your company."

Her heart fell into her stomach. "No, no, there must be some mistake! I have the purchase order right here!"

The man on the other end of the telephone took the information and promised to get back to her.

After fifteen minutes, he called back. "Mrs. Rausch, this is Ed from Earnaster Cabinets. I found your purchase order, but you don't have an open order here. It looks like the order you placed on the sixth was canceled. Paula made a note in the file, 'Order canceled by Mr. Rausch on the twentieth.'"

"What?! We never canceled that order!"

"I'm just telling you what I see here, ma'am."

"Well, well, let me talk to Paula! I'll straighten this out!"

"Won't do any good to talk to her, ma'am. We can't get those particular cabinets from that order any more. That order hadn't been delivered to us yet when your husband cancelled it, but we were able to sell them to another company. I personally made that sale. And since we don't normally carry that style in stock, would you like to place your order again? We might be able to get them delivered in another three to six weeks."

"Three to six weeks?"

"Only one company makes that style. It will be three to six weeks, and that's assuming they don't have a backlog. Oh yes, here's something else, there's another note here. The deposit you made on the cabinets, it was forfeited when your husband canceled the contract. They were a special order."

"What? There is no way!"

"Ma'am, don't get upset with me. Your husband agreed to it."

Openly panicking, she tried to figure out what to do. "I've got to call my husband. I'll get back to you."

Eunice tried to radio Tim, without success.

When Tim got home that evening, Eunice was in hysterics. They had pledged their current home and their anticipated profits from the Elkora Hills contract as security for the loan on the home they were building. Now, their Elkora Hills contract was falling apart. They stood to lose everything.

Krodder Construction finished the cabinet work at Elkora Hills. They completed the job without a hitch.

SHORTLY AFTER THE cabinet work was completed at the resort, Steve called his mother just to talk. After the usual pleasantries, Dyna asked about Steve's personal life.

"How's Rene?"

"She's fine."

"Steve, why don't you ask Rene out sometime?"

Steve got quiet at that point. "I'm not sure she would go out with me now. She's seeing Bart Krodder now, he's one of our contractors. I may have missed my chance with her, Ma. I really blew it with Rene by doing nothing."

"It's never too late, Steve. If you want her, go after her. The best marriages come from good relationships and love. You two get along so well, I would just hate to see her marry someone else. Your dad and I were friends before we were married. We got to know each other first. We planned together and did things, you know, we went for our dreams." She sniffed and added, "I miss your dad, I really do. We had a good marriage."

Steve and Dyna sat silently for a few moments.

"Anyone else?"

"No, nobody serious."

"Well Steve . . . ."

"Ma!"

"Son, I just wanted to—"

"Fix me up? No thanks Ma!"

Out of the blue, his mother asked about his past acquaintances in Cellis. "Steve, have you seen very many of your childhood friends since you've been back?"

"Sure, Ma. I've seen a few. A couple of weeks ago, I saw Eunice and Tim, you know, Eunice Driver and Tim Rausch. They're married now and have a construction company here."

"Steve, those names sound familiar. Were they children that I knew?"

"I don't think so, Ma. But those two are in hot water financially now, something to do with being unable to finish their contract work."

"Well Steve, I'm sorry to hear that. Maybe your company can do something for them."

"Probably not Ma. We've helped them enough. I've got to get going now. I love you. Goodbye."

"'Bye Steve. I'll talk to you later." As Dyna hung up the telephone in her Ohio home, she remembered who Tim and Eunice were. Long ago, she had called their parents to complain about their children's teasing Jacob and to ask their parents for their help. The calls must have helped, for Steve expressed no anger at those two. He even mentioned that his company had helped them. Dyna smiled, happy that Steve had resolved his anger at those two.

In Indiana, Steve was glad to tell his mother that he had seen Eunice and Tim. But unfortunately, he could never tell her all of the details of his most recent encounters with them.

DR. TANNER WAS one of the first to buy into the resort at Elkora Hills even if the resort wasn't even completed. But Brian could see that resort time would be useful. He planned to use the two weeks he had bought at Elkora Hills for business and for pleasure. Trading his time for reservations at other resorts, or giving a week or so to his daughter, were choices Dr. Tanner had considered in making the purchase. He paid cash; he had plenty of money from the insurance proceeds from Sierra's death.

ON HER FORTY-EIGHTH birthday, Dyna expected that the ringing telephone would be the first of the calls from her sons. But the first call that day was from Regina Carselli, one of Aunt Alicia's children.

"Happy birthday Dyna! How are things in Ohio?"

"Regina, is that you? It's been a really long time, cousin! And thank you!"

"You've been on my mind lately, and this morning, I remembered that today was your birthday. How are you? I haven't had a chance to talk to you in years."

"I know, I know. Time has been flying for me too. I'm fine. I guess I should be grateful for how well things have turned out. Despite everything that's happened over the years, I'm still around. You know, a weaker person might have committed suicide, gone insane, or turned to drugs or alcohol. But your mom helped me to become strong. She had a lot to do with my survival, you know that."

"I'm glad to hear that. She really loved you, Dyna. How are your boys?"

"Benjamin, Alfred and Steve finished high school. Steve is doing exceptionally well. He's the manager of the big, new resort, Elkora Hills, back in Cellis."

"That's really impressive! Any of them married yet?"

"No, but I'm not worried about them. Steve will get married

when he's ready. With him, some lucky girl will get a hardworking, goal-oriented, devoted husband." Dyna laughed. But she thought to herself, that is, unless that girl seriously ticks him off. If she does, that woman will get some major grief from a vengeful and very determined Steve.

Dyna added, "Too bad that he and his nice assistant, Rene, don't get together. They seemed to work so well together."

"And the twins?"

"The twins are out of jail now and look as if they finally want to be decent and law-abiding. I know prison reformed those two, and I'm grateful for that."

Regina asked, "Where are the twins?"

"They live here in Ohio. They're working in construction now. Both learned how to weld and in any event, seem to have no problems with any kind of manual work."

"Any grandchildren yet?"

"Not that I know of. At least, no woman has ever come here with a baby claiming that I'm the grandmother." The women laughed.

As Regina gave an update on her life and the lives of their family members in New Jersey, Dyna thought about Javier. Dyna had finally come to grips with the death of her eldest son. While he was alive, she worried about him for seventeen years. From time to time, over the years since his death, Dyna remembered the old woman's saying. She could repeat it word for word now, "Seventeen but not eighteen. Seventeen but not eighteen. Seventeen but not eighteen. Beware of the healer and the one of blood and cloth."

Dyna finally decided the old woman was just plain wrong or just plain crazy. Those words probably meant nothing after all this time. But she could never put those words, and what had happened, to rest. But one thing she could be grateful for—at least her sons hadn't turned out to be as rotten as Brian Tanner.

"Dyna? Dyna, are you still there?"

"I'm sorry, I was thinking about our mothers. I just remembered what my ma and yours used to say all the time, and it's so true, what doesn't kill you will make you stronger."

"So true! Well Dyna, happy birthday again. I've really got to get going."

"Thanks Regina, for the call. Let's stay in touch, okay?"

"Sure cousin. Bye."

"Goodbye, Regina."

After Regina hung up, Dyna thought back on the tragedies of her life. Coping with Brian Tanner's cruelty, the deaths of her parents and her husband John, the old woman's words, Jake's injuries and even Javier's death had been hard. Now she knew deep in her heart, those events had in fact made her stronger. She wasn't glad they had happened, only that she had survived them all.

AN INVESTIGATION SEEMED unlikely since Sierra's death took place almost a year ago. Brian began to freely spend the life insurance proceeds. Some of the money went to buy a bigger stake in the partnership. He made some improvements on his home. He gave some of the money to his daughter, Andrea. And he bought some new toys, including new golf clubs and a mountain bike, to help him over any grief he might have possibly felt.

With some of the money, Brian enjoyed a gambling junket to Las Vegas. He lost big, but he didn't really care. Brian still had plenty left. And with the rest of the money, he made plans for future activities. Being married to Sierra did have some special benefits, after all.

CHAPTER 46

A YEAR TO the day when Sierra Tanner died, Everett stopped by his nephew Dieter's home on the way home from one of his shops. He routinely stopped by Dieter's now. After the deaths of his wife Ellen and son Zachary and the rapid departure of his mistress Gina, Everett went back to the life he once knew. With the help of his nephew Dieter, Everett hoped to build a criminal empire that reached far beyond that of his former boss, Mike Hoffer.

Everett and Dieter were in the middle of planning a job to generate plenty of money for their enterprise. They had argued about a hit, then boom—Everett was writhing on the floor, gasping desperately for breath. He felt as if an elephant were sitting on his chest, a really heavy elephant.

Sometime between dropping to the floor and arriving in intensive care, the elephant got off Everett's chest. He was alive, but just barely. He opened his eyes to see Dieter in a chair, sitting near the head of the bed.

"Almost lost you, Uncle. How are you feeling?" He took his uncle's right hand. It was weak.

Everett tried to laugh, then winced. "Take a guess," he whispered hoarsely.

"You talked a lot while you were under."

Everett's hand locked onto Dieter's hand. He was afraid of that. He worried that he might have implicated himself in a few of his crimes while he was unconscious or semiconscious. Maybe it wasn't so great to be alive. He might have to spend the rest of his life in prison.

"Did you take notes?"

"No. Most of it had to do with dry cleaning. What did you do, memorize your customer mailing list?"

Everett relaxed his tight grip on his nephew's hand.

"You did say something I know didn't have anything to do with the dry-cleaning business. Something like 'brakes, Doctor T., brakes, that dark-haired boy,' then you said something else that I couldn't make out."

In fact, Dieter heard his uncle say the words "Mitchell," "car wreck" and "dead" quite clearly.

"Some doctor walked into the room then, so I pinched you and you finally shut up. I don't think he heard what you said."

"Good. I'd have to kill him too. Remember the rule. Leave no unnecessary witnesses." Everett told his nephew about the job he had done for Brian, but he gave Dieter no names or dates. Dieter needed to learn how do this kind of hit, if it ever came up again in their business. But Dieter didn't need to know who the customer was. Everett had promised Brian Tanner that the services exchange would be their secret forever.

Dieter Hunt had learned something more valuable that day. He learned his uncle had orchestrated the death of a dark-haired boy by the name of Mitchell by tampering with his brakes, and that a Doctor T. was involved. He didn't know Doctor T. or the Mitchell kid, and he couldn't ask his uncle right then. But he planned to ask him in time.

Everett Sears died that night.

Dr. Tanner rejoiced when he saw Everett Sears' obituary in the *Cellis Courier*. Glad Everett was dead and their arrangement was still a secret, Dr. Brian Tanner didn't even send a card.

Within a week, Everett had a rather showy public funeral. His nephew Dieter watched carefully to see whether any doctors would show up or at least send flowers or cards. There would be no graveside services; they might interfere with his plans.

"Put that bunch over there. Yes, there. Give me the card." The ashen-faced funeral director turned over the mint-green envelope to Dieter and placed the large, ivy-covered arrangement to the right of the coffin. Dieter opened the envelope and looked at the enclosed card. Closing it, he put the envelope and card into his pocket, along with the other sympathy cards he had collected so far.

"Any more?" Dieter asked impatiently.

The director looked carefully through the flowers, green plants and other arrangements that filled the end of the room. "Here," he kept poking and lifting through the greenery, "Oh and here's one more." He pushed a plant stand back in place after handing the two cards to Everett's nephew.

The first card was from an insurance company. The next came from the Tanner, Meyer and Smertz Clinic.

Rosalie Franson, the clinic's office manager, had sent out the floral arrangement. It was her job to send out cards and flowers under circumstances like these. The partners never knew exactly to whom or when the cards and flowers went out, they just trusted Rosalie. Rosalie had done this job for over twenty years and she enjoyed doing it. Plus, none of the partners wanted to do it.

No other doctor whose last name began with a "T" sent a card. Dieter guessed Dr. Brian Tanner had to be the one. But he didn't know enough yet to be able to effectively use the information he had so far against Dr. Tanner.

But Dieter was a patient person. After the lawyers finished with his uncle's legal matters, the dry cleaning chain would be his. Dieter would have plenty of time to figure out which of his uncle's customers he could blackmail or otherwise use to his advantage. He would make sure that Dr. Tanner would be among those that he would consider.

WITH THE START of the new Police Chief Jerry Unger in

1985, Sledge watched the Cellis Police Department transported from the 1950s to the 1980s in just under two years or so. The new guy got into scientific evidence—all kinds of tests Sledge had never even heard of—to prove cases.

For years, Sledge was sure that the tampering with the Mitchell boy's brakes had occurred at the Tanner home or nearby. But without more proof or even a motive, Sledge faced a roadblock. To make it worse, former Chief Gardener had been absolutely clear about his ban on further contacts with the Tanner family on the matter.

But with the new guy, maybe it was time to try again. Maybe he could get some proof from the note about who was involved in the Mitchell kid's death. Sledge convinced the new chief to let him submit the old note and envelope to the crime lab for the first level of testing—just to see if the spot was blood and its type. Sledge brought the scorched note and envelope from home, carrying it in the same sandwich bag he had put it in years before.

The envelope and note went to the state crime lab later that week.

THE TELEPHONE RANG in the Tanner exercise room around seven that evening. Brian stopped riding his stationary bike to answer it.

"Tanner residence?"

"Yes."

"Is this Brian Tanner?"

The caller sounded familiar, but Brian couldn't place the voice. He mopped his brow with the green bath towel that dangled from his neck. "Yes, it is."

"Brian! How are you doing? This is Merritt, Merritt Hughes from college."

"Wow! It has been years since the last time I saw you! How are you?"

"Well, I'm fine. I saw your picture in the newspaper here in Enid and I thought I would give you a call. Congratulations on receiving the humanitarian award from your club." Sitting at his desk, Merritt had the newspaper spread out in front of him.

"Thank you. So, how many years has it been?"

"Quite a few. I called your home a couple of times. Did you know?"

"I'm sorry, I never got any of your messages. I wish I had known you were trying to reach me. I wondered what had happened to you."

"I even came to Cellis a couple of times, right to your house, but you weren't at home."

"When? When was that?"

"Oh, the last time was about two years ago. I worked full-time driving a truck for years so that I could go back to school. It took a while. I could go to school only part-time."

"You drove a truck?"

"Yes, I had to pay for school myself and had to take a job that would give me some flexibility. The last time I had a run near Cellis, I came right to your home."

"I don't understand why no one told me."

"Well, don't worry about it now, Brian, that's okay." Pausing now, Merritt had to ask about her. It wouldn't seem right if he didn't. "How is Sierra?"

Brian hesitated. "Merritt, Sierra's dead. She's been gone more than a year now."

"I'm sorry, Brian, I'm so sorry to hear that." Neither said anything for several seconds, then Merritt asked gently, "Brian, are you all right?"

The front doorbell rang, the sound echoing through the house. "Yes, I'm fine now. But I have to go, someone's at the door." Brian hung up without taking Merritt's telephone number or address.

CHAPTER 47

S LEDGE DIDN'T EXPECT the testing to take so long. When the envelope came from the State Crime Lab two months later, he was a little anxious. After Callie logged the letter in, he got it. He looked over the envelope, turning it from side to side in his left hand while he ran his right hand back and forth slowly over his chin. After walking slowly back to his locker, he placed the envelope there and closed the locker slowly.

Even with all his anxiety, he decided to wait until the end of the shift to read the results. If the tests showed the spot was blood, he still had to figure out who the note-writer was. If the tests were inconclusive or showed the spot was not blood, he didn't want to let the disappointment ruin his whole day.

THE TWO TELEVISION camera crew members from station WZXZ21 who introduced themselves to Andrea as Randall and George arrived that morning right after the caterer and hours before the first guests. The newscaster would arrive just before the guests. But Randall and George wanted to make sure that they could conduct a site survey and set up for the field production, including laying down power cables and taking corrective steps for lighting.

The crew had their work cut out for them. The forecast for that day in June included sunny skies and few clouds. The sun would act like a giant spotlight, creating dense shadows and high contrast. With Andrea leading the way, they went to the rear of Brian Tanner's home.

"Why not use this area next to the house?" Andrea asked, "With the white stone, it ought to make a nice picture." The two men nodded politely but continued looking.

"What about the area near my father's roses? They're not too tall, and the colors are nice and bright." She gestured out over the lush green lawn in the direction of the fence. But over that area, the sun shone down harshly. The men shook their heads and continued to look around.

"Well, if you don't like it there, maybe you should set up next to the pool. The water is really sparkling today. The blue should make a nice scene." She turned to point behind them. "If you want to set up there, we'll have the crew move a few tables."

Eventually, the two men chose a site near the garden, where a large white arbor stood at the entrance. The area behind the arbor had some exposure, but the arbor sat in the shade. "Miss, uh, Andrea, we would prefer to set up here. George, two large reflectors should do for this area, and maybe a spot for the background. Let's use the light meter and check."

Andrea got out of the way to let the men start setting up. She had plenty to do in the hours that remained.

While Andrea busied herself with the caterers, the telephone rang in the Tanner home. Brian answered it.

"Brian, this is Merritt."

"Oh, I'm so sorry that I didn't get back to you. After I hung up the telephone, I realized that I didn't take your name and number."

"Well, I was going to call back. I still wanted to talk to you anyway. Life is strange, Brian. You know, I dropped out of school, but in time, I did go back. I'm a doctor now too, but not the same as you."

"What do you mean?"

"I got my doctorate in theology less than three years ago. I'm Reverend Dr. Merritt Hughes now."

"You are kidding! Say, didn't you say that you drove a truck?"

"No, it's true, I'm the pastor at a church here. And yes, I drove a truck. I did that while I went to school. After I finished with school, I kept driving a truck until I found and accepted the right pastorate. It surprised me that it was right here. I had expected to relocate."

"Merritt, I still can't get over it. First you were a medical student, then you were a drug rep. Next you were a truck driver, and now you're a pastor? Forgive me Merritt, but I can't imagine you in the last two roles!"

"When we were in school, I felt something was missing in what I was doing. I'm a new man now, I'm totally changed. I'm really glad it turned out this way. Let me give you my address and telephone numbers at home and at the church."

Grabbing a notepad and pen, Brian jotted the information down. While Brian wrote, he thought about a troublesome matter that still remained. He figured that this might be his only chance to wrap up this part of Sierra's past. "Thanks for the update. One personal question, what did you do with your collection?"

"Collection?"

"I know about your trips with Ricky. You know, your home movies."

After a long silence, Merritt finally answered. "Ricky got those from me years ago. I needed some cash and he said that he had some plans for them. I never asked what he did with them."

But Merritt didn't tell Brian about his private films involving Sierra. He had destroyed those years ago.

Brian didn't know what to do at that moment. He wanted to know whether any more films of·Sierra as Boom-Boom Betty existed, but didn't want to arouse any suspicions.

But his opportunity to ask more questions from Merritt without raising suspicions had just slipped away.

"Brian, I'm really ashamed about that part of my life. I'd greatly appreciate it if you would keep that information to yourself and, uh, don't ever bring that stuff up again."

"Understood. By the way, whatever happened to Ricky?"

"I haven't spoken to him in years. But I understand that he lives there in Cellis. I really hope that he has gotten rid of those trashy movies by now." Uncomfortable now, Merritt decided to end the call. "I've got to get going now. I'll keep in touch. Nice talking to you."

"It's been nice talking to you too, Merritt. Hope to see you soon."

"Daddy, can you help me please?" Andrea touched his arm and Brian turned to see what she needed. With the party starting at noon, it would be a very busy day in their home.

AT NOON THAT same day at the twins' duplex in Todda, Steve, Alfred and Benjamin Mitchell gathered around the open hood of Benjamin's car in the garage. The twins had worked on the car for hours before Steve's arrival. The car was one of the last things they had to work on that weekend.

The twins were preparing to move back to Cellis, Indiana, where they hoped to find jobs in the RV trade and get a new start. "New state, clean slate," they told their mother. But they had other reasons for wanting to go back to Cellis.

"What else is there, Benjamin?"

"Steve, we still think Dr. Tanner had something to do with it."

"Who else was involved Benj—clearly involved and not just who you think was involved?"

"We don't have anyone else, Steve." Alfred answered as he wiped the black motor oil from his thick hands. "So what do we do now?"

"Realistically, without more proof of wrongdoing, this is going nowhere."

Benjamin looked into the engine and didn't move. "I just want to know what really happened, Steve."

"Me too," Alfred added.

"Steve, you can stop thinking about Javier, but we won't. Not ever."

Pangs of guilt and doubt left Steve quiet. If Dr. Tanner did murder Javier and got away with it all this time, he would be a tough man to take down. Dr. Tanner had too much to lose, and he would play for keeps. And Steve wondered whether he and his brothers had what it took to do the job. There could be no mistakes in pursuing Dr. Tanner; any mistake might prove to be fatal.

Steve finally answered, "I don't want to go after the doctor unless he's guilty and we can prove it. But like you, I just want to know the truth, no matter what it is or who it might point to."

"No question, Steve. And I won't give up on it either." Benjamin made one quick adjustment under the hood. He pulled a 38-caliber semi-automatic from the spot under the hood where he had hidden it and checked it. Satisfied it was in good working order, Benjamin put it back into its hiding place and carefully covered it with the piece of black felt he had glued in place to conceal it. "Dr. Tanner thinks that he got away with killing Javier, but he has another thing coming!"

But without more information, they had reached a dead end. Javier's death would remain a mystery, unless fate intervened and the truth somehow came out. Among themselves, they vowed that if they could find out for a fact that someone murdered Javier and who the killer was, they would get revenge on that person. The Mitchell brothers would get revenge, no matter what it cost them personally, or how long it took.

NEAR THE END of his shift, as he got ready to go home for the day, Sledge opened his locker and pulled out the State Crime Lab envelope. He pulled the report out of the envelope, paused and took a deep breath. He read the report and letter slowly, growing angrier by the second.

"So Danny, what was the result?" Dean Forsythe had joined Sledge as he stood by the open locker.

Sledge didn't look at his partner, he was so furious. "The test was inconclusive. The only fingerprints on it were from Chief Gardener and Javier. There should have been a smudge from the side of the hand when the person wrote it, but there wasn't. I expected something, a fingerprint or other evidence would have been left when he put his hand down on the paper to write the note."

"What about the spot? What was it?"

"The spot was blood, but it was too degraded to be of much use due to improper storage and other factors. Can you beat that?"

Sledge crumpled the report and letter into a ball. He threw the ball into his locker and slammed the door so hard it could be heard outside the locker room. Sledge hit the locker with his fist as hard as he could while he exploded from the tension he had held in for years. "Inconclusive my foot! I know in my gut that Dr. Tanner did it or he had someone do it for him! I've got three more years until retirement and I'm going to find out what really happened to Javier Mitchell, if it's the last thing I do! Dr. Tanner thinks that he got away with killing Javier, but he has another thing coming!"

"WILL YOU LOOK at this? There must be over two hundred people here!" Looking over the crowd, Herve Meyer bit into a pâté hors d'oeuvre and chewed slowly.

"More like two fifty, and that doesn't include the television and newspaper crews." Taking a long sip of his drink, Bill Smertz corrected his partner's estimate.

Herve washed down the rest of the goose liver tidbit with a drink of water. "Anyone from the *Courier* here?" He asked.

"Look over there, to your left."

Herve turned his head and whistled. "They didn't send enough people, did they? I recognize the photographer and the reporter, but who are the guys in the dark suits?"

"Top brass. You know the editor, the others are some of his assistants. I invited them especially, I figure they've done a whole lot for the clinic over the years." Bill took a sip. He wanted to make his drink last for a while. He had work to do even at this party, like socializing with select guests and checking with the caterer and with others. His drink was lemon-flavored tea, poured into a highball glass. He looked over the crowd and tried to figure out which ones he had to mingle with. Some of them he could safely ignore.

"Have you seen so many pastel suits? Looks like a regular Easter parade out here." For this party, snazzy day wear ruled. Silk and linen outfits in colors like pale ice cream predominated. Creamy vanilla, frosty peach, sugary mint, buttery tan and even one in a raspberry ice, the men's suits made the event look like a wedding.

The women were decked out even more, as if they were in a fashion show. Sheathes, column dresses, A-lines, skirt sets with pleats, popover dresses, the outfits were beaded, embroidered and fringed, and many had trim of lace appliqué, rhinestones and pearls.

This crowd knew that they were making news and that they would be seen all over Cellis and beyond. No one wore jersey or piqué knit shirts. And only the photographer for the *West End Gazette* wore blue jeans.

"Well, let's get this show on the road." Herve whispered to Bill. By now, they had walked to the front of the yard near the white canvas tent. The brightly decorated head table held place settings for the partners and select guests. Herve's wife, Grace, and Bill's wife, Sofia, sat chatting with Andrea, who sat in the chair at the end. Dr. Tom Swanson, Andrea's new husband stood behind her, listening to the women talk. Only the birthday boy was missing.

"Where is he?" Bill peered at the crowd, looking for Brian's familiar face.

"I don't see—no, look over there! I see him. He's with the reporter from the *West End Gazette*." Herve gestured and fortunately caught Brian's attention. "Okay, he's on his way."

"Good."

While they waited for Dr. Brian Tanner to make his way through the crowds, the partners exchanged pleasantries with their wives and with Andrea and Tom.

As soon as Brian cleared the last row of white cloth-covered banquet tables, Andrea looked up, exclaiming, "Daddy's here now."

"Fine with me. Start tapping." Bill and Herve reached for their teaspoons at the same time and began tapping on their water glasses. Leaning forward over the small stand in front of him, Bill flipped on the power. Having the portable microphone was a good idea.

"Quiet! Quiet please! I'd like to make a toast." Bill tapped against his water glass until the group grew quiet. Eventually, the crowd of doctors, families, socialites and well-wishers got quiet.

"Thank you all for coming," he started. "This toast is for two happy events, the fifty-sixth birthday of my good friend and partner, Brian, uh, Dr. Brian Tanner, and his receipt of the Professor Gesaw Francisio House Humanitarian Award. He has helped hundreds of children and contributed to area charities over the years. Dr. Tanner was recently honored for his humanitarian efforts by one of our local service agencies, and we want to honor him too. He's a really outstanding pillar of our community and more of us should be like him. Dr. Tanner has touched the lives of so many in this region . . . ."

Someone in the crowd interjected, "Yes, and he's made you and Dr. Meyer rich too!"

Bill couldn't help smiling. "True, how true!" he laughed. "I could brag about him all day long, but I won't. Brian, here's to you and happy birthday! Cheers!"

The group joined in the toast. After the noise died down, Tom walked over to the microphone stand.

"I'd like to make a toast too." After Tom Swanson cleared his throat, he started. "To the man who created the most beautiful woman in my world, who will someday be a grandfather to our children, and who was brilliant in choosing the best person to be the new team leader at the clinic, namely, me! Cheers, Dad!"

Most of the guests joined in the toast, laughing and cheering. But one woman, a doctor from the clinic, turned beet red, appeared aggravated and quickly left the party. Herve and Bill huddled together, whispering. Brian smiled and took a slow sip of his drink while watching Tom Swanson the whole time. He stood, thanked his guests simply and sat down.

Some time later, after the birthday song and squares of fluffy German chocolate cake, Brian looked for a chance to get away, even if only for a few minutes.

While his guests continued with their revelry, Dr. Brian Tanner slipped away from the group and headed toward the rear of his flower garden. He could meditate there alone. Few people would venture out that far uninvited.

As he stood near the outer boundary of his garden, Brian leaned on an oak tree. He picked up a leaf that had fallen and turned it over, finding several galls on the back. The galls reminded him of Everett Sears and his work. Brian began pulling the leaf apart slowly.

To Brian, the best reasons for celebrating were ones he could not openly talk about. He had gotten rid of that punk, Javier Mitchell. Brian believed Javier had been involved with his wife Sierra and his daughter Andrea at the same time.

Everett never bothered Brian after the extermination job. And he never tried to extort money for his work. Now Everett Sears was dead too and Brian didn't have to think about him anymore. For all Brian knew, that man had died without telling a soul about their special arrangement.

As for the clinic, it was doing well, and so was he, in more than one way. Among some of the hidden fringe benefits he enjoyed from the clinic, Brian had all the sex he could handle—and with no personal commitments to the women involved. And he regularly received money from the insurance scam that he and Alma Hormiga ran.

Most important to Brian, he was free of Sierra, who had cheated on him indiscriminately during their marriage. She had been dead for years now and he was very glad. Dropping the rest of the tattered leaf, Brian looked out over the huge, flower-filled yard. When he got to the roses, Brian thought about his time with Sierra.

He had enjoyed being with her, especially when he tortured her with the letters over the years. After seeing Sierra as Boom-Boom in that tacky film years ago and with her infidelity and abuse of him during their marriage, Brian figured Sierra deserved anything he could do to her.

Brian had handled that murder on his own. While he was grateful for the professional services Everett Sears had given many years before, the threat of exposure or blackmail had convinced him to do this job himself. He felt proud Sierra had died without any apparent clues as to the real cause of her death.

THE DAY THAT Sierra died, Andrea had early morning classes at college. Brian picked a fight with Sierra to upset her, but made sure that the fight was over long before Andrea left. Next, Brian made sure that he was ready for work with his briefcase on the counter. He sat in the kitchen before Andrea came through on her way out. For Andrea's sake, he had to appear calm, as if nothing had happened. He had to leave the impression that today was just another day, that the fight was just another fight. After chatting briefly with his daughter, he watched as Andrea pulled her car out of the driveway.

After Brian finished his coffee and toast, he checked on Sierra. As he predicted, Sierra started drinking right after their fight and by 8 A.M., she was sprawled out on the sofa in the recreation room. Her glass was half empty, her liquor bottle tipped over, and she was too drunk to care.

Back in the kitchen, Brian opened his briefcase and pulled out a plastic bag. So far, he had been able to retrieve the package from the mailbox without leaving any fingerprints. Still using the plastic bag, Brian put Sierra's unopened package to the blackmailer on the table by her glass. From his jacket pocket, he pulled out a syringe and a single vial of potassium chloride. He gave her an injection right into her shrunken rose tattoo.

With the last two letters he sent to Sierra, Brian set up her death to look like a suicide. That is, if anyone had figured out Sierra Gleason Tanner had not died of natural causes.

Having Andrea find the blackmail package was a stroke of genius. With it, he gave himself an alibi and provided an alternate theory for her death in case of an investigation.

NOW IN THE garden, Andrea slid her arm into his. They stood silently for several moments, with the muffled sounds of the party behind them.

"Daddy, were you thinking about Mom?" Only she would know where to look for him. She noticed that he was very quiet as he sat at the party and that he had slipped away without telling anyone where he was going. "I miss her too, Daddy," Andrea said.

He kissed his daughter's forehead and smiled as he gazed into her unsuspecting eyes. "Of course, dear. I miss her," he lied.

To Dr. Brian Tanner, life was good, and the best was yet to come.

As Brian and Andrea emerged from the shadows at the rear garden, Randall, the camera operator from the television crew, turned the field camera on them. The footage looked great, some of the best that they had shot that day. With the distinguished doctor and his daughter walking arm in arm, chatting peacefully, the footage could be useful in future stories about the doctor.

Randall commented to the technical director at his side, "Just think George, with this footage, we might even win some kind of award! You know, a human interest story about the doctor and what a good man he is."

AUTHOR'S NOTE

THIS BOOK IS one in the series entitled *A Promise of Revenge,* in which key characters face moral questions. The first question involves what each would be willing to do for a family member. The second is what each person would do if he or she believed that he or she wouldn't be caught.

Please read the upcoming book in this series entitled "The Secret at St. Sans," if you want to know more about the Mitchell and Tanner families. This book is scheduled for completion in 2003.

In "The Secret at St. Sans," mysterious women in the clinic after hours, suspicions of fraud and other irregularities make rich Dr. Brian Tanner a prime target for blackmail by his disgruntled son-in-law, Dr. Tom Swanson.

But Brian is a target for other people too. When the Mitchell brothers, Steve, Alfred and Benjamin, uncover that Brian murdered their brother, Javier, more than two decades ago, rage and determination lead the brothers to seek revenge.

Anxious to silence Tom, Brian follows him to the vacation resort where Steve is the interim manager. When Tom dies mysteriously, most clues lead to Brian. Was Tom's death an accident or was it a murder?

Following this page is a sample section from that book.

Terri Kay

Excerpt from "The Secret at St. Sans"

CHAPTER 1

FROM HIS OFFICE behind the newsroom of the *Cellis Courier* chief editor Ed Corbal telephoned the desk of reporter John Waters for an update on the article Waters was working on. "Waters, are you ready with that piece on the doctor yet? I need it for the next edition."

"Almost, I'll be right there."

Within minutes John stood in the chief's door. "Here you go," John said as he handed the draft article to his supervisor. "I'm still waiting for the photo of him, but Bert in records said he was pretty sure that we have an archive photo."

"Mmh, let's see," Ed began reading, then stopped, and began rubbing his eyes. "Wait, my eyes are really hurting now." He handed the article back to John. "Read it to me please."

"Local Doctor Drowns . . ."

"Maybe we can do something with the title, like jazz it up or something," Ed interrupted. "Sorry, go ahead, keep reading."

John made a small mark on his copy, then continued reading. "The body of Dr. Thomas Swanson of Cellis was recovered on Saturday from the Ketchetaw River just south of St. Sans, Missouri. Preliminary reports indicated that Dr. Swanson died of asphyxiation due to drowning. Dr. Swanson was a surgeon with the Tanner, Meyer and Smertz Clinic in Cellis, and was the son-in-law of Dr. Brian Tanner, one of the owners of the clinic. Funeral arrangements are pending. Other details will be provided as soon as they become available." John looked at Ed. "How does that sound?"

"Okay so far. Do you have anything else?"

"Not yet, but . . . ."

Ed interrupted again. "Do you know why he was in Missouri?"

"Not yet. The office manager at the clinic called the story in this morning." John hesitated, "I'm still waiting for more. I've called and left two messages for that woman, but she hasn't called back yet. Oh, wait, I did find out that Mrs. Swanson is still in Missouri though."

"Follow up on it—maybe there's a story behind this, something more than a drowning death. But for now, get your piece in on time for the next edition."

ALMOST ONE MONTH earlier, on a Wednesday evening in September, as Dr. Thomas Swanson checked the Tanner, Meyer and Smertz Clinic's billing printout, he found no unusual orders for scheduled drugs—those would have triggered a Drug Enforcement Administration investigation. But two entries for trihyperboodiol appeared in February. Three entries more were made in March and the last prescription was issued in April. In the clinic's billing statement for the first quarter of the fiscal year, a total of six prescriptions for this expensive drug appeared, and all were from Dr. Brian Tanner. Tom noticed the drug entries quite by accident; he was looking for something entirely different. The name of the drug caught his attention, especially since one entry was for a patient whose last name matched the name of one of the women he was looking for.

Were there any other links to the mysterious ladies? Tom decided to check the patient records. He flipped on his computer and entered Melanika Gissellera, the name of the first woman whom he'd seen Brian with long after the clinic was closed. Her name appeared, along with her telephone number, but in the column for the address, the word "archive" appeared. Could he get any more information? He tried to access her records in a different way. No luck. He tried a third way, but got the same results as the first. On a hunch, he entered her telephone number. Following her name, six other names appeared as linked files. No addresses appeared on this screen either, just the word "archive" over and over in the address column.

Tom tried to open each file in succession, but just like before, he was blocked. Getting the files from the archives might give him the information he needed about Brian, but the request might alert the wrong people that he was investigating his boss and father-in-law, Dr. Brian Tanner.

Tom had gotten the billing statement by accident. Someone had carried it into the employees' lounge and left it momentarily. It should have never left the billing office or the hands of one of the clinic owners, Dr. Tanner, Dr. Meyer or Dr. Smertz. But whoever left it was bound to be looking for it, and Tom wasn't about to pass up the chance to look at it, even if only for a little while. The report could give patient information that he had no other access to.

But now that he had it, he could see that he needed the patient files as well, especially if he wanted his plan to work.

Tom couldn't pull the records personally; the clinic had strict rules on who could retrieve patient files. And he couldn't sweet-talk the records clerks into pulling the files immediately; both had left promptly for the day at four thirty, and it was close to seven now.

Tom had hit a roadblock that evening; he would have to order the files the first thing in the morning and wait until they arrived. He chose three records to start with and stuffed the bulky quarterly billing statement into his duffle bag to take home.

ON FRIDAY MORNING of that week, Rene Dezza piled the ten yearbooks from Pye Academy onto the desk of her boss, Steven J. Mitchell. Six of the books were from the 1971-72 school year; the rest were from the prior school year. It had taken three months and about $1,000 to collect them all. In her usual efficient manner, she had managed to get them. But months after getting the order from Steve to round up the old yearbooks, Rene still didn't know why or what Steve planned to do with them. She knew her boss well enough to figure out that something big had to be up. Steve was planning to do something to someone, and whatever he had in mind wouldn't be pleasant for the recipient. But what was Steve planning, and for whom? And how did the Pye Academy yearbooks fit in?

"Pye Academy, Cellis, Indiana, right?" She hoped that Steve would tell her how the yearbooks had anything to do with the resort where they worked now. Roger's Hideaway Resort in St. Sans, Missouri, was hundreds of miles away from the northern Indiana town of Cellis. Although she and Steve had worked in Cellis years ago for the same resort company, these books were from a period many years earlier.

Steve didn't say anything but sat motionless, staring at the pile.

Rene slid into one of the chairs in front of Steve's desk and picked up one of the yearbooks. As Rene turned the pages of the 1971 Pye Crust, she ran her fingers across some pages and flipped quickly through others. One face caught her attention, prompting a comment from her. "This guy isn't bad looking. I wonder whatever happened to him?"

Steve now stared at her but still didn't say anything.

Rene kept her head bowed over the yearbook. She felt his stare but didn't look up. "Steve, I've worked for you for a long time. Usually, I understand what you want or I can figure it out on my own."

"Mmmh," Steve sniffed. You don't know the half of it, he thought.

"I know that you didn't go to Pye Academy. And I know that you didn't graduate in 1971 or 1972, you were just a kid back then. So why did you send me out to look for these? What are you looking for? Just give me a clue Steve." Rene looked up quickly, hoping to catch his reaction.

But his face gave no clues to his intentions. Without saying a word, Steve got up from his chair and stiffly walked over to the file cabinet. After fingering through the files in the top drawer, eventually, he pulled out a single thin folder. Dog-eared and dirty, the file bore the simple label "Javier." From the file, Steve pulled out a single sheet of paper, a yellowed copy of a handwritten note and placed it on the desk before her. "Rene, I need you to find out who wrote this."

Steve sounded as if he were trying to hold back tears. Puzzled, Rene wondered what was wrong. She looked at him, then immediately looked at the note. Maybe she would find a clue in it. She read the note aloud. "I don't love you anymore and I never want to see you again. I'm going with someone else. Forget me. Goodbye."

She frowned, "No signature, no date? It doesn't even say who the note is for! How am I supposed to find out who wrote this?"

"I think that it was a student at that high school."

"So? I mean, what difference does it make?"

"This is only a hunch, but I think that the person who wrote this note might know who killed my brother Javier."

LONG AFTER THE rest of the Tanner, Meyer and Smertz Clinic staff had gone home that Friday, Dr. Brian Tanner sat in the lower level of the clinic, in the records room. Normally, by this time in the evening, he would be at home, asleep. With a cup of water in front of him, he sat at a long table, skimming through patient files and a printout of the current monthly billing statement. He flipped through the top file quickly. For the next file, he took a little more time. Occasionally, he consulted the payment ledger beside him. As he reached the last file in his stack, he decided he needed to talk to the billing manager, Alma Hormiga, first thing on Monday morning. From the last four files, Brian could clearly see that Alma could have been more aggressive in billing.

BY 7:30 A.M. on the following Monday morning, five telephone message slips were waiting for Dr. Tom Swanson in his mailbox at the east wing nursing station at the Tanner, Meyer and Smertz Clinic. He had stopped by to pick them up on his way to his office. As Tom walked down the hall, he flipped through the slips to see which he would call back in the few minutes before his first appointment.

He flipped through the telephone slips. Patient, patient, patient, Alma, pharmacist. Tom decided to call the pharmacist first. He'd waited a week for him to call back.

Down in the pharmacy, at the left-side counter, K.C. Glade picked up the telephone on the first ring.

"K.C.? It's Tom."

"Tom, that drug you ordered is in. Three single-use injections of trihyperboodiol."

"I'll have Audrey pick it up sometime today." He made a note to call Audrey.

"It'll be ready for her then. Wait a second," K.C. leaned over and reached under the counter. From a bin under the counter, K.C. pulled out the invoice and the packing slip. He looked them over and whistled. "This stuff is pretty expensive. At this price, I'd hate to stock it unnecessarily. Do you think that I need to order any more?"

"Well, maybe you should," Tom replied.

"Are you sure?"

"Well, just wait then, K.C. I don't know if the patient will respond very well to this. I'll let you know. Thanks."

After he hung up the telephone, K.C. put the invoice back on the counter and made out the drug order with Audrey's name on it. She would have to sign for these injectables; they cost too much to lose track of.

TOM PUNCHED IN the number for Audrey Pelson's extension. "Good morning, Audrey."

At the first nursing station on the east wing, Audrey sat, making chart entries. She hadn't seen Dr. Swanson go by her desk yet and two patients were already waiting there for him.

"Hi." She lowered her voice. "I'm glad you called in, Tom. You've got two here already. Where are you?"

"I'm here—I'm in my office. The Milleson script is in."

"Milleson?"

"Yes, you remember, we needed that special injectable for her. Please pick it up at the pharmacy and set up the appointment for her. Thursday or Friday would be best for me."

"Boy, what took so long? You saw her more than a week ago. You would think that they would keep that stuff on hand."

"I don't know. Get back to me after you've set it up. I've got another call to make, then I'll be right there. Thanks, Audrey."

But the telephone rang as soon as Tom hung up.

"Dr. Swanson, this is Crystal from the Records Department. The three files that you asked for are in. Do you want them by interoffice mail or will you have someone pick them up?"

"I've got something to take care of near there. I'll pick them up myself. Thanks Crystal."

He wouldn't send anyone else to get those files. Calls to Alma and the three patients would have to wait for now. To avoid going through the east wing nursing station, Tom took the back stairs near his office. He cut through the side hallway to bypass the waiting room in front of the imaging area. Too many people would be there this early in the morning. His boss, Dr. Brian Tanner, might be among them.